Agents of Chaos

Marc L. Abbott

Danielle Ackley-McPhail

Rachel A. Brune

James Chambers

Teel James Glenn

Maxwell I. Gold

Carol Gyzander

Jeffrey Lyman

Will McDermott

F.R. Michaels

Bernie Mojzes

Jody Lynn Nye

Hildy Silverman

STEAMPUNK TITLES BY eSPEC BOOKS

THE CLOCKWORK CHRONICLES
The Clockwork Witch
The Clockwork Solution
The Clockwork Discovery (Forthcoming)
(MICHELLE D. SONNIER)

Baba Ali and the Clockwork Djinn
(DANIELLE ACKLEY-MCPHAIL AND DAY AL-MOHAMED)

A Curse of Ash and Iron
A Curse of Time and Memory (Forthcoming)
(CHRISTINE NORRIS)

Spirit Seeker
(JEFF YOUNG)

Sherman's Last Round-Up
(DAVID SHERMAN)

Esprit De Corpse
Aeros & Heros (Forthcoming)
(EF DEAL)

Crimson Whisper
(KEN SCHRADER)

STEAMPUNK ANTHOLOGIES BY eSPEC BOOKS

FORGOTTEN LORE
A Cast of Crows
A Cry of Hounds

After Punk:
Steampowered tales of the Afterlife

Gaslight & Grimm
Grimm Machinations

Grease Monkeys:
The Heart and Soul of Dieselpunk

The Weird Wild West

Other Aether: Tales of Global Steampunk

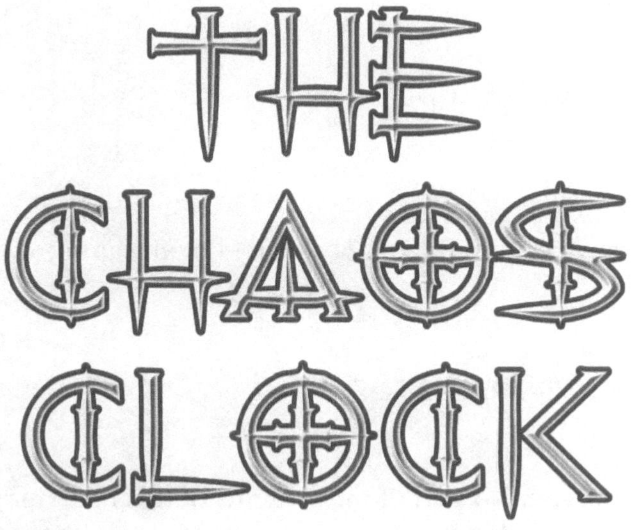

TALES OF COSMIC AETHER

EDITED BY
DANIELLE ACKLEY-MCPHAIL

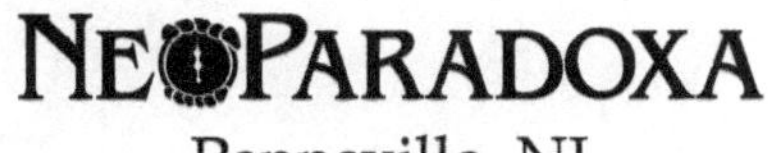

NEOPARADOXA
Pennsville, NJ

PUBLISHED BY
NeoParadoxa,
a division of eSpec Books LLC
Danielle McPhail,
Publisher
PO Box 242,
Pennsville, New Jersey 08070
www.especbooks.com

ISBN: 978-1-956463-35-4
ISBN (ebook): 978-1-956463-34-7

Cover and Interior Design: Danielle McPhail, McP Digital Graphics
Cover Consultation: Mike McPhail, McP Digital Graphics

Cover Art Credits - www.shutterstock.com
A cosmic horror concept. Of a alien monster with many eyes floating above a figure at night © Raggedstone
Infinity time spiral in space, antique old clock abstract fractal spiral 3d illustration, time travel concept © Svarun

Interior Art Credits
floral_lines © sanyal, www.fotolia.com

Surreal sketch art © Crystal Eye Studio, www.shutterstock.com

For James Chambers,
Thanks for always pushing me to up my game

12
3
6
9
FRAGILE

Contents

THE BIRTH OF MECHANICAL THINGS
Maxwell I. Gold 1

THE THIRTEENTH HOUR
Hildy Silverman 3

ON THE FACE OF IT
Danielle Ackley-McPhail 13

LIGHTHOUSE AT THE EDGE OF TIME
Teel James Glenn 33

ACCELERANDO
James Chambers 47

THE LAST FLIGHT OF THE ONE-EYED JACK
F.R. Michaels 65

THE RING OF HOURS AND SECONDS
Jeffrey Lyman 89

SAVING TIME
Jody Lynn Nye 119

REIMAGINING THE MECHANISM
Bernie Mojzes 135

SKY RIVERS OF GRAY
Will McDermott 145

THE RECLAIMING OF NEW YORK CITY
Marc L. Abbott 159

VISIONS OF THE MANOR
Carol Gyzander 181

TICK TOCK
Rachel A. Brune 195

THE EYE AT THE CENTER OF EXISTENCE NEVER BLINKS
Maxwell I. Gold 206

ABOUT THE AUTHORS 209

OUR CALM AMIDST THE CHAOS 215

THE BIRTH OF MECHANICAL THINGS

MAXWELL I. GOLD

Cradled in brown, dirty, and spike-covered canyons of manufactured entropy against the hot, flaming bosoms of industrial masters; silvery oil belched from molten stomachs—unable to be contained in the old, glass-bodies whose wings shimmered in shadow and ash below old cities. There were those who spoke in muddled tongues, of metallic forges packed deep under the cement bottoms of nameless cities and bemoaned the horror of the Mechanical Things. Worse than the fear-drunk delusions of an old world, standing taller than everything, a clock like stereopticon whose puckish crystallizations of time haunted the ruins of the present with ghosts of what used-to-be.

The awful bastards of gods older than the oldest stars, fourteen billion years at the beginning of existence, rose higher over the emerald skies whose unsettling particulates discolored the world with the music of something tenebrific and wild. The weary clock face flickered in and out, unable to hold the terrible burden any longer—stale light crashed with explosive relief throughout the putrid air.

Few remained after the clock fell, deserted and empty, the cities became bleak monuments doomed to oxidize beneath a cruel daytime star, once the forges collapsed, wrought by some splendid, winged death. Cold, filled with dust and regret, the sand and shadow asphyxiated any remnant possibility of sanguinity, replaced by the demented muddled tongues—cackling through broken glass and bent dreams inside the ruins of metallic forges lost under the cement bottoms of nameless cities.

The Thirteenth Hour

Hildy Silverman

My Dearest Etta,

The dirigible has delivered me safely to Greenwich. I am, as of this writing, in the back of a marvelous horseless carriage on my way to the Royal Observatory. The conveyance they kindly sent to fetch me is an amazing piece of work. One loads coal into a bonnet hopper for conversion and the internal workings are driven by the steam created thereby. The wheels are *[crossed out text illegible]* … ha, but I digress, as you are all too aware is my habit when presented with miraculous advancements. Such times we live in, my heart!

I shall arrive at the observatory soon, after which my letters to you are bound to become infrequent, as I fully immerse myself in the project. I know you shall forgive this, as you swore to me you understood my apprenticeship with the estimable J. Pond, Astronomer Royal, must come first. Our entire future together depends upon the success of this project—indeed, it might just change everyone's future.

The magnificent campus is within sight now. Oh, if only I could capture this first impression in a daguerreotype and somehow instantly transmit it, so you could share in my amazement! Alas, I am limited by my inability to paint images with my words like a Brontë or Poe. That said, I shall do my utmost to describe it as we approach.

We have just passed through ornate iron gates, which cranked themselves open after my driver presented his credentials. A great brick building looms over lush green lawns and old-growth trees. We pass large domes that contain retractable brass-encased telescopes for observing the heavens. Astronomers and staff hurry along cobblestone paths, most carrying books and various equipment. I imagine those in pairs and small groups are holding lofty discussions on subjects like temporal mechanics and the possibility of life beyond our world.

We approach the main entrance to the observatory. I must reluctantly turn my thoughts from your beauty, your patient devotion, and dreams of our delayed—temporarily, I promise—life together and focus on presenting myself as a suitable apprentice to the A.R. First impressions are everything, as you well know! I shall write again whenever I have a break between assigned tasks.

Most affectionately yours,
Thomas

Dearest Etta,

Please forgive the gap between missives—I assure you it does not mean I have stopped thinking of you. As evidence, I share that I have read your three letters received in the interim so often, the oils from my fingertips have yellowed their edges.

My time has been very well spent in pursuit of A.R. Pond's extraordinary project. He assigned me several tasks soon after our formal introduction, which I accepted as a compliment, not a burden. Apparently, he considered my top marks at Davy-Herschel University more than enough to recommend me as a suitable apprentice.

I am finally at liberty to reveal the premise of our extraordinary endeavor: completing construction of the most accurate chronometer ever developed! All timepieces 'round the world will soon be set according to it. Indeed, all time down to the smallest increment will be measured by it. Think of the possibilities, my love—no longer shall a dirigible captain keep to Solar Time while the submariner observes Lunar. Imagine consistency across all lands! All timepieces, from pocket watches to clock towers, local and global, shall be set according to our new chronometer! This shall revolutionize travel, commerce—I could go on and on.

I imagine your rosebud lips pursing in doubt reading this. "How?" you may well wonder. While I cannot wholly satisfy your curiosity due to your inexperience with the subject matter, I can relay the following insight, trusting in your ability to keep my confidence.

You see, the A.R.'s predecessor, the rightly lauded, if unfortunate, A.R. Maskelyne, discovered something most extraordinary during a joint expedition with a New England uni's geological team to distant mountains in Antarctica. Snaking through a cliffside cave was a vein of the rarest of elements, perhaps the only vein of the stuff on our planet. Whether it was some accidental natural occurrence, or the residue of an extra-planetary meteor embedded in the mountain ages ago remains undetermined. Frankly, its origin is the least important feature of this chronoaether, as Maskelyne named it upon his return to the observatory and before his descent into [crossed out text illegible]. To protect his memory and your delicate sensibilities, let us just call it the sad conclusion to an otherwise exceptional life. The chronoaether is now in the keeping of my benefactor, who has already carried Maskelyne's research beyond mere comprehension of its fundamental abilities to the application of them.

I bemoan my lack of ability to make the complexities understandable to someone lacking my education in the alchemical and astronomical sciences but shall do my utmost to explain plainly.

Simply put: the chronoaether can be used to power time. Well, timekeeping devices, to be more precise. It senses global meridians, latitude, and other necessary measurements with uncanny accuracy. And once we have completed the aetheric converter and attached it to the chronometer, it will run unceasingly and with absolute accuracy for... well, we do not know exactly how long a measure of it will last just yet. We hope to discover a way to replicate it, should our supply run out. Certainly, a return to the source in Antarctica would be challenging, given there are apparently no surviving members of the discovering party to provide guidance, may they rest in peace, nor did they leave any maps to it unburnt. However, the A.R. remains confident we shall discover an answer to this challenge in short order.

I miss you terribly, my sweet Etta. But I cannot regret taking this opportunity nor all I am learning under Mr. Pond's tutelage!

Most affectionately yours,
Thomas

Dearest Etta,

I hope this finds you well and that your pining for me is not overly distressing. Your last few letters describing your loneliness made my heart ache. The tenor of the last one in particular was so hopeful, focused on my anticipated return next month... which makes what I am about to share particularly difficult.

I expect to remain in Greenwich for a bit longer than originally planned. You see, although the aetheric converter has been constructed and the (as we have dubbed it) Universal Mean Time Chronometer is functional, Mr. Pond and I have encountered some, let us call them anomalies, which will necessitate our continuing efforts to unravel. I shall share some of these with you, again trusting in your ability to keep my confidence, as much as I have trusted you with my heart since I was but a poor student, and you, the young proprietress of my favorite teahouse. As first, you were merely a lovely distraction from my studies, but once I came to know your tender heart, your supportive nature... how could I not fall hopelessly in love with you? I yearn to feel your gentle embrace again, your *[crossed out text illegible]*.

Forgive my tangent. Besotted fool that I am, memories of our time together, combined with general weariness, distract me from my narrative.

Do you recall what I told you about the chronoaether, that we did not know how long this unique element would last? Well, it is the most extraordinary thing — it does not burn away! Rather, a single infusion of the stuff, which gives off a sickly yellow glow and smells like (forgive my indelicacy) decaying meat while processing, has not stopped fueling the Chronometer since first loaded into the converter! This is no jest, and I am not mocking you, as you have likely concluded. We truly cannot fathom how just yet, but it is as if the substance regenerates like a phoenix rising again and again from its own ashes.

Imagine the implications, my heart! If it may be adapted to replace coal as a source of fuel... but that would require deeper understanding of its temporal properties and how to filter them out, so it could be used as mere energy without risk of disrupting *[crossed out text illegible]*. My mind races with the possibilities, when it should remain focused on the already world-changing use at hand.

The U.M.T Chronometer remains in the testing phase. We have discovered another irregularity... one Mr. Pond reassures me is merely a temporary issue, quite minor really, and that shall soon be corrected. Anyway, once the A.R. is confident that the Chronometer is completely accurate, we shall formally declare Universal Mean Time the official time by which all timekeeping devices should be set worldwide. I expect that will mark the end of my apprenticeship here at the Observatory, and though I eagerly await my return home to plan our wedding and alleviate your loneliness, I confess a part of me shall miss the intellectual stimulation, fellowship, and sense of accomplishment discovered here.

Most affectionately yours,
Thomas

Dear Etta,

I have been remiss in updating you on the progress of our grand project, though according to your last letter, you already know what has been shared publicly. You said you read in the papers about the official establishment of Universal Mean Time and applaud that our Chronometer has been hailed as a groundbreaking achievement. While all that is true, the irregularity I alluded to previously—or did I, I cannot recall for sure what I wrote in my last—never mind, I shall tell you now, for I must tell someone and the A.R. continues waving it off as if… well, he is not overly concerned. This is only one of the odd reactions he has demonstrated of late; such a precise scientific mind as his, one would think he would be more perturbed—

My thoughts meander. Apologies, I shall try to remain focused despite the exhaustion that plagues me of late due to the *[crossed out text illegible]* … no, never mind my childish complaints.

As you, as everyone knows, there are twelve hours we call day and twelve hours assigned night. Twenty-four total, midnight to eleven fifty-nine. Of all things, the most accurate chronometer ever developed should know this too. However, for some reason, it has been… I don't know quite how to describe it clearly, but it has been <u>adding time</u> that simply does not exist. I realize this will make scant sense to you, to anyone really, but it is the only way I might describe what is happening.

At first, it was just a second, a tiny error that we dismissed as one would a hiccough. We tried a simple resetting, adjusting the amount of chronoaether in the converter, more involved tinkering with the gears and works... "A second is nothing," Mr. Pond insisted finally, when we were unable to resolve the issue. "Certainly no reason to delay introducing Universal Mean Time to the world."

I confess I was shocked by his, shall I call it, cavalier attitude. I understood his eagerness to bring our good work to fruition and present it to the world, but surely a man of science should... no, it is not right for me to denigrate the mentor who has provided me with such an opportunity... I shall criticize him no more.

The fact remains: since the formal launch, we have observed the extra tick of time has expanded, and even more concerning, continues to do so. Time is being inserted between 11:59 and midnight specifically — we are tracking it to the best of our ability as 11:59:59, 11:59:60, and so on. As of this writing, the gap has expanded to a full minute.

I very much fear that it shall continue, which of course will render the entire project — if only Pond had waited until we could resolve it! Now everyone, everywhere, might have to be told that the most accurate measurement of time on Earth is, in truth, incorrect. The shame of it, the humiliation, should this become public knowledge... Again, darling girl, I am trusting you with this potentially explosive revelation. <u>You must not reveal it to a soul!</u> The consequences, oh the —

Hopefully, it will not come to that. We work tirelessly to ensure it shall not come to that. Indeed, my slumber has become as disrupted as the Chronometer, especially around midnight... I pray tonight to only dream of you instead of [crossed out text illegible] anything else.

Affectionately yours,
Thomas

Dear Etta,

My concern for you now distracts me throughout the day nearly as much as the nightmares torment my nights. Your most recent letter — was that a month ago? More? I can no longer accurately judge the passage of time. Regardless, your account of what is occurring back home to our friends and family — to you — distresses me greatly. I wish I could set your mind at ease with this tardy response but fear that instead it shall only deepen your woe. However, I must be honest with you, for without truth between them, how is a couple to remain steadfast in their devotion?

The nightmares or visions or hysterics or whatever they might be, given they occur whether one is asleep or awake during the new span of time 11:59-11:90 P.u.M., or post-unknown meridian, as the A.R. dubbed it *[crossed out text believed to be 'before his erratic behavior worsened']*, are beginning to afflict more than the United Kingdom; indeed, we are receiving reports from nations throughout our hemisphere that their people are being tormented by such images of debauched sadism and glimpses of creatures that, to merely gaze upon their misshapen forms, incites madness. Outbreaks of violence — self-inflicted wounds, suicides, and murderous sprees — are spreading. I fear this plague of the mind shall spread until it afflicts the entirety of the world's populace, from the smallest of babes in a hovel to the eldest of elder statemen in his manor.

For my role in this, however unintentional, my guilt also grows exponentially.

I hesitate to even share the next with you, but I still endeavor to trust… despite dreams in which you show me your true wicked na *[crossed out text illegible, paper torn]* No, I shall not give credence to these delusions! <u>Someone</u> besides me must know, must believe, and tell others… assuming there will be any left capable of listening.

Pond has gone mad. This is not hyperbole; I swear it on the life I still pray we shall live together someday despite… He raves about the revelation of U.M.T. and the great power of the Chronometer, which he says has revealed to us the reality about time and space and our existence within — and the existence of things without. Understand these are <u>his</u> ravings, not mine. I merely relay them.

Pond insists that humanity is entering into an era pre-destined from before the beginning of time as we once comprehended it; before the familiar gods worshipped around the globe were even conceived. He rambles on about elder gods returning from beyond our realm that surpass our ability to conceive of their great and dreadful majesty. Our collective suffering is merely part of an evolution — or perhaps more accurately de-evolution — preparing us to serve them.

His lunacy, the constant night terrors, and fear for their families have driven away the Royal Observatory's surviving staff. Some resigned, others simply fled or vanished. I fear an untold number may have met grimmer fates — genuinely, I no longer know. As for me, I have done my utmost to remain a viable aide to Pond and to continue trying to puzzle out the reasons (based on science, not deranged fantasy) for the ever-expanding thirteenth hour… alas, to no avail. I have scrutinized the Chronometer's components and samples of the chronoaether under the most powerful microscope lenses, studied the movement of the stars and planets, poured over maps — <u>nothing</u> explains this phenomenon!

I even sought to remove the chronoaether converter, in which the disgusting stuff continues to burn and renew itself like the blessed oil in the ancient Hebrew tale, but Pond drove me back. It is true — my one-time benefactor, that wise and gentle soul, came at me screaming and thrashing until I was driven from the tower room in which the Chronometer resides. He has barricaded himself within, wholly absorbed by his psychotic delusions. When I tired of banging on the door and leaned against it, exhausted, I could hear him jabbering to himself about "outer darkness" and "the city shall rise from the ocean's depths," and "those who will come."

Oh, God, <u>what is coming?</u>

Lately, as I lie exhausted in my room fighting sleep and the dreams for as long as they might be staved off, I find myself questioning… what if Pond is not mad after all? Given there is no logical, no scientifical, explanation for the expansion of time and the window into darkness it has somehow opened, forcing humanity to gaze into an abyss beyond comprehension and bear witness to the horrors eager to enter our crumbling domain… perhaps the only sensible thing to do is give in. To despair, and to await the eldritch ancients who will soon claim us as their own.

But then I remember you, my love, my innocent, and kind… and no, I cannot, <u>must</u> not yield. I must fight this darkest hour that plagues us all. I shall, I swear it, I shall fight on for you… even if it means battering through the tower room's door and *[crossed out text, might be 'slaughtering']* subduing my former benefactor. It would be a mercy, really — if he could comprehend that his great mind has been rent by insanity, he would no doubt beg me to end his misery. A kindness, yes, I can save him, and in doing so, perhaps save you and the entire world as well.

Stay strong, my beloved, my heart, my reason.

Yours,
Thomas

My Etta,

Why am I writing this letter? A waste of time—ha, a pun without humor or intent! Doubtless you are no longer in this ruined world to read it or if you are, incapable of doing so. Yet here I am, spending the last of my sanity and likely my existence on this clearly fruitless endeavor because... well, at least I can pretend it will reach you, whole and healthy and safe... a comforting lie I shall tell myself for as long as possible.

In distant lands where they did not reset their clocks to Universal Mean Time, some survivors might someday find this and understand that I tried, I swear that I did. Of course, I failed, as you and millions of others know only too well. Knew, I suppose, or perhaps know... did <u>They</u> let you go, I wonder? Do you rest in a peaceful oblivion, devoid of the visions that singular hour inflicted upon us all... or do the sources of those nightmares yet hold you fast, trapped in an everlasting thirteenth hour of agony and screams?

I did get through that tower door, my darling, my lost love. I found a fire ax during my frenetic search of the observatory campus and used it to split the door apart, just wide enough for me to squeeze through. I found... oh, God, the poor wretch! Pond was there, curled upon the floor beside his greatest creation, groaning and clawing at his empty sockets, the jelly that remained of his eyes dripping through his fingers. The bones of his face were crushed to bloody pulp; broken teeth scattered along the floor. Judging by the blood and flesh stuck to the walls, he had smashed it against them repeatedly. Yet, somehow, he still drew breath through his torn, blood-filled maw. He chanted— prayed, more accurately—his voice hoarse from repeating words in a language I could not recognize, but when I heard it, it made my ears bleed and my mind retreat into a place without sense or reason or hope...

I did the only thing, the merciful thing. A single blow with the ax and the grey matter of the once most respected astronomer in all the kingdom, if not the world, lay exposed and stilled.

I turned to the U.M.T. Chronometer next. Oh, my heart, you would have been so proud of me! I did not hesitate—I swung the ax until every component that housed it, every clockwork that made it run, lay broken upon the floor next to its damned creator. I dumped the chronoaether out the window and destroyed the converter too. I know not how long it took, only that by the time I was done, my shoulders and back screamed in protest against my taking another swing and my chest heaved as I struggled to draw breath.

"Done and done," I said and laughed, fool that I was, thinking I had stopped it somehow. That it would be so simple.

Perhaps it would have been, had we destroyed the thing as soon as we realized it was marking time out of time, when we noticed the extra second. Or perhaps we were doomed the instant we added the infernal chronoaether to fuel the clock. I suspect that once all timepieces were reset globally to obey UTM that the die was cast, permitting a new, distorted version of reality to seep in and warp our perceptions, our minds. Likely it would not have mattered whether we discovered the stretching of time and it all would have happened anyway without our realizing it. There is just no way to discern correlation from causation when it comes to an event so outside human experience.

And it does not matter, does it? Not to Pond, not to you, not to the world. Certainly not to me.

The last newspaper I saw relayed tales of mass suicides, whole families killing themselves, their neighbors. Dire predictions were made that open warfare across continents would soon follow as civilization buckled worldwide. That was quite some time ago, I think. I can only assume it has all come to pass, and worse.

I have survived so far by rationing what food I could find, but without steam in the pipes, everything has shut down including the iceboxes, so soon even what remains shall rot. Chaos reigns just outside the main tower in which I am holed up. The screams echo through these walls, sometimes punctuated by explosions and… other sounds… like the skies themselves are being rent apart. Blood drips frequently from my ears, my eyes… I try to stop my ears hearing, to stop seeing what They show me, but nothing works, for Their whispers and Their visions come from within my head… rending my sanity and my self until nothing remains but a husk in service to…

At least I still have the ax. I have only to figure out how to employ it to end my suffering and join you, my beloved, wherever you might have gone. I hope and pray that we shall be reunited, not as slaves to those unbound by time and space, but in a paradise far beyond their reach.

And there I shall drop to my knees before you and beg forgiveness.

Thomas

On the Face of It

Danielle Ackley-McPhail

"It began… with I…" his voice rasped from the deep shadows of the drawn bed curtains, breaking on the softest of syllables, only to ring out with the sharpness of honed steel, "but it ends with me.

"Oh?

"By God… it… did. It must! It will!

"One way or the other, aye?

"No! In a manner of my own choosing!"

I would have thought no less than three people conversed… or better to say, squabbled, had I not sat witness and heard each utterance pass the same man's lips. His head — or perhaps just his hair — thrashed, the bright glow of his bandages remaining turned away as he went on in mounting vitriol, seemingly arguing amongst himself.

Again, subtle and peculiar modulations of tone caught my ear.

I shifted in the chair I had pulled up beside the bed, leaning ever so slightly closer, rapt by his diatribe. My efforts to glean the discourse for details of significance had thus far yielded nothing, until I grew desperate. Reckless, perhaps. The man stilled, his muscles taut, of a sudden alert, where before his attention turned only inward to his ever-fracturing turmoil. With slow deliberation, his head rotated in my direction. I swallowed a gasp at the two spots of faint rose hue seeping to the surface of the stark white gauze in mockery of what had once been his eyes.

A low, harsh rustle came from the bedding as the patient shifted.

"Oy! Back yerself off," the orderly barked, his rough hand grasping my shoulder and yanking me away, chair and all, even as the damaged soul on the mattress lunged forward, his equally gauze-wrapped hand grasping for my arm. For the briefest of moments, the skin of his bare wrist brushed mine before the burly attendant drew me out of reach, depositing me safely behind him, close to the grandfather clock standing sentinel in the corner. My flesh burned like the cold of deepest winter, nay, like the everlasting void seeping into my soul. I shuddered and rubbed at my skin, the sensation dissipating as if it had never been, a fancy of the mind built upon rumor and speculation.

"Right, off with ye then," the orderly pointed at the door, brooking no argument.

If he knew who I was, he never would have spoken so abruptly or without deference, but my... patient's family wished none to know either their son's standing or my own, lest their reputation be tarnished.

"But..."

The man's broad brow furrowed into deep valleys, his eyes aglint with annoyance. "Ye weren't to rile him. Ye has, so out ye go. It'll take all day an' half the night gettin' him settled again."

Quite uncustomary to my usual nature, my blue blood rose to the surface, a kindling flame that warmed my cheeks but left my gaze cold. I stood, shoulders back and spine straight, as only the strictest of Dunaway upbringings could instill, honed through twelve generations. Slowly, my head tilted just so as to gaze down the slope of my nose at this common man. The essence of a sneer toyed with the corner of my lip, but I did not indulge it. Without further word, I strode from the room, distinctly unsettled.

On the desk in my study lay a daguerreotype of Edward Moreton, first son and heir to his family's fortune. A well-manicured gentleman of not much greater years than myself, slight and studious, I would hazard a guess, based on appearance. Until now, we were not acquainted, though in truth I could not claim to know the man he had been, only familiar with the fragmented remains I had so far observed. My brow furrowed as I noted a peculiar emblem pinned to his lapel. I could make out a small circle atop a larger rough circle surrounding a six-pointed star, but little else of the clearly ornate icon. It bore some faint familiarity to me, though I could not say why. Something from my studies, perhaps? Yet another puzzle to solve amidst all this madness.

No one could tell me what fractured my patient's psyche. Or perhaps, no one *would*, to be more accurate. What horrors drove him to the depraved acts he'd committed I could only guess at, but for the mutilation of his features, which I am told were self-inflicted. The family—as old as my own, but of lesser standing—refused to furnish details, preferring to bury their shame. To pretend it had never been. Though how they expected me to proceed uninformed I could not say.

They had engaged my assistance by unofficial means, knowing, through our families' shared circles, of my penchant for psychology. Long had I studied the works of Wundt and Freud and Titchener, among others, out of personal interest, rather than intent to practice. My devotion to this science had, in fact, brought me to reside—until now—in Boston, where I studied at Harvard under William James, who some already called the father of American psychology.

I found the workings of the human mind, both hale and broken, of particular fascination. Of late, I had also immersed myself in the study of brass instrument psychology and had even procured for myself a chronoscope and kymograph, along with assorted pendulums, gravity fall devices, and such, to better understand their function.

I would have perhaps rethought such dedication, had I known where it would lead.

Beneath the print bearing Moreton's image lay a scant page or two of observations from the local inspector, written in broad, clean strokes, studiously vague on any details the family did not wish revealed. Regardless, I had requested more. The peculiar, the unsolved. Beginning from when the foundation of Moreton's reason grew unstable. Anything I might connect with what transpired. I could not say if the constabulary would go against the family to honor my request, though I held high expectations, having consulted for the department in the past. For now, I poured over what I did have in the hopes of gleaning more understanding.

I found it difficult to reconcile that image, those accounts, with the individual I had myself so recently monitored. And yet, reconcile I must if I was to help knit the fragments of his mind back into one. Picking up the daguerreotype, I considered Moreton as he had been. We were contemporaries, by age and birth and standing. What happenstance led us each to this point, both divergent and unified at once? By what stroke of fortune had our paths not been transposed?

I shuddered as well-founded unease gripped my being.

And this is why I stood, at morning's darkest hour, in the simple gardens of Pike's Cliff Manor, the retiring house where Moreton's family had sequestered their former scion, staring up into the sky in search of direction. I found a faint flicker of green light tickling the fading stars, but no more. Breathing a sigh, I slid my hands into the warmth of my trouser pockets and strolled the shrouded paths letting the cool darkness soothe my anxious thoughts before retiring to bed.

A futile effort.

Braced by a night of fitful sleep and a rather strong cup of tea, I entered Moreton's chambers with strides both determined and confident. I was no dabbler. I had studied at the highest institutions of learning; I had consumed volume after volume on the science of psychology and was noted among the educated for my discourse on those studies. Cradled in my arms, the stout wooden box I bore contained the finest precision instruments of my chosen discipline.

I quite nearly dropped them.

Moreton's chambers more resembled a tavern after a barroom row. My patient lay in his bed, unmoving, for once in full light, the torn bed curtains puddled on the floor, along with most of the bedding. On the far side of the room, by the seating area arranged before the fireplace, the orderly cleaned up the remnants of the grandfather clock that had stood in the corner. The clockface, with its hands bent awry, had been perched on the mantle, with the weights and their chains pooled around it, like an octopus nested among its tentacles. The rest of the cabinet lay like so much kindling on the hearth. Actually, nothing else in the room looked damaged, or so it seemed, until the orderly turned at my entrance, revealing bruises of deepening hue along his swollen jaw and climbing toward his ear. A single tendril of color crept out beneath his eye, which was not quite blackened but clearly tender.

"What happened?"

He gave me a look that bordered on stark hatred and his words of the night before echoed in my memory: *Ye weren't to rile him. Ye has, so out ye go. It'll take all day an' half the night gettin' him settled again.*

All he said now was, "T'were a bad night."

I shifted my burden, my confidence momentarily shaken, but I had a task, and I would not retreat from it now.

"All right…" I responded in even tones as I set my box of precious instruments out of the way on a table beside the door. "Let's get things into order and get to work."

The orderly grunted and glowered and continued with his labor while I restored the bedding and tucked the drapery out of the way until the household staff could deal with it.

"Has he eaten?" I asked, trying to gauge how the morning would proceed.

"That blighter don't eat."

I frowned, all must eat and drink. Moreton looked haggard, tortured even, but not gaunt, and clearly had the energy for tantrums. My determination returned tenfold. Today I would take Moreton's measure with my devices.

"Help me move him to the chair," I said, pointing toward the seating area, where the side table by the wingback chair would serve nicely to hold my equipment.

"Nah, m' shift's done. Yer on yer own 'til Layton shows his face." Without an ounce of deference, but a healthy dose of insolence, the man strode from the room.

Though I highly doubted he was meant to leave his charge — even if not strictly unattended — before his counterpart relieved him, my employer's directive of anonymity stayed my objection as the orderly departed.

I would swear I heard ticking, though the clock lay shattered.

Turning, I considered my situation. With the bed curtains gone, the light from the window shone full on Moreton and if I moved the table from the seating area to the bedside, I could proceed even unaided. My course determined, I began my work, first arranging things to my liking, then retrieving the kymograph from the box, electing to leave the rest well distanced from potential harm. Setting the device on the table, I examined the workings closely, making sure the drum and the stylus were properly aligned with the paper, and winding the clockwork that propelled them. Lastly, I inspected the tube connected to its rubber membrane for any imperfections before running it along the table and applying the membrane to Moreton's carotid artery.

As I leaned over him in my efforts, casting him once more into shadow, I would swear I saw the faintest of movements beneath the encrusted gauze that hid his ruined eyes. Just a flutter, caught in the corner of my gaze. A green shimmer, there, then gone. A moment of fancy, perhaps? For when I looked full upon him, I saw but the indentation of the empty, sunken pits I knew lay hidden there. Returning to my task, however, I could not help but cast a sideways glance, looking without looking as best as I was able, and I would swear to the Almighty that something writhed beneath that stained cotton, coiling and probing, testing the bounds constraining it.

Slowly—ever so slowly—I reached out a finger to determine if my eyes had lied, my chest inexplicably tightening the closer I drew.

"Here! What is this about?"

I may have cried out.

I most certainly jerked away, my arm snagging the tubing and pulling the membrane askew.

Even so, I heard a skritching at my back, faint and rapid as the stylus etched white lines across the soot-coated paper installed for the purpose of recording.

Banished once more from Moreton's chambers, I tempered an increasing desire to flee the premises by ordering my steam-powered velocipede readied for a trip to town. I needed details, and with Moreton all but senseless, I had only one other source to tap. So far, my request had gone unanswered, but perhaps paying a call on the inspector would advance my efforts.

The further I traveled down the road leading from the manor the more my muscles uncoiled fiber by taut fiber. I would not say my tension left me but, without doubt, it loosened its grip. By the time I pulled up to the local ward my breath came much easier. Until that moment, I had not realized how scarce a full inhalation had been at the manor.

Climbing from the velocipede and leaning it out of the way beside the building, I extinguished the boiler for safety and went inside. The bustle of central processing assaulted my ears after my solitary drive through the countryside. I felt my muscles tighten once more, until I almost turned and fled, overwhelmed by the resurgent desire to drive off into the wilderness, never to return to Pike's Cliff Manor.

But such would not do. Honor demanded I complete my task, no matter the obstacles before me. Drawing up my noble manner like the armor it was, I approached the registrar's counter. The officer on duty was unfamiliar to me.

"Sir Gyles Dunaway to see the inspector," I said, presenting my card.

The man scarcely looked up from the paperwork before him.

"He's in a meeting." The deflection would have borne more weight had I not a clear view of the man in question through a gap in his office door. "If you have something to report, the forms are right there. A constable will be with you shortly."

Though his tone was more of overwork than disrespect, my ire rose. Stiffening my spine and hardening my gaze, I gave a sharp rap on the counter, commanding the man's full attention, since manners had failed. The room fell silent around us.

"The inspector, if you please." My tone brooked no argument.

Open-mouthed, the officer half rose. Before he could speak, the inspector left his desk and crossed the station to stand at the man's back, lightly touching his shoulder.

"It's okay, Burnell," he murmured in a calming tone before turning to me. "Sir Dunaway, it's good to see you. Shall we take this to my office?" With one hand, he gestured the way he had come.

With a curt nod, I preceded him, my thoughts and mood in such sudden turmoil I dared not speak. I had never in my life subscribed to the gentry's entitlement, yet I found myself sliding into such manner more and more. I did not care for this.

Stopping abruptly, I turned. "My apologies, Mr. Burnell," I said with a brief bow. The officer just stared at me, his expression shifting from anger to perplexity. Slowly, he nodded back.

A brief touch at my elbow moved me toward the office, where I sat in the chair set before the inspector's desk. The door closed with a soft *snick*. The inspector resumed his seat and waited for me to speak, giving ironic truth to Burnell's lie. I, not yet in command of my behavior, remained silent.

"Are you all right, Gyles?"

Drawing a deep, steadying breath, I met his gaze.

By long association over the course of several years and over a dozen consultations, I had come to count this man… well, if not a friend, something more than a professional acquaintance. And even so, the concern I saw in his gaze unsettled me, much as my current manner clearly unsettled him.

"By what definition?"

His brow furrowed even more.

I shook my head and drew another steadying breath. "More apologies are in order, clearly. I am sorry, John. I am not myself of late. Stress. Frustration. The most peculiar nature of my… patient."

"Ah," he murmured. "Now we get to the meat of it."

"They will tell me nothing! I am more in the dark in possession of both eyes than Moreton is blind."

The inspector shifted uncomfortably behind his desk, tensing in anticipation of my next words. I gave them voice, nonetheless. "I need details, John. All I know of is that poor sot Horton... gouges above his right eye and his left hand hacked off. Good Lord, they could not hope to cover that mess up, but that is not enough for me to base informed decisions on. I must know what I am dealing with. It is more than needing to know how to help him. How am I to protect myself if I am unaware of the risks?"

"The family..."

"I am aware, I assure you." Grimacing at my continued lapse in manners. "My apologies. Let us set Moreton's infractions aside. Is there aught else you can share without violating these vexing limitations?"

The silence in the wake of my words drew on in fragile filaments until I wondered would it shatter under its own weight. John defused the mounting strain with a slow, soft sigh. Without taking his gaze from mine he leaned to the side and opened his desk drawer. He withdrew a sheath of pamphlets and laid them before me.

My brow furrowed. The top pamphlet read *Theosophy and the Mission of the Theosophical Society.* I barely noted this, however, on seeing the crisp, clear icon above those words. I had seen this in Moreton's image. When I reached to turn the page, John stayed my hand.

"Some reading for later. I believe you'll find it most interesting," he murmured with a slight frown, as if anyone were about to overhear. I nodded, acknowledging the care a public servant must take when dealing with the entitled. Though rank bore less weight in the Americas, the power of wealth still held sway.

Collecting the pamphlets, I slid them into my jacket for later perusal. As I did so, a possible path forward came clear to me.

"Inspector, I wish to offer my services... to consult on current cases for which your fine officers are at a loss on how to proceed. The bizarre, the peculiar, cases you have all but given up on... unsolved and unlikely to be..."

John's frown eased and his gaze brightened as he nodded.

"I will see what cases might benefit from your... analysis."

Accepting his word with grim satisfaction, I took my leave, turning the velocipede toward the Manor, still fighting my earlier impulse to fill the boiler to the brim and flee.

⌘

Though the hour was late by the time I reached Pike's Cliff Manor, my curiosity would no longer be stayed. I ensconced myself in my study, locking the door and stoking the fire before withdrawing the pamphlets John had provided and spreading them across the surface of my desk. Lighting a lamp, I began to read.

The first few bore nothing extreme. Official tracts issued by the Theosophical Society touting high-browed mysticism and spiritualist palavering of the sort popular with the idle gentry around the civilized world. I dare say, I myself had attended one of their meetings in London — strictly out of academic curiosity — before leaving for Boston. Their philosophies did not mesh well with my own, but each to their own enlightenment.

By the fourth or fifth pamphlet, issued independently by a local chapter of the Society, the tone began to change, taking on a more occult nature, putting a whole new slant on their mission to prepare the world for the coming of the 'World Teacher.'

Despite the fire's warmth, I felt chilled, my nerves pricking along my skin like a train of angry ants. Wondering what Madame Blavatsky thought of the more extreme offshoots of her Society, I pushed the materials aside and contemplated the darkness encroaching on my thoughts.

Perhaps I should have saved such reading for the daylight hours.

⌘

I was informed, on the morrow, that Moreton's family had ordered one Hydro-Electric Chain, the cure-all contraption touted by the wealthy and the broadsheets alike, reportedly employed by Dickens himself! I was also informed said device had arrived. I had heard of Isaac Pulvermacher's "magic band," and had even been trained in its operation, but must admit I had my doubts as to its effectiveness. My cynicism aside, what they thought such a device would accomplish for one whose senses were scattered, I could not say. The man's condition was scarcely on par with headaches or palsy, particularly in light of the… spiritualist influences at play.

As I entered Moreton's suite, I spied the broken soul bound into what I could not help but think of as a Bedlam coat, though most would call it strait. He sat slumped into a ladder-backed chair with his bandaged eyes angled toward the ceiling and one pallid bare leg resting in a basin of water. On a table beside the chair were arranged a series of electrodes connected by sturdy cables to a leather battery belt around Moreton's waist.

A sense of uneasy relief coursed through me at the sight.

"Why is he restrained?" I asked the orderly, a different man than either of the others I'd seen before, but of the same burly stature.

"Fer protection." The man did not clarify whose, though he too bore the shadow of what might have been a bruise at his temple.

I turned my attention back to the patient.

Moreton's black hair resisted any sense of order, and the faint rose hue that had stained the gauze over his ruined eyes had darkened to an oxidized brown. I would have thought him a particularly macabre mannequin, poorly posed and lifeless, only as I moved closer, he tensed and drew upright, his half-blank face turning in my direction.

"It began with I…" he muttered, leaning toward me, the words altogether more sinister than before. They seemed to echo in my mind as if uttered by a mad horde and not a solitary shattered man.

Rattled though I might be, I did not engage him, instead turning my attention to the device, a single brow raising in uninhibited skepticism as I ran my hand over the casing, reacquainting myself with the buttons and toggles gracing the top.

"They must not be wasted," Moreton hissed barely at the level of a whisper, low enough I would not have heard him, had I not been inspecting the contraption. "I won't be made to begin again! Souls fighting their vessel. Marking time in frantic pounding. Like a heartbeat… faster… faster… You cannot stay the hands… Make it stop! Uncoil the spring! Pluck out the bright jewels of the movement!"

My brow furrowed at an unexpected change in the timber of his voice at first, before it fell into his usual cadence. I lost focus of that observation, however, as my own heart sped up to the rhythm of his words, my ears straining to catch each one. I gasped, wondering if I mistook his meaning or not, envisioning how he'd come to lose his sight.

"Quickly, man, before it's too late!" his last words came on a stronger breath, desperate, insistent.

"Too late for what?" I murmured, not really expecting him to note my presence, let alone the question, any more than before.

Looking his way, I fumbled the electrode I had just picked up. Moreton's shocking mimicry of a gaze locked steadfast upon me. In entreaty or calculation? I dropped the lead and rubbed the wrist he'd grazed that first night, suddenly as searingly cold as if I had brushed against M. Thilorier's 'dry ice.' Was Moreton about to speak? To engage me directly? I leaned closer almost without realizing.

"Don' just stand there! Get it done so's I can bundle him back in bed. I'm due my tea in an hour."

I jumped and straightened at the brash words, my gaze snapping to the orderly waiting with fisted hands to Moreton's other side. With a sharp nod but no words, I took up the electrodes once more and approached Moreton. Though he clearly could not see, he stilled and went taut. The voids pulsed.

Did a bare whisper cross his lips? The fading echo of a plea? I dare say the words, 'unseat the lodger who is in me' taunted my ears. Imagined? Perhaps. Perhaps not. But those words were passingly familiar, though I could not pinpoint the source. The pamphlets, perhaps? Either way, the insight they might give to Moreton's current madness disturbed me.

Again, the illusion of movement beneath that gauze. I recoiled, averting my eyes.

Before he could thrash about, the orderly moved behind the chair and planted his beefy hands one on either of Moreton's shoulders, pinning him in place. Quickly, I stepped forward and placed the electrodes around his head, managing to do so without once touching the man's flesh.

It is quite possible I drew not one breath the entire time.

Before I could rethink my purpose, I took position beside the Chain and flipped the toggle. The indicators on the gauges pinned all the way to the far side.

With a yipe the orderly stumbled back, shaking his hands and glaring in my direction. I barely noticed. A sharp sizzle and the scent of scorched hair filled the room as Moreton stiffened, his back arching impossibly. The water in the basin splashed with vigor as his foot twitched, and his unruly tufts of hair fairly stood on end. His mouth fell open, releasing an eerie undulation the likes of which I had never heard before.

I scrambled to disengage the machine. At the halting of the current, the patient slumped back in the chair, falling silent. What I could see of his expression seemed nearly peaceful. No movement at all, expected or otherwise. I released a quavering sigh on observing that his chest yet rose and fell with life's breath. Such a charge had been known to stop a hale man's heart, let alone one in such a poorly state.

Slowly, his head swung in my direction. "Not enough, damn you… you stopped too soon…next time…" His words trailed off.

Falling back from him and the machine, my head shook of its own accord, first slowly, then with building vigor.

Never. Again. *Never*. Again!

"Here! Warn a bloke!"

I turned to look upon the orderly, noting in both horror and fascination that his cheek yet jerked and twitched with the remnants of the current from the Chain until it seemed he parodied a wink. I had not anticipated the current traveling so, or I would have warned him to stand back. Even now, his face stood out bright red with the features limned in white, all his muscles clenched and poised, as if he barely restrained the urge to knock me arse over tea kettle.

I could not blame him.

I had no words to say in my defense. I had no words at all. With trembling hands, I removed Moreton's leads and left the room.

I woke with an ache in my bones and the scent of scorched hair flooding my senses. Sweat beaded every swath of bare skin and elsewhere soaked the fabric of my nightshirt. The remnants of a screech echoed from my dreams to tease my ears as I pushed myself upright against the pillows. It took several long moments to calm my breathing as fragments of images tormented my sleep-clouded brain, of staring into a writhing, green-tinged darkness and having it stare back. Images that slowly faded as the room beyond the bed curtains lit with sunlight.

A quiet masculine humming came from the direction of my dressing room, its bright cheer chasing away the final shadows of my nightmare. I drew back the bed curtains and swung my bare legs to the floor just as my valet, Malone, entered the chamber. He had drawn the drapes, allowing the sun to stream through the French doors leading to the balcony. I squinted against the light. By the angle, it seemed closer to noon than dawn. My grip on the curtains tightened in an effort to still the tremors in my limbs.

"Good morning, sir," Malone murmured, his eyes thoughtfully averted. "There's warm water in the basin and cold in the pitcher. Will you be shaving?"

I blanched at the thought, though my own hand would not wield the razor. I could see no course where blood would not flow as his steady ministrations met my unsteady flesh.

"It can wait until later," I murmured as I pushed to my feet and moved to the basin to begin my day's ablutions. With no further discourse, Malone helped me dress.

"Would you like me to fetch you a meal?"

The mere mention wracked my body with shudders.

"Are you all right, sir?"

I waved him off as he reached to steady me.

"It's nothing, just a chill."

"Very well, sir. Some chowder, perhaps?"

"Just some coffee." A rare indulgence, but I felt the need for something more bracing than tea and less scandalous than spirits.

In Malone's absence, the faint ticking of the mantel clock plucked at my nerves. Moreton and his bloody mutterings. *Uncoil the spring, pluck out the bright jewels.* I shuddered. *Unseat the lodger…* Most would not have noticed, but to my reluctant ear, three steady, incongruent rhythms seemed to compete, forcing my heart in step until my head pounded threefold with their separate and varying beats. Until all I heard was the clicking gears advancing those unrelenting hands.

Again, Moreton's manic muttering taunted me, *"You cannot stay the hands…"*

Whether inspired by my reading, or Moreton's muttering, I found myself overwhelmed by the sense of something ominous looming. I stepped out onto the balcony to escape the sound, closing the doors behind me. Storm clouds moved steadily to obscure the sun, roiling low in the sky. In an echo of my dreams, they seemed tinged faintly green. I pushed that thought away and drew the crisp New England air into my lungs, willing the thunder of the waves below to drown out the intonation of the clock, only to find those three beats trapped within me. I fought to return my functions to a more natural rhythm, to some success, but only by fixing all my will upon the task.

In all confession, I startled like a young faun at a sudden gentle tap upon the glass behind me. Only my grip on the rail kept me steady. Turning, I spied Malone, his carefully schooled expression giving way to apprehension. I made no acknowledgment of his concern. My eye went from the steaming cup of coffee in his hand to the carafe on the dressing table beyond him.

I waved for him to step back, my free hand going to the handle on the door.

"God bless you," I murmured as I accepted the cup, draining it dry in one gulp before moving to refill it.

Malone nodded but said nothing. His features returned to a pleasant neutral mien, though his eyes remained watchful.

I savored the next cup, only then noting a thick stack of folders beside the carafe. It had not been there before.

"Malone?"

"Sir?"

"The folders?"

"Oh! Yes. The local inspector delivered them this morning. Said you requested to see anything… unusual."

The coffee cup clattered as I set it down. I had not expected John to act so swiftly.

I reached for the top folder, chagrined to note my fingers still faintly trembled. My heart seized on my distraction once more and took on the erratic rhythm of the clock, or perhaps it merely galloped and stuttered all on its own. I could no longer say. My focus locked upon the folder as I turned the top leaf to reveal a letter written in the inspector's familiar hand and, beneath that, a stack of reports and what looked to be albumen prints.

Dunaway,

As discussed, enclosed you will find those cases that defy our explanation. As in the past, it is our hope your unique perspective might prove instrumental in their solving. Some, we have discussed in passing. Others, not. The murdered. The missing. Disfigurements enough to drive one to despair. Also included, please find another noteworthy volume I feel might be of interest.

For whatever good it may do you, I wish you well in your efforts.

Inspector J.R.L.

I moved the letter aside to gaze upon the reports beneath it. I had not anticipated the photographs. The first startled a gasp from me. I stood there staring at the remains of a young woman, my breath arrested. Again, it was as if a presence loomed over me, poised and ready, but for what I knew not. My head filled with the ticking of the gears until I clenched my teeth and forced the sounds away. My jaw still set, I flipped the photographs face down and focused on the reports. Not all of those provided had the feel of what I was looking for. Those I set aside, drawn by what, I could not say. But by the time I was done I had two piles, one thicker than the other by at least a factor of two. Dry accounts written by jaded men. Officers of the law who had clearly seen more than their share of the worst of humanity cataloguing details and moving on. Even so, upon occasion, some faint essence of their unease crept between their judiciously worded lines. Like the very edge of madness they carefully tread.

As I immersed myself, Malone retreated to the other room. I hardly noticed.

The barest shiver skated across my shoulders as I read those reports. And read them again. And again, until I could not say how many times I sifted them for details and patterns and relevance otherwise gone unnoticed with no path to clearly link one to the other, save for some sense that they were relevant. Tossing aside the reports in vexation, I took up the prints, steeling myself for their macabre images.

My weary eyes blurred and shifted. Or perhaps they merely sought to evade the horrors I demanded they observe. Details bubbled up like from a caldron, sickening. Bursting forth with a stench of pending decay.

With a shudder, I set them aside to take up the volume of which John made particular mention. On seeing the gilded title embossed upon the leather, I gasped. *Isis Unveiled,* a controversial tome penned by Helena Petrovna Blavatsky, the founder of the Theosophical Society, of which I was now more acquainted than I wished to be.

The lodger that is in me… Words heard most recently from Moreton's lips, but first uttered by the Madame herself in regard to the book in question. Words perhaps holding a more literal significance for Moreton than one would expect?

No… surely not. Surely…

Casting the book away, I turned my attention back to the reports. Somehow less disturbing than my current thoughts. I ran my finger over those dull images of doomed faces, my subconscious clattering to the rhythm of my heart. Measured. Constant. Ticking up a beat, like a clock running fast, when instinct told me 'this one.' I nearly missed the pattern; it was so subtle. Anabel Lawson… her parents' only daughter.

Geoffery Taylor… the younger half of a set of twins. Henry Jacobs… the third in his family to bear that name. The others were trickier. More difficult to discern. The next was Francis Murphy. Frank, to his men, the foreman at the local lumber operation. Fore-man. *Four.*

My jaw clenched as my head throbbed. My normally neat hair stood out in tufts from raking through my fingers, looking for the pattern most diabolically hidden in these gruesome accounts. A pattern I would have had no hope of spying if not for my desperate grasping for sense in chaos.

Five about broke my reason, if not for that niggling instinct telling me Jack Turner was one of mine. For such had I come to think of them. And then the twisted sense hit me. Who but a Brit like me… and Moreton… would know a Jack for a five-pound note?

Why the progression I did not know, but now that I had clued to it, my mind sought the connections like an unhinged game. Six was a coal miner known simply as Augustus, a correlation no one but a well-read man could make, based on Moseley's recent discovery of atomic numbers. Seven… Seith, a local Welsh farmer with an unfortunately numeric name. Eight was Sally Acher, who had celebrated her bronze anniversary. And nine… by all that was unholy… nine was one Father Patrick, doomed, for all I could determine, because the nineth hour was the hour of prayer.

The next brought bile to my throat. Beyond weary with the horror, I lay my head down and cried for little Milly Patterson, all of ten years old. Which brought me to Handy Horton, a sorry sot born with eleven fingers, who died with only five.

Eleven horrific murders, beyond disturbed. On the surface, nothing to connect the cases, but for superficial damage to the faces and hands. All unsolved, but for the last, which had been the pinnacle of Moreton's downfall. And all for what? I may have deducted the pattern, but there remained no sense to it. Or did there…

Again, Moreton's recent words whispered through my thoughts. *"It began… with I…"*

I.

I.

I stared at the prints, flipping from one to the next and back again, fanning them like a child's kineograph… the images in my hand creating a depraved flipbook no sane mind had ever intended. I noted for the first time, a pattern overlooked, on the face of it. *On the face of it…*

my voice cracked on a barking laugh. With a finger, I traced the gouges marring the face of each seemingly unconnected victim. Never the same mark, never in the same place. Shoving aside the reports covering the dressing table, I searched in vain for a writing implement.

"Malone! A fountain pen and a sheet of foolscap, now!"

I all but snatched the items from his grip when he brought them from the other room as urgency drove me. Clearing a space, I carefully scribed a circle on the page and added the marks from each victim's face in as precise representation as I could manage in both placement and shape. My hand trembled as I completed the last one, coming not quite full circle on the page.

My gaze went from my drawn image to the mantle clock, elegant with filigree and gilded roman numerals.

"It ends with me!"

Eleven… he stopped at eleven.

"One way or the other, aye?"

A peculiar, horrifying sense began to surface.

"You can't stay the hands…"

My finger traced the damage on the top victim's limb.

I could not say what I feared would happen, but I had a feeling it went well beyond murder and mayhem. Unholy, indeed. My battle against the sense of something… *other* looming faltered, then failed.

Dropping the pen, I scrambled from the room, the ticking, or my heartbeat, I couldn't say which… thundering in my ears.

The hour had grown late without my notice, yet I rushed through the sleeping household, unmindful of the noise I made. Drawn to my charge's rooms, I cursed the dimmed corridors lit by the barest glow of gas. My heart pounded and raced until my chest felt battered from within, until all of me felt battered from within. As I ran, my beleaguered vision insisted a greenish mist thickened at the corners of my gaze, like a foul and writhing miasma driving me forward.

As I approached Moreton's chambers I stumbled and fell, tripping on something large and unyielding shrouded in the shadows at my feet. I turned to look, my head spinning as I peered into the gloom. Swallowing a cry, I scrambled back, only just noticing a heavy scent pinching my nostrils, like old copper pennies and sheer terror. I raised my hand to the orderly's torn neck as if I might still find a pulse, only to snatch it back as something viscous dripped from my fingers, belaying any hope of life. I stared at the man's face, puzzled to see no mark such as the ones that sent me rushing here.

Jerking to my feet, I backed away, sense telling me to run. To leave this place and never look back.

Honor — or insanity, more like — had me turn and creep toward the just-cracked door of Moreton's chambers, with no thought but to end this, *"One way or the other..."*

More fool, I.

As the door creaked open, I stared, aghast.

Moreton stood before the cold hearth with his back to me. His head hung forward as he moved from side to side in a languorous sway, surrounded by a nimbus of eldritch light in a room otherwise steeped in darkness. Faint, smoke-like whirls wove about him and the stench of burnt sulfur competed with the metallic tang of fresh-spilt blood.

I must have gasped or made some other sound of which I had not realized, for the man stiffened and stilled his swaying. Slowly, his head rolled toward me, the motion disjointed, like a marionet with tangled strings.

At the sight that met my gaze, all breath arrested, silencing the scream now trapped within my throat. Where before I saw the implication of pulsing, swirling motion beneath Moreton's gauze, I now spied bare flesh, the skin rent and putrid, pushed beyond the orbit of his eye sockets, exposing bone. And from those voids, and every other opening both natural and inflicted, phantasmic tendrils of celadon hue reached and thrashed, eager to break free of their vessel.

Moreton's body twisted around to join his head in facing me, revealing the gauze wrapping his hands had likewise been torn away. I stumbled back at the sight of a poker brandished in his grip, the hook coated with blood and shreds of skin. A rictus twisted his lips until his bloodied teeth glistened at me in a grim display. Though his expression remained fixed and unresponsive the rest of him fair vibrated with energy, coiled, ready to be unleashed.

"Come, Dunaway, let us have done..." Moreton... or... something called out to me, the voice rasping. The tone, the cadence, oddly offset, as if formed by a mouth unfamiliar with the words.

"Have done?"

The eldritch glow in place of Moreton's eyes flared and brightened. "Do not play the fool, sir. The portal is cracked enough to let our light shine through, not enough to cross. This one has proven unequal to the task. You shall shatter the barrier for us."

My gaze skimmed the room looking for anything in reach I could use to defend myself, asking, half as a distraction, "But what of the orderly…?"

"It wasn't his hour."

I stilled in my search, my gaze snapping to the abomination. Me. This *thing* — the lodger within Moreton, be it World Teacher, or something *other* — from a dimension clearly not our own intended *me* to be the twelfth hour. It intended *me* to open this portal giving it free rein of our world.

Like Hell!

As the lodger sprang forward, translucent tendrils reaching for me, I allowed it to latch on as I lunged to the side, grabbing for the electrodes on Pulvermacher's Hydro-Electric Chain. I flipped the toggle and slapped the electrodes on Moreton's head, holding them in place as if the world, my life, and all I held dear depended on it, though I knew what was to come as the current hit.

For an eternity, our bodies jerked and thrashed in fading force, until with a final gasp Moreton's fell motionless. And still I held steady, though my own heart stuttered and my vision dimmed. I waited for the final whisp of green to fade from the pits of Moreton's eyes. Only then did I slap the toggle off, loosen my grip, and let the scion… the first son and heir of the Moreton family fall.

For an instant brief enough that my kymograph could have scarce captured it, I felt a sense of triumph, mingled with relief. And then, as if a stylus drew across Moreton's flesh, a crooked X and two I's etched the center of his forehead and the broken clock chimed the twelfth hour.

It ends with me…

My vision hazed in increasing shades of celadon hue, and the true horror of my failure took hold. First son and heir Moreton may have been, but, as myself, of the twelfth generation.

I stumbled back, but no distance would have been enough to save me. From the broken body rose an entity beyond my ability to describe. Solid and unearthly, lashing and thrashing tendrils wrapping around me, drawing me in. The trifold pulsing rhythm drowned out my screams as I knew everything and nothing and then no more.

Lighthouse at the Edge of Time

Teel James Glenn

"Ghost ships, you say?" I asked my companion in the passenger section of the steam-powered paddle wheel ferry. I had an odd sensation at that moment, as if I had said it before, but shook it off and raised my voice because the rough seas outside roared with a banshee wail of wind. We were steaming toward Old Grimsby settlement on the Isle of Tresco in the Scilly Islands, some twenty-four nautical miles off the Cornish coast.

"Aye, ser," said the bearded old salt who had confided his experience to me. "Last month it was, ships disappearing. Two I knows of fer sure. A packet and a ferry." I could scarce make out what he said, between the clay pipe clenched precariously in his mouth and the wheezing and hissing of the steam-powered limb that had replaced his right leg. "And worse—reappearing in a strange fog but not quite—phantom ships seem to sail along the shoreline with the screams of those on shipboard."

Most would take his story as a tall sea tale, but I had come to appreciate such things as more omens than imaginings. It might be the year of Our Lord Eighteen Hundred and Ninety-Four, but superstitions of ages gone lived long. My name is Jack Stone, Captain of the Horseguard, and currently seconded to Dr. Augustus Argent. The Doctor is Minister Without Portfolio for the Crown, charged with investigating occult affairs. Phantom ships were exactly the sort of thing to interest him. And with the odd occurrences happening recently in other corners of the Empire, it behooved me to look into his tale.

"You've seen these things yourself?" I asked the codger.

"Aye, ser," he said. "There were thirty souls on that ferry and nay a single one of them's been heard from again."

I found this revelation most disturbing. I knew, of course, of the history of wreckers along the Cornish coast, and the wild waters legitimately claimed their share of souls, so ships disappearing was not an unknown occurrence. Still…

"Has the Admiralty not investigated?" I asked.

The old fellow gave a snorting laugh.

"Them swabs could nay find their own stern without help," he said. "They dismissed it all. said I was over my rum ration, and claimed it was bottle-born bilge." He all but chewed through his pipe. Setting his jaw, he seemed to decide he'd talked his quota for the trip and took to staring out the porthole to the churning sea.

It was just as well. I was set for Old Grimsby on a somber mission, escorting the remains of an old regimental chum to his birthplace in Dolphin Town on the island, and it was best I kept my mind on it. We had served together in Afghanistan, and on his deathbed, he asked me to return him home.

We came in sight of the long-disused, 16th-century blockhouse at the southern end of the harbor. As we pulled into the quay, we beheld a crowd from Old Grimsby, locals awaiting the weekly ferry for supplies and news from the outside world. There was a dirigible station on the island, but with the weather's uncertainties, they only flew for a few months of the year to monitor the seas to the west.

"Captain Stone?" A thin, grey-haired gentleman met me at the dock. "I am Vicar Whytte of Saint Nicholas parish." He extended a bony hand to shake mine, his grip surprisingly firm.

"What gave me away, sir?"

"If not that you are the only unfamiliar face," he said with a smile, "your military bearing, even in civilian attire, betrays you."

"Did you bring a wagon for Tommy's remains?" I asked.

"Aye," he answered, indicating a steam cart with a mechanical driverbot at the end of the pier. We walked to the cart while several of the stevedores loaded the coffin. "Tommy, like all of them, came home eventually," he said with a little sadness. "Though most wait too long like he did."

We rode along a coastal path to the graveyard outside his tiny church, sitting in reverent silence while the clanking of the wheels and the hiss of escaping steam filled the space.

I cast my eyes out at the choppy seas. I was thinking about what the old mariner said, so when I saw the vague shape on the horizon, at first, I thought it a daydream.

A four-master seemed to be moving in and out of a fog several miles out to sea, but not in any way I had ever seen before, in that the craft wavered — now solid, now translucent, all with a strange iridescent glow surrounding it.

I blinked and shook my head. The ship was of an older type indeed; I doubt its like had seen service since the Armada sailed. *This is wrong,* I thought, but even as I thought it, the image of the ship was gone, and the horizon was bare.

I most certainly need to contact Dr. Argent.

My whole being felt uneasy for the rest of the trip and kept me much on edge.

The ceremony to send Tommy on his way was a somber, quiet thing, with only the vicar and two locals there to say their goodbyes. Afterward, one of the attendees, a bearded salt of a man, approached me, introducing himself as a childhood friend of Tommy's who had stayed behind on the island as a fisherman.

"Jeremy Karn," he said, holding out a hand to me, "and you're Captain Stone." His grip was firm, and his palm calloused from a life of hard work. "Tommy described you to a T in his letters."

"Guilty as charged, sir."

"Jeremy, please." He walked with me back toward the cart the vicar had brought. "You're heading back with the ferry when it leaves?"

"Yes," I said. "But I heard that is not for some hours."

"Aye," Karn said. "It waits for the tide. I'd be glad to stand you a pint or two while you wait."

"That sounds like just the thing."

The vicar let us take the cart, telling us that the steamboat driver would return it to him when we were done.

The fisherman was an amiable companion, and on the way to the town pub in Old Grimsby, we traded stories about Tommy and our lives in general. I could not tell him of my missions with Dr. Argent, of course, but he was an easy, uncomplicated man to talk with.

By his third pint at the pub, Karn started telling me sea tales about the island, and I asked him if he had any encounters with phantom ships.

"Aye, true it be," he said, "out of the fog it came, a full-rigged vessel, it was, but old design, and well… not so substantial. I know, I know, sounds like bunkum, but I seen it. All misty and waving it were."

I felt the same chill I'd had seeing that phantom ship on the way to the funeral. It was the sort of feeling I often had when encountering the extra-normal under Dr. Argent's tutelage.

"I don't doubt your word," I said. "Just where did you see this ship?"

"Out by Wolf Rock it was," he said. "There's a fishing ground not far off that lighthouse."

"Have you seen this ship again?"

"Aye," the fisherman said. "Two more times in the last month, always in the morning mist just as the sun tops the horizon." He finished his pint and looked up at the clock over the mantle. "Best be heading to the ferry, Jack, if you don't want to be marooned here a week."

I made a decision then. "Will you take me to where you saw this phantom?"

"What?"

"I'll charter your boat to take me there," I said. I smiled at his look of incredulity, so added, "I work for a government department, and they'll foot the bill at a fair rate. The Admiralty will want a report on that phantom."

Karn looked at me, apparently trying to decide if I was mad or in my cups, but after a long moment nodded. "Well, since I can't take you out till morning, we've got time for a few more pints."

I laughed. "Well, that sounds good to this Edinburgh lad. And from now on, The Crown will be buying."

I took a room upstairs from the pub and retired after a full meal and several more pints, ready to be up before dawn. There was a Marconi set at the harbormaster's quarters, and I was able to use my credentials to send a coded transmission via relay to Dr. Argent in London.

I found myself with a premonition that this side trip was important. There had been a number of events across the Empire, disappearances, odd weather occurrences, and reports of strange lights in the sky. This could just be connected, so I had to be alert.

Then it was early to bed for me, as the local grog was good enough to put this Scotsman in need of sleep.

We were up and off during the false dawn, sailing Jeremy's little sloop into the gathered mist and heading east toward Wolf Rock Lighthouse. My companion was a solo sailor, eschewing a navigational robot or star guider, and was grateful for the company and, to be truthful, for the Crown fee I promised him.

We had a good wind, and he'd brought a wineskin and a basket of food, so we had our breakfast as we sailed, both none the worse for our drinking the night before. I relaxed and enjoyed the open sea as the morning mist burnt off. All in all, we had a pleasant trip.

"It be in these waters I seen it both times," Karn said a few hours into our trip. "We've just entered the fishing grounds. Wolf Rock is just over the horizon."

The stone spire of the lighthouse just peeked above the rim of the sea, looking lone and forlorn in the vast, empty ocean. Yet there was some sense working on my mind that I felt oddly ill at ease.

I looked at the ocean differently now, studying it as if it were a predatory beast. It was then I noticed that while the surface lay calm, there was a change in the color. When I remarked on it to Karn, he just nodded.

"Aye," he said. "Been that way for a few weeks, a strange color it be — happened around the time I first saw the — there!"

His exclamation drew my attention to a low bank of fog crawling across the distant surface of the sea and coming our way. More to the point, I beheld a shape in that fog, indistinct and wavering in the bilious, green mist.

"There it be!" Karn whispered, awed as I was by the sight. "Are we looking at the Flying Dutchman?"

It was a large ship, an old square-rigged three-master. Indeed, it looked to be a ghostly apparition of another age, for it was almost transparent, wavering in and out of substantiality like a desert heat mirage.

"God's garters," I gasped, "it's coming straight for us!"

"But that's impossible," Karn said. "It's moving directly against the wind."

Impossible or not, it traveled at a good clip against the wind, straight at us — I saw distinct figures moving on its deck, scurrying up the sheets and generally performing the duties of swabbies of times past.

"It's going to ram us!" Karn yelled as he swung the boom to tack, leaning hard into the tiller to move us out of the phantom's path. His efforts were to no avail; all it did was move us so that the phantom bow raced at our midship, broadside.

I was about to leap overboard to escape when the square rig plowed into us — and went through! It was as insubstantial as a puff of smoke, but as the massive vessel passed through our boat, I felt a bone-chilling cold pass through me.

There was a strange electric charge, one that carried aetheric emanations such as I had felt before. I went lightheaded so that I fell against the sail boom. I saw that Karn also fell over, gripping the gunwales of the sloop.

In a few moments, the phantom moved beyond us, the luminous mist moving with it, and then, as I watched, it seemed to evaporate. Suddenly, we were alone on the surface of the ocean.

"Saint's alive!" Karn gasped. I made my way to him, for he was still shaking, though whether from fear or the paranormal chill, I could not say. It was not my first encounter with things outside the norm, and while I was upset, he seemed more than unsteady.

"Easy, man," I said. I took the tiller from him as he cowered on the deck.

"I swear I've never seen anything like that," he managed. He was pale and wild eyed, not steady on his feet at all.

"Take it easy, Jeremy. Break out the 'emergency' rum I know you fellows always have and relax."

He barely managed to crawl to a locker, pull out a bottle, and take a healthy swig, before muttering, "Make for the lighthouse. It's an easy channel. I feel the need to be on solid ground."

Having no desire to repeat our encounter with the phantom craft, I turned our boat toward the lighthouse, as instructed.

Wolf Rock thrust up directly out of the ocean in seeming defiance of the waves pounding around it, the lighthouse itself a marvel of human versus nature's extremes. This third iteration of the structure rose forty-one meters above the ocean, a solid bastion built from Cornish granite brought from Penzance and erected over eight years for the challenges of the weather and location.

Its light was a lance of brilliance visible for over twenty nautical miles, cutting through the salt spray day and night. A keeper manned the light, keeping constant vigil on the bare rock of the island.

I shared Karn's sudden need to feel solid ground beneath my feet. And the fisherman looked to need real help, perhaps more than I could tender.

The pier lay just around the point and, as he had indicated, was easy to reach as the ocean bottom dropped away sharply from the rock — which contributed to the violence of the churning waters. I steered the boat up to the stone jetty and pier and managed to tie up alongside. Then I jumped back aboard to get Karn. He lay against the gunwale shivering, his eyes wild and manner distracted. He was a big fellow and dead weight, so it took all I had to hoist him over the side of the boat to the dock without falling.

The lighthouse and a cottage beside it were several hundred yards away, a farther distance than I could carry the fisherman.

"I'll be back for you in a bit, Jeremy," I said as I set him down against a stone outcropping at the foot of the jetty. "Hold on, mate, I won't be long."

He stared up at me with an odd expression, almost as if he could not see me — as if he were looking at some far-off vision. His lips moved, but no sound came out. He was in a bad way.

"Easy, mate," I said, not knowing what else to do. He gestured beyond me out toward the ocean, and I looked, half expecting to see the phantom ship again, but there was nothing there. At least nothing I could see save a darkening sky that foretold a storm coming in.

I had no choice but to leave him and race toward the cottage near the lighthouse to try and get help.

The building was rustic, a single story with a tiled roof and shuttered windows. When I reached it, I found the door locked. I pounded on it.

"Hallo," I shouted, "I need help."

After several fruitless moments with no response, I left the cottage and headed for the lighthouse itself.

At the base of the massive tower, I was about to reach the door when the portal swung open, and a man stepped out.

"Who's this?" he asked. "What are you about?" The man was thin with a high forehead and narrow, birdlike features. He was dressed in an old-style frock coat in a vivid hue of red with a black knit watch cap barely stretched across his balding pate. He waved an augmented left arm at me, the gears grinding, the hiss of the steam-powered limb somehow sinister.

"My apologies, squire," I said, "But there is a sick man on your dock, and we seek aid."

He looked at me with a neutral expression, his eyes regarding me as if he doubted I was really there. He blinked like an owl, pulled out an oversized pocket watch, looked at it, and then up at me again. "Aid?" he asked.

"Yes, he's not in a good way," I said.

He regarded me like a bug under a microscope for a moment, then nodded.

"Let's see this fellow, eh what?" The red-coated man brushed past me and walked back toward the jetty with a peculiar bent-kneed gait that made me think of a sailor who hadn't regained his land legs.

The two of us made it to the dock in no time, but Karn was nowhere to be seen.

"I left him right here," I said. Then I called out, "Jeremy? Where are you, fellow?"

I looked all around, even leaping back on the boat, but of my friend, there was no sign. When I looked out toward the sea, the storm clouds roiled thicker now, a grey mass moving toward us in a solid line, but there was something else, a strange verdant glow coming off the ocean at the horizon.

"I've seen Saint Elmo's fire," I said as I stared at the odd glow, "but nothing like this."

"You really had a fella here?" the lighthouse keeper asked.

"I realize I have been rude. I'm Jack Stone," I said, "my friend is Jeremy Karn—that is his boat."

"Well, where is he?" The red-coated man's voice was shrill, and his tone annoyed.

"I don't know," I said. "He couldn't move when I left him."

Indeed, I was at a loss to think what could have happened to Karn, for the fisherman had been barely conscious when I set him down.

The storm now approached with force, the raindrops almost horizontal and the wind whipping the waves to white-capped hills.

"We'd better get inside," the lighthouse keeper said, raising his voice to be heard above the howl. "It's gonna be a hard blow."

He spoke the truth, for the wind raged strong enough that I had to fight to stay upright. At the same time, the wind was making the rock live up to its name, howling like a pack of wild wolves.

"We can't leave Jeremy out here," I yelled.

"But he ain't out here," he called with a wave of his augmented arm. "You can stay if you want, but I don't have time to waste freezing for a figment of your imagination." With that, he turned and headed back toward the cottage.

I stood for a moment, unable to bear the idea of leaving Karn to whatever fate had befallen him, but the violence of the wind forced me to reconsider. The sky was as dark as night, and visibility was rapidly dropping. I realized I would have no chance of finding the fisherman in the gale as it was. I fought the wind all the way to the cottage, falling twice, but reached the door not far behind the keeper.

Once inside, the fellow closed and barred the door behind us. The cottage was rustic with a roaring fire going in the hearth, but few other conveniences save that there were a dozen clocks of different types all around the room.

My host doffed his frock coat, and I could see the full extent of the mechanical arm; it replaced his entire limb. He adjusted the gears, then went to the hearth to warm himself, pausing to also adjust one of the clocks.

Being soaked to the skin as well, I removed my jacket and joined him.

"Dyowl," he said when I crouched down by the fire.

"Say again, sir?"

"Dyowl Hobbson," he said. "That's my name."

"Pleased to meet you, Mister Hobbson." I warmed my hands for a moment, then rose. "I'm sorry to impose further, but do you have a mackinaw I can borrow? I really must head back out to look for Jeremy."

Outside, the wind still howled but seemed, from the sound, to be letting up.

"Ye can't go far in that," Hobbson said. "Nothing to do till it passes. In time, all things do. So far, anyway."

"But Jeremy can't—"

"You'll not find him out there, fella," the keeper said. "But you're welcome to my mack over there. I gotta get back to the lighthouse. I just came out for this—" He held up a silver and brass device with clockwork gears the size of a hen but brightly colored.

The keeper went to the back door of the building, donned a cloak, and then, with not even a backward glance, went out.

I put on the offered rain gear, including a hat, and went out the front door into the maelstrom in search of my friend.

The nature of the storm had indeed changed in the few minutes I had been in the cottage. It still rained, but the wind had died to almost nothing, making me recall what I knew of hurricanes, massive storms with a calm center.

Could this be such a storm? The sky had lightened but still had that odd green glow behind the clouds.

"Jeremy!" I yelled. I raced toward the jetty to where I'd left the fisherman, initially thinking to start a search with that at the center of a pattern.

Imagine my shock when I reached the foot of the jetty, and Karn sat exactly where I'd left him! He was unmoving, propped up against the low stone wall of the jetty, but otherwise, exactly as I had last seen him.

I started to run toward the man, calling his name, but before I was twenty yards away, he began to glow a strange green and waver like a mirage, his form blurring at the edges. Then, to my shock, he simply blinked out of existence and was gone.

I skidded to a halt. "Jeremy?" I yelled. When I reached the spot where he had been, I felt that same odd tingling as when the phantom ship had passed through our boat, becoming disoriented, spots appearing before my eyes, and it was a few moments before I could stabilize myself. When I did, there was no sign of my friend. I looked around, frantic to find him or some other trace, but there was nothing.

I looked back toward the lighthouse, shocked again to see that the tower was bathed in the same eerie glow that had shrouded the phantom ship and Karn.

The beacon atop the tower alternated a white lance of light and a red, but the overall glow of the building was as if it was backlit by the fires of hell.

The whipping rain gained force again, the storm's fury growing once more. I knew now that I indeed dealt with something of Dr. Argent's realm, like the strange weather events across the empire, this was something beyond the normal.

I fought the wind and raced to the lighthouse. If I was to find Jeremy, I had to know what was actually going on.

I reached the building just as the fury of the storm exploded again. A slash of blinding white light cast my shadow on the lighthouse tower ahead of me, so I had the sensation of fleeing into my own umbra.

Finding the door unlocked, I yanked it open and raced in, grateful to be out of the wind, but I stopped short, shocked by what I saw inside.

A spiral staircase wound around the wall of the tower. The central space, left open almost all the way up, over forty meters, held the strangest mechanism I had ever seen, filling the space.

In the center hung a long, bronze pendulum enveloped in an odd green shine. All around it ran a dazzling array of gears and clear tubes through which multicolored liquids flowed and bubbled. It cast bizarre luminous patterns across the walls of the vertical space creating a dizzying, hallucinogenic display.

More than just the light show, a strange humming emitted from the odd mechanism, a deep, vibrating sound that seemed to press against my diaphragm in a way that taxed my breathing.

I yelled, "Hobbson!" but the mechanism before me dwarfed my booming voice. "What is going on?"

I did not wait for an answer. Racing to the spiral steps, I sprinted up, careful not to look down, for while there was a handrail, the gaping maw of the central shaft was a frightening thing, made more so by the lightshow and the hypnotic hum of the infernal device.

I reached the apex of the stairs and was confronted with an ornately carved wooden door that looked completely out of place in that tower. It looked more like something one would expect to see on some Middle Eastern tomb.

"Hobbson!" I yelled. I tried the knob and found it to be locked. "Hobbson!" I repeated and pounded on the door with both fists. "Let me in!"

For long moments, only the humming of the strange device throbbed against my eardrums. Then came the sound of a bolt being thrown, and the door flew inward.

"I cannot be annoyed now," the lighthouse keeper sneered at me. His eyes were wide, his expression angry. "I am close now, finally, close."

"What madness is this?"

"Madness?" he shrieked. He gave a sweeping gesture at the space behind him. The beacon was there but with strange prismatic mirrors angled to reflect the rays from the mechanism below into the tower's light. That newly refocused beacon now flashed out as a strange, greenish glow.

Beyond, I could see the horizon of the sea, and what I beheld took my breath away. There were ships there, at least three, but from distinctly different time periods: sail and steam powered, a ferry, a man'o'war, and the square rig I had seen before. I saw the ferry, much like the one I'd taken to Old Grimsby, solid and real, begin to waver out of solidity to become like the other phantom shapes, etched in green.

"What devilish thing is this?" I accused.

He laughed like a damned soul. "Not devilish," he proclaimed, "godlike! I have cracked the code and found the secret. Time is now my toy."

The enormity of what he said struck me like a physical blow. From the wide windows, I could see all of Wolf Rock set out below us, and on the jetty, I could see Jeremy Karn again, glowing green and wavering in and out of existence.

"Stop this," I said. "You have no idea what terror you are unleashing. The Aether is a power beyond control. You can't possibly foresee the repercussions."

"I *can* control it, only I!" he cackled. "I can gather the threads of the cosmos and reweave them to my liking. I will prove to the world my greatness! Damn them all."

"No," I said. "Those forces are beyond anyone to control, you fool. Others have tried and paid the ultimate price. You have upset the very balance of reality, not only here but across the Empire." Before he could argue further, I moved to lunge toward him, but abruptly, he had a revolver in his hand.

"I cannot be stopped—not now, I am so close." He tried to raise the gun to aim at me, but I moved with the speed of desperation, throwing myself at him. I got my hand on the cylinder so he could not fire.

"I must complete my work," Hobbson screamed. Though thin, he had the strength of madness, and it took all my power to keep the barrel pointed away from me.

"You have to stop this," I yelled, "you are destroying lives."

He made inarticulate snarling sounds, his teeth grinding, his eyes bulging.

Outside, the ships moved on the waves, all more solid now, as if each time period were giving up their prisoner ships to this, our own time. Karn, below, was fully here and now again. He rose on shaky legs to stare around him in confusion.

"This… must… stop!" I screamed with my own mad strength. With a final surge of desperation, I threw Hobbson back the way I had come, through the open doorway and out, over the stair railing and into the infernal device.

The mad keeper screamed a long, undulating cry of pain that ended abruptly when he smashed into one of the clear, liquid-filled tubes, bursting it to drench him. His flesh sizzled where the liquid touched him even as he continued to fall, bouncing off the various mechanisms like a game ball, ricocheting back and forth until he thudded onto the tower's stone floor.

The kaleidoscope of lights now flared into a blinding, green fire, and I staggered back into the prisms in the light room. As I fell into them the crystals shattered, and I swirled into a rainbow of madness, reaching out, grasping for any anchor.

Finding only blackness…

I fell into a seemingly infinite, swirling maelstrom of light, and from that whirling reality, I could see across a limitless space. I saw the ships again, but somehow could also see the individuals on them, all screaming in agony. I also saw dozens of other ships on other seas than the Atlantic. All were wavering in and out of tangible reality.

I felt a force then, clawing at the edges of my mind, a remorseless, impersonal force, bending reality into shapes I could not comprehend. And somehow, I knew it was a force in direct opposition to the thing we called life.

I screamed a soundless cry of terror then, lashing out against this force, and my hand made contact with some of the crystal prisms. My knuckles smashed into them and then everything exploded into a thunderburst of color.

"Ghost ships, you say?" I found myself asking the old sailor in front of me. I sat in the passenger section of the paddle wheel steam ferry where it had all begun. I stopped speaking and looked around me in confusion.

"Aye, ser," the old sailor said. Then he looked at my odd expression. "Be ye alright, lad?"

I found myself breathing hard, looking around with a vague feeling of dread. Then I looked down into my hand and saw that I had a faceted prism of crystal in my hand.

"Time," I said aloud with the beginning of understanding. "Yes, time. Fluid."

"You need to sit down, fella," the one-legged sailor said. "You need get yer bearings."

"Yes," I said, "bearings. I'll get my bearings sure enough."

I knew then that I would put Tommy to rest as I had before and meet Jeremy Karn and Hobbson. But now, now, perhaps not the way I had. But could I change what had happened? Did I have any chance against such eldritch forces?

Only time would tell.

Accelerando

James Chambers

I am the last. I will tell the audient void.

The surrounding gloom opens its multitude of eyes to watch, tilts its shadowed ears to hear. Unseen pipers fill the air with faint melodies that follow no earthly scale, while maddened, many-armed drummers rattle and tap the tempo from a place beyond space and time… time… time… the time… each note a second, each bar a minute, each movement an hour, a day, a month, a year, a millennium, an epoch, counting down the dreamer's slumber to the awakening of the nuclear chaos at the center of the universe. Do those around me hear the music's pitch and timbre and tempo?

Flutes and pipes whistle, shriek, and sob a primordial lullaby to the rhythm of countless drummers and demon dancers tapping their hideous feet, clapping the time with their monstrous hands. These invisible things I have heard, oh, how I have heard them filling my skull, resonating in my brain, trapped inside me since the day I walked out of the city, alone, the last, the last, the last…

I am the last. I will tell the audient void.

Do they yet hear the music? Do they see beyond the darkness-draped stage to the dancing abominations it conceals? I hope to spare this city the fate of my own. Around me, people shuffle and shift in their seats. They whisper and point, laugh, cough, and sigh with anticipation, innocents gathered before an altar of slaughter not for the slaying of their bodies, but of their minds and souls, of that integral component of men and women that when lost shows only in their eyes… eyes emptied of humanity, eyes that have glimpsed other worlds where reality lays bare in all its grotesque and vast excesses, like the eyes of the people of my lost city.

Ah, a skip in the rhythm! The tempo rises.

The shrillest of the demoniac flutes wails. It pierces me, dizzies me, sickens me.

A signal from beyond this world that the show is about to begin.

I would swear myself to my mission upon the memories of those most dear to me if I only could remember them. Had I a wife in the old city? Children? Siblings? Parents, surely, as all humans do, but their faces, names, tempers live nowhere in my mind, erased by the same sights and expositions about to unfold in this darkened theater. I would warn these watchers who fill the air around me with the earthy scents of their breath and sweat. I would chase them to the street, but none would believe me.

Far better to rob the pharaoh of his uraeus, extinguish the flame from his brow, and sever the head of chaos's wandering dream here where it crawls upon the earth.

I slide my hand into my coat pocket and grip my revolver, seeking reassurance in the cold solidity of its iron and the potentiality in its ammunition. Hope springs from the tiny explosions they contain.

Ensconced gaslights flickered then dimmed before a crackling streak of electricity shot from the stage to the balcony of the Old Pharoah's Odeon, drawing gasps and muted shrieks as it sizzled over the audience's heads. Morris Garvey's hair stood on end. Betsy Carpenter clutched his arm and pressed herself against him for reassurance. The pair sat third-row, center, with a clear view of the stage, which descended into impenetrable blackness in the aftermath of the blast. As their eyes recovered from the shock of brilliance, a troublesome hum filled the theater — a deep, pulsating *thrum* that rattled Morris's nerves and made his teeth vibrate.

A towering figure emerged from the stage dark as if from blackness itself. He stood on the edge of a spotlight beam, his features hidden in shadows.

"Ladies and Gentlemen, welcome!" The man's accented voice spoke of forgotten, exotic lands and ancient sensibilities. "My name is Nyarlathotep. I have come to New Alexandria to spread wisdom recovered from the blackness of twenty-seven centuries, to share messages from voices beyond this world, and to open your minds to cosmic vistas outside human experience. I applaud your curiosity and your *courage*. The secrets I shall reveal this evening may shake the very foundations of your beliefs. The portents and prophesies I display may change you forever. Those gathered here tonight shall witness wonders beyond your most fevered imaginings. When you leave you will tell the people of this city, so that they too may come and look upon my miracles. Open your eyes, now, and *see*."

The spotlight blanked out. A resounding *clink*, as of a massive lock falling into place, drummed the air. Center stage, a great glass globe, larger than a cask, ignited with miniature lightning. Streaks and ribbons of white and purple energy stormed within it and shot sparks swimming into the air around it, creating a crackling, amethyst aura. Into this light stepped Nyarlathotep, revealing himself in full.

Near seven-feet tall, gaunt and bony, his complexion olive dark, the sharp geometry of his features reminded Morris of pharaohs in hiero-glyphs and statues he had seen in the great tombs and pyramids of Egypt. A platinum uraeus glittered above his forehead, sweeping back hair black as the night sky. His robes, woven with some special silk and dye, scintillated in the globe's flicker-flick light. The sight of him filled Morris with unwelcome coldness. More than anyone else in the audience, except perhaps Betsy, who held her breath as tightly as she clutched Morris's hand, he understood the mechanisms of electric-ity. The founder of New Alexandria's biggest business, Machinations Sundry, inventor of the steam-powered chimney sweep and many other revolutionary steam-powered devices, Morris did not fall easily under the sway of parlor-tricks and theatrics. He had seen his hometown, New Alexandria, through more than a few crises that had steeled his nerves. Yet he found himself forced to concede the man's showmanship and talent, which placed an icy knot of dread inside him, unnerved by the performer's utter control of the forces he deployed and his mastery of his audience, who sat in total, rapt silence.

Nyarlathotep raised one dark, knobby arm and waved his fingers. Tiny lances of lightning danced from the globe to his blackened fingertips. Nyarlathotep smiled, and in the strange light, his teeth glowed, and currents raced across his long, wrinkled lips. Coruscations filled his eyes with riotous, swirling flashes.

Had the performer mesmerized them all by some secret means?

No, Morris thought.

His head remained clear, and he felt no resistance when he twisted in his seat to glimpse the audience behind him. Men and women in their best evening attire sat at perfect attention, light dancing across their fascinated faces. Perhaps the only one among them distracted, Morris missed Nyarlathotep's next words, and when he righted himself, he faced a stage now exposed and lit by a panoply of sparking, buzzing electrical devices choreographed around a climbing arc device, a Jacob's Ladder, nearly as tall as its master. He worked them like a maestro, gesturing and adjusting dials, flipping switches, as he danced from machine to machine and played them in a visual symphony, a virtuoso of natural forces, light and sparks flashing at his fingertips in perfect time — until a sphere materialized in the air above him.

Morris spied no obvious means to produce the effect. The blank sphere simply hung there as though conjured by the power of Nyarlathotep's machines. Then it widened. Its perimeter rippled with electrical force, while the inner disc paled to a grainy mist contained by the shock-white outer ring, which coruscated around it like a ticking dial. Within the disc appeared a shape, a living thing of hirsute limbs, chitinous joints, and arachnid eyes. Citrine ichor dripped from its mandibles. Then it scurried across the face of the light and vanished.

The best industrial designer at Machinations Sundry, Betsy studied the demonstration with the same analytical eye as Morris, and yet even she whispered in awe, "My God, Morris, what was that awful thing? How is he doing this?" Her short, fast breaths tickled his neck, transmitting her excitement and heightening his own rising anxiety. This surpassed even the marvels of the cinématographe and the kinetograph. Morris had no answer. He only squeezed Betsy's hand tighter and redoubled his exertions to decipher the onstage theatrics.

A landscape appeared in the pale disc, now grown twice the size of a wagon wheel. Stone ruins took focus. They prodded up from desolate ground littered with the ashen remains of plants and trees. Among the stones, which echoed some grand, fallen architecture, hooded figures walked an unseen path on the blasted earth. Nyarlathotep's machines gave them buzzing voices, chanting in ancient tongues. The sky above them cracked apart, illuminating them for a moment in crimson light, enough for Morris to spy the scaled texture of inhuman hands protruding from their robes. The scene vanished, replaced by the vision of a city of wood and paper buildings where a giant, dark bird crossed the sky moments before light flashed then coalesced into a mushroom of violent smoke and flame ravenous to devour the world.

The succeeding visions revealed monstrous, yellow faces peering from grimy, broken tenement windows. The drained and empty-eyed faces of people surrendered to terrifying secrets that liberated them from their humanity. The skyline of a city Morris faintly recognized appeared. Two ruined towers striking upward into the greenish night provided background to columns of people plodding from its streets onto the open land beyond, draped in a greenish, unnatural snow, gathered in great drifts along the edge of a yawning gulf into which the people disappeared, step by step, marching to the beat of unknown drums, the monotonous whine of blasphemous flutes, a rhythm, time, and count beyond human music. The image shifted skyward, soared through the night, beyond Earth itself, toward some dark, pulsing heart of the universe where the music intensified, and black figures danced and frolicked, visible only where they blacked out distant stars, circling, circling around the suggestion of some vast, slumbering, inhuman monstrosity…

Morris clamped his eyes shut and planted his hands over his ears.

Betsy pressed her face to his shoulder.

"Hang on," he said, his jaw tight. "It can't last much longer."

The pair pressed together while gasping, gurgling sounds rose from the audience. A woman moaned. A man sobbed. Someone shrieked, cut off in an instant by unknown means. The electric droning that filled the auditorium reached such a feverish intensity that Morris's ears grew hot from it—

—and in a moment of thunder, it ended.

"False prophet!" a man screamed into the stunning quiet.

A second clap of thunder, now recognizable as a gunshot, followed the declaration.

Then another. Its crack reverberated with the force of a collapsing building.

Screams of fear and shock rose from the audience.

Morris opened his eyes as he pushed Betsy down in her seat for cover.

Two rows behind him a pale man with wild, uncombed hair and deep rings under his eyes, aimed a revolver at the stage and fired a fourth shot. Nyarlathotep jerked as another hole appeared in his robe. Rage twisted his face in a furious grimace. He lashed out with one arm, sending an electrical blast at his attacker, who fired once more before the bolt struck him. The last round hit Nyarlathotep on the chest, punching him backward, and, finally, shattering his conjured illusions. The pale disc vanished. The machines died and darkened. Nyarlathotep toppled backward, a giant plunging into an ocean of night.

The gunman screamed and twitched in place for several seconds before he collapsed.

The houselights flared. Bystanders seized the dropped revolver and pinned the shooter to a seat. In moments, New Alexandria Police Department officers hurried in from the lobby, summoned by theater staff. They urged everyone to remain calm and stay in their seats.

Two men, announcing themselves as doctors, leapt onstage to help Nyarlathotep, but he waved them away, snapping sparks from his fingers to drive them back when they refused, then with a swirl of his now-tattered robe, he vanished.

⚜

"He won't give us his name. All he says is he is the last," Inspector Daniel Matheson said.

"The last what?" Morris said.

"I was hoping you and Ms. Carpenter might shed some light on that given you witnessed this whole rodeo." Matheson tipped his bowler to Betsy. "Much obliged to you, ma'am, for answering my call at this late hour."

"It's no trouble, Inspector." Betsy shuddered. "It's not as if I was going to get any sleep."

"No, I suppose a lot of folks are going to struggle with insomnia tonight."

"How can I help you, Daniel?" Morris said.

"Don't let me down. You never have before when weirdness rears its ugly head, don't start now. Tell me, how'd this Nyarlathotep fellow put on his show? What even was his show? The statements from the audience sound, well, they sound like everyone went to a different barn dance and some left their wits at their last camp. I want to understand what all took place on that stage tonight. I want to know what our would-be assassin is ranting about because all I can rustle out of him is a lot of nonsense."

"Would-be assassin? Then Nyarlathotep survived?" asked Betsy.

"Yup. Shot five times but refused medical attention. He would only jaw with me through the cracked door of his dressing room. Claimed he takes precautions before each performance because his displays affect the mind so profoundly. He wouldn't tell me what they were. Reckon he wears some kind of leather or silk anti-ballistic vest. You'd never catch me relying on one, but some folks do."

"A plausible theory, but I fear that's not the answer, Dan."

"Why not, Morris?"

"I can explain confidently about half of what we witnessed in that theater. I'm familiar with the means and mechanisms of electricity. What I can't account for are the sensory effects of Nyarlathotep's demonstrations. I can't explain how he projected such stunning, horrible visions into the air, seemingly onto a disc of controlled electricity—or what those scenes mean. It was like looking through a hole in the world at other worlds that don't yet exist, or maybe existed a long time ago, or perhaps will never exist. Betsy and I looked away before the sensations could overwhelm us. Others watched everything until the gunshots interrupted. Their lack of our knowledge of the mechanical aspects of the performance made them more susceptible to its effects."

"Can you two give me a statement that makes some sense?"

"We'll do our best, but first, perhaps, I should talk with the gunman."

Matheson led Morris into the depths of New Alexandria Police Department headquarters, to a row of holding cells, empty except for one, where the haggard gunman sat on a bare cot. He flashed Morris an expression of sullen contempt. Ground-in stains spotted his thread-bare suit. His salt-and-pepper hair stuck out in rough tangles rising from patches matted to his scalp.

Morris introduced himself. "I'd like to help you," he said, but the man ignored him. "Do you know who I am?"

The man only snorted.

"All right, then, what's your name?" Morris asked.

The man sniffled and dragged the back of his hand across his runny nose.

"Tell me why you tried to kill Nyarlathotep."

At this, the man jolted upright. All color drained from his face. Shock and anguish widened his eyes. "Try, you say? *Try?* Then I failed? And he still lives?"

"Yes. Apparently unharmed too."

"Oh, no, no, no," the man said. He rocked himself and shook his head. "I am the last. I will tell the audient void. I am the last. I am the last. I must be the last."

"The last what?" Morris said.

The man ceased speaking, then lifted his head to meet Morris's gaze. "The last of the great, old, terrible city of unnumbered crimes. The last to leave its weed-cracked alleys and ruined towers. The last to speak to the audient void. I am the one left behind to expose the true message of the dark messenger."

"The terrible old city," Morris said, low-voiced, apprehensive.

"You know it?" asked Matheson.

"Maybe," said Morris.

He spoke the name of a port city to the north, long derelict and shunned, a place he knew by reputation, though several times his travels had brought him near enough to view its corrupted skyline and the jagged steeples and broken towers that defined it. At the city's name, the man leapt from his cot, thrust his arms through the space between his cell bars, and grasped Morris by the coat, yanking him against the iron cell door with extraordinary strength.

"Don't say it! For the love of all that is human, *don't*! I can't bear to hear it!" he cried.

Matheson thrust his nightstick into the man's belly, knocking the wind out of him and breaking his grip on Morris. "Back off, now, partner. Stay back if you know what's good for you."

"I am the last," the man whimpered. "I will tell the audient void — but, for pity's sake, why won't they *listen*?" He fell to his cot, curled into a ball, and wept.

Morris met Matheson's befuddled stare.

"We'd best talk a bit, Dan," he said. "This could be serious."

"You know I'm not superstitious, but even I don't like to say the name of that place," Morris sat in a chair facing Matheson's desk. Betsy sat in its twin. Matheson occupied a rolling, leather high-backed chair opposite them behind his desk. "If someone has brought what happened there to New Alexandria, we may have little time to avert catastrophe."

"What in tarnation happened there? A plague?" Matheson said.

"That's one theory," Morris said, "Most investigators favor mass delusion. The place bore a foul reputation for years. A political machine built on extortion and intimidation rotted the civil government from within. Murder investigations routinely ran cold within hours. Compromises in construction of the natural gas system caused leaks that affected people's mental faculties then culminated in a subterranean fire that still burns today for all anyone knows, filling the metropolis with an unhealthy and unseasonable miasma of heat. People stopped moving there. Those who visited on business made sure to leave before sunset, driven out by screams that resounded through the streets beginning at twilight and continuing until dawn. People stopped leaving too—as if some force bound them to the place. Until one early winter night some years ago when every last citizen vanished, apparently having marched into the sea. No one knows for certain because no bodies ever surfaced or washed ashore, but that's the theory that best fits the facts. The times I passed the place by rail or coach, the sight of it filled me with such antipathy and dread, like gazing at one's own corpse, that I slept poorly for weeks and still wake from the occasional nightmare of it."

"That's one doozy of a yarn," Matheson said.

"Morris," Betsy said, "what if this man only believes he came from this city?"

"I'd like to think that if not for rumors of the mysterious Egyptian wizard who set up shop there and gave dazzling performances of electricity and instruments of glass and steel in the weeks before the people disappeared."

"You mean Nyarlathotep," Matheson said.

"I'm not sure. I never knew his name before tonight." Morris rubbed his forehead and sighed. "His show has been selling out the Old Pharoah's Odeon every night for two weeks now. If a mass delusion claimed the people of that abandoned city and Nyarlathotep had a hand in spreading it, how many people must he contaminate with his ideas and illusions before the good people of New Alexandria reach their tipping point into madness? The clock, as they say, may very well be ticking."

Matheson stood behind his desk. "I reckon, then, we ought to pay a visit to this electric wizard."

⁕

The Old Pharoah's Odeon sat closed and dark, not surprising for the late hour, but Inspector Matheson refused to let it deter him. Locating a door with a lock in desperate need of repair, he jimmied it and let them in via a backstage entrance. Silence filled the air. Their soft footsteps echoed.

"Is anyone here? This is Inspector Daniel Matheson of the New Alexandria Police," Matheson called out. "Hello?"

No one answered. The three exchanged glances then spread out to look around. Betsy slid through an opening in the curtains onto the stage. "Morris, come here," she called.

They gathered by the tall climbing arc device, where Betsy crouched, pointing to the wires that ran from the base of the mechanism. They snaked out perhaps eighteen inches from the steel foot and lay loose on the boards, their frayed copper windings licking out from crumbling insulation.

"It's not the only one," she said.

Rising and walking to several other devices, she indicated similar wires that connected to nothing. She removed a plate from the base of a spinning disk that, during the show, had created a pinwheel of brilliant sparks, and revealed an empty machine box.

"I don't get it," Matheson said.

"There's no mechanism," said Morris.

"I see that," Matheson said. "I thought electricity required a power source. A battery or a generator. Even if these were connected to one, where are the moving parts?"

"I don't get it either, Inspector. Betsy and I saw these devices in full operation only a few hours ago, sparking, whirring, humming with undeniable energy."

"Props," Betsy said. "They're only props. He did the tricks another way. With lights and mirrors or lantern projections. Sleight of hand on a grand scale."

Morris shook his head. "What we saw and heard went far beyond that, Betsy." She frowned and lowered her eyes. Morris gripped her shoulder, reassuring her. "Don't take it so hard. I can't explain it either. Nyarlathotep is a genuine wizard of some kind, whether its electricity or stagecraft."

"Hush, there, you hear that?" Matheson said.

They held their breath and listened. A whisper of flutes haunted the stage. Matheson raised one finger to his lips, then crept backstage with all the stealth his stocky frame allowed, passed the ropes and levers that controlled the curtain riggings, and tracked down a narrow, lopsided corridor The fluting grew louder with every step. Shriller, too. It drilled Morris's ears with the persistence of uncontrolled tinnitus.

Betsy grimaced and pressed the heels of her hands to her ears.

"That music is sickening," she said.

They came to the doors of two dressing rooms, one bore a star in faded gold paint.

Sweat beaded Matheson's brow as he knocked on it, and Morris knew the music put it there. It made his guts churn the way the deep, penetrating hum of certain massive machinery sometimes roiled his innards. At the first crack of Matheson's knuckles, the music ceased. The door, ajar, creaked inward on its own—

—then Betsy screamed.

A coruscating electric light filled Morris's vision. It flowed out from the dressing room like liquid. Every hair on his body rose to flagpole attention. His mouth filled with a coppery taste and turned dry as sandpaper. The floor beneath his feet seemed to soften, or maybe his legs went rubbery, he couldn't tell, but the world spiraled and rippled in disorienting waves. His awareness seemed to part from his body as if he rose toward the ceiling and looked down on himself; on Betsy, who dropped and placed her head on the floor, arms clutched over it as if willing herself to turn to stone against the overwhelming sound and light; on Matheson, face pale as fresh paper, one hand firm against the wall to brace him, the other clutching his bowler to his head, his eyes clamped shut. How long this lasted, Morris couldn't measure. Time stretched then lost its elasticity then retracted then hastened, slowed, hastened, and ticked, ticked, ticked, measured in the tempo of the ghastly music of flutes and drums resurgent from within a dressing room far too small to contain the infinite crowd of musicians required to raise such cacophony. Morris's body pulsed to the music's time. His heart beat in sync with it, and his awareness snapped back into his physical form as if retracted by a coil. The wooden walls and floors vanished, becoming an abyss with no boundary through which he plummeted toward a dense and secret core, where the music originated, following the metronome pump of an infinite beating heart—the heart of a thing beyond his power to conceptualize or identify, a thing bathed in sound, soothed and calmed by the noxious composition.

The dressing room door slammed shut.

Reality crashed back into place, leaving Morris short of breath. Matheson's arm folded, and he toppled against the wall to keep his balance. Betsy cowered on the floor. Nyarlathotep stood in front of the door, towering, dark-skinned, slender, draped in a black robe of no material Morris knew.

He said, "You don't belong here. The theater is closed."

Flustered, Matheson gasped several times and waved a hand as he regained his composure.

"Now you hold on there a second, fella," he said. "We're here on official business. You're part of an active investigation, and I want some answers."

Morris knelt beside Betsy then helped her to her feet. He expected the worst when he looked upon her face, shock, terror, or despair, but instead he found it filled with fury and determination. She regarded Nyarlathotep with dreadful anger.

"Now is not the time, Inspector," the tall man said. "Come back in the morning."

He took two steps forward, his stride forcing them all to retreat halfway down the corridor. His pace quickened as he drove them back the way they'd come, directed them toward the backstage door, all of them too disoriented and weakened to protest, until he opened the door and, with a sweeping gesture that sent his robe swirling from his arms, ushered them out. Morris spied the delicate flicker of electrical sparks in the cloth before the door slammed shut. The lock mechanism sizzled and glowed, and when Matheson tried to open it again, he found it fused and immovable.

"What the hell just happened?" Matheson said. "Tell me, Morris, please, tell me what the hell was that?"

Morris met the inspector's eyes, then Betsy's still full of rage.

"I'm afraid I can't, but... maybe our nameless friend in a holding cell can."

⋇⋇⋇

"Help me kill him, and I'll tell you all I know," Nameless said.

Matheson laughed. "Out of the question, you maniac."

Nameless retreated from the bars of his cell and settled on his bunk. "Then your city will fall to his influence like mine did. It's only a matter of time."

"What happened in your city?" Morris asked. "I've heard rumors and speculation, but what are the facts? Can you tell us that much?"

"I am the last. I will tell the audient void," Nameless said. A tense quiet followed, then he stood again and pointed at Betsy. "He almost took it away from you. I can see it in your eyes. He almost got yours, but you resisted. You felt it, though, didn't you? The loss it would mean. The void it would leave in you."

"What's he yakking about?" Matheson said.

"I can't explain it," Betsy said, "but it's true. I sensed a part of me being drawn out like sawdust into a vacuum. I knew if it left me, I would never be the same again. I don't know what it means or how it could happen, but I experienced it."

"Like your humanity being yanked out of your body?" Morris said.

"Yes."

"You both felt that back at the theater? I just felt sick and sweaty like I'd eaten too many chili peppers," Matheson said. "How d'you reckon that?"

"Isn't it obvious?" Nameless said. "He focused his efforts on those who pose the greatest threat to him as well as those who offer him the most to gain. Imagine, two of the city's best and brightest subjugated to him, spreading his message to others. He started like that in my city, with invitation-only previews of his show for people in authority, people with social influence. Once he won them over, others all but offered themselves up to him. It was the fashionable thing to do, after all, see the great show, how shocking could it be? The people in my city had seen it all, hadn't they? It came easy to him there. It was already a corrupt and dehumanized place."

"Mumbo-jumbo aside, what the hell does he want out of all this?" Matheson said. "Sold out shows? Command performances for royalty? What makes this guy more than PT Barnum with crazy fireworks and bad music?"

"PT Barnum is human," Nameless said.

The words hung in the air, leaden and startling even though Morris had already reached the same conclusion. Some things had to reveal themselves on their own to be fully accepted, though, and so he'd waited for the discussion to lead there naturally. Matheson turned to him with a look that said: *Can you believe this guy? Help me out here with this insanity.* But Morris's expression only confirmed the man's words. Deflated, Matheson pushed his bowler back on his head and rubbed his scalp.

"He took five rounds and walked away unharmed," Morris said.

"He produced that lightning show without any working machines," Betsy said.

"Well, then." Matheson ground his teeth as he thought. He pulled a keyring from his pocket and unlocked the holding cell. "I guess it wouldn't be murder if we send an inhuman varmint to Boot Hill before he messes more with my adopted hometown — but we only get lethal if there's no alternative."

After leaving New Alexandria Police Headquarters, they detoured to the Machinations Sundry workshop, where the morning shift coming on eyed Morris and Betsy in their rumpled evening clothes and wondered. For an hour, Matheson and Nameless waited while Betsy and Morris tinkered in Morris's personal workshop until they emerged with a rough-forged assembly of brass and steel, clinging to Morris's back on leather straps. A pipe rose from the mechanism two feet above Morris's head, ending in a fluted horn encased in a perforated cap of bronze.

"What is that contraption?" Matheson said.

"Something I've been field-testing for the New Alexandria Fire Department. It's meant for mounting on machinery, but in a pinch, I guess the human machine is as good as any," Morris said.

"What's it do?"

"Maybe nothing, Dan. It's only an idea I've got, but it's all we have for the moment."

They found the Old Pharaoh's Odeon as closed and still as the last time they'd visited. Matheson knocked at the front door. They waited, but no one answered.

"Let's get some men out here and break the door down," Betsy said. "Shouldn't we rouse a posse or something? Isn't that what they do in Texas, Dan?"

Matheson raised an eyebrow at her. "This ain't Texas. With what we're contemplating the fewer eyes the better. Human or not—and I ain't decided on that question, yet—this fella looks like a man, and that's going to raise questions if we take any sort of permanent-type action."

"The fewer people exposed to him, the better. We must contain the mental contamination he breeds. Reaching weak minds will only make him stronger," Nameless said. "Show me the door you used to enter last night."

As Matheson led the group through an alley to the rear of the theater, he said, "I still don't see what he gets out of all this. No one goes around ruining cities for fun, do they?"

"He is the messenger of the Old Ones. In places outside of time and space, in cities sunken at the bottom of the ocean, at the heart of the universe, they sleep, and sleeping they dream, but one day when the stars are right they'll awaken," Nameless said. "It is written in the *Necronomicon* that with strange aeons even death may die. When the stars are right, the clock of the cosmos will chime their return. Each city and soul Nyarlathotep takes under his influence speeds the pendulum toward the time when the Old Ones will reclaim what they once possessed. First our minds, next the Earth, the outer planets, then other worlds and times unknown to us — before ultimately, the nuclear chaos at the heart of the universe, Azathoth, who slumbers to the demoniac music of countless dreadful beasts who drum and pipe and dance for him to the measure of all time, ceases to dream reality. Each note of his servants' music ticks another moment toward that day, and the faster their tempo, the sooner it comes."

Matheson stopped dead in his tracks, whirled, then grabbed Nameless by his dirty suitcoat. "Are you pulling my leg? This is insanity. Nonsense. Bull-pucky. Morris, Betsy, tell me this can't be true."

"I don't want it to be true," Morris said, "but I've heard of the *Necronomicon*, attributed to the mad Arab, Abdul Alhazred, around 730 A.D. Anna Rigel, the Queen of New Alexandria's witches, speaks of the tome with fear, and you know there is almost nothing in this world that truly frightens that woman. Betsy and I witnessed Nyarlathotep's power last night. And… I've seen the lost city. From a distance, true, but its atmosphere of dread was unmistakable. Can we risk what happened there happening here? Do you want to watch one cold night as all of New Alexandria marches hollow-eyed into the sea?"

Matheson shook his head. "It's too incredible, too… outlandish." He released Nameless. "Guess I'm having second thoughts about premeditated murder if this hombre turns out to be more smoke and mirrors than monster. Can you promise he isn't?"

Morris parted his lips to speak. An ear-shattering burst of sound stilled his words before they left his mouth. Noise cascaded around them, filling the alley, shaking dust and debris loose from brick and wood walls. A thousand, a million, even more flutes shrilled clashing notes into the air, accompanied by seemingly infinite drumbeats and footfalls, all wrapped in the crackling hiss of electricity unfettered. The back door of the theater flew open, slamming against the wall before cracking from its hinges and falling to the alley stones. Nyarlathotep emerged to his full, intimidating height. Morning light only deepened the shadows of his complexion and robes. Darkness writhed at his feet as if he stood upon a nest of squirming snakes and cockroaches.

"Welcome. Please, come in, come in, and see what I've prepared for you. The time is now," he said.

Unable to do otherwise, they entered. The door vanished behind them, replaced by a solid wall as if it had never existed. Nyarlathotep pulled back a curtain and ushered them to the stage. Morris tried to stand his ground, lock his feet in place, but the rhythm of the demoniac music forced movement into his bones and muscles as if it combined with the ambient electricity to stimulate his body against his will. The pale disc of electricity rotated above the stage. All Nyarlathotep's devices leapt with flashes and sparks of light and energy as if animated by the same irresistible power that carried Morris to center stage.

The quartet took equidistant positions beneath the electro-disc, puppets whose strings dangled from Nyarlathotep's sinister fingers. Shapes formed in the charged air. Visions of abominable musicians and dancers, so hideous Morris could only perceive them as glimpses of body parts — mouths, hands, feet, and other appendages beyond anything human. His brain struggled to make sense of the perversity flooding it even as he fought to hold onto what Nyarlathotep tried to pry out of him. His awareness began to drift, to rise. He clutched onto it with all his willpower, clung to his body.

"Betsy, now, please, if you can, do it now," Morris said.

Betsy took three steps toward him then stopped as if paralyzed. "I'm trying, Morris. It's so hard to move."

The maelstrom of sound and light cycloned around them.

"Whatever that thing does, now's the time," Matheson shouted.

Nameless moved then, seemingly less controlled than the others, perhaps from his longer exposure to the powers in motion or to his seasoned acceptance of the madness. He seized the tall climbing arc device, the Jacob's Ladder, at its base, raised it, and thrust it into Nyarlathotep's face. Electric ladder rungs lanced the dark man's flesh. Showers of electrical sparks ignited and fell on the stage. Locked into place by the circuit he created, Nameless quivered and twitched in his threadbare suit as smoke rose from his body. Tongues of fire licked at the mechanism. Electricity coursed into Nyarlathotep's uraeus until it seemed as if the snake's mouth spit fiery venom. Nyarlathotep staggered, startled, even as Nameless's teeth brightened with electric light and gray wisps trickled from his lips.

I am the last. I will tell the audient void.

I will tell. I will… Karolina, my wife! Muriel, my daughter! Oh, how I have missed the memory of you. But I must tell. I must. I must.

I am the last. I will tell the audient void.
I am the... I am... Richard.
Richard!
Oh, I am complete again!

Freed for a moment, Betsy rushed to Morris's side and fired the miniaturized steam engine in the device on his back. Pressure built, and the bronze cup atop the fluted horn whirled. From his pocket, Morris withdrew the control mechanism wired to the engine and pushed a button. A howling whistle blasted from atop the fluted horn. The bronze cap oscillated, warping the sound, which rose and fell in pitch and volume. Designed to be heard through stone walls, through several floors of a building, the warning siren tore a sonic rip in the audible electric cloud pouring through the electro-disc. The rhythm of those inhuman players faltered. Their music struck even more sour notes. Morris worked the controller, pressing its buttons, turning its dial, sending disruptive peals of random sound in chaos time into the electro-disc, forcing sound waves into conflict, pushing back on the mad music from the heart of the universe until the sizzling lines around its circumference flickered and broke.

The disc snapped shut. The music from beyond ceased.

Betsy and Matheson dropped to their knees, hands clamped to their ears, screaming without voices, their words erased by the wailing of the siren until Morris switched off the steam flowing up the pipe and silenced it.

"Are you okay?" he said.

He shouted without meaning to, all sense of volume gone. So did Betsy and Matheson when they replied. Thick silence filled the theater. How much genuine, how much the result of the assault on Morris's ears, he couldn't say.

Nameless lay on the stage, face blackened and blistered, smoke wafting from his head with the awful odor of burning hair. His hands remained clutched around the climbing arc where his fingers had fused to its metal. At the end with which he struck Nyarlathotep there remained only a deep, dark stain seared into the wood of the stage, and no sign at all of the tall man.

"Did we kill him?" Matheson said.

"I don't know," Morris said. "Maybe we only sent him back somewhere."

"To the dreaming thing?" Betsy said. "To… Azathoth?"

"I… don't know," Morris said.

"Wherever he went, I hope we never see him again," Matheson said.

"You and me both, Inspector," said Betsy.

"Me, too, but, even the poorest clock sometimes strikes the right time, and the universe is one enormous mechanism. How much could we have disrupted or delayed it with our little cry against its encroachment? I fear only time will tell."

The Last Flight of the One-Eyed Jack

F.R. Michaels

Romilda Gunn wore black against the soot and filth of the Aerodrome. Her mind swam, haunted by the visions she'd seen over the past few months: a figure, wreathed in shadow, standing at the foot of her bed, its eyes reflecting the light of eldritch stars back at her.

Not a dream, she thought. *It was Derrick, or his specter, trying to reach me.*

Romilda walked the narrow causeways between the hangars, jostled by groups of rough-looking aeronauts and mechanics, lost in her thoughts until she was nearly trod upon by some clanking metal monstrosity that stomped past her, hissing steam, carrying a pallet of storage barrels toward one of the docked airships.

Romilda resumed her trek to the docking gantry disheveled but in one piece. An airship floated above the platform, moored like a whale on a leash, complete with rounded nose and pointed tail, and a spruce-wood cabin slung beneath. Masts fitted with triangular sails jutted out like flippers along the fuselage, and four great fins stabilized the rear. She spied the enormous playing card painted on the tail, the Jack of Hearts, cunningly wrought but faded and chipped, just as the harbormaster had said. Romilda mounted the stairs leading up and scaled the tower.

At the top, a man in a weather-beaten frock coat sat with his boots up on the rail by the gangplank, idly flipping a throwing-knife.

"You want something, miss?" he said, without pausing his knife-play, peering at her from beneath the lowered brim of his leather coachman's hat.

"I'm looking for Captain Finch."

"Are you with the Air Guard?"

Romilda blinked. "No."

"Then you've found him." He touched the brim of his hat, hard blue eyes peeking out from beneath. "Alton Finch, Captain of the *One-Eyed Jack*, at your service."

"*Acting* Captain!" came a shout from somewhere up in the rigging.

"My name is Romilda Gunn," she said. "I'm looking for my brother, Derrick. The harbormaster said you might know him."

Finch sheathed the knife and swung his feet off the rail. "Well, Miss Romilda Gunn, sorry to disappoint, but I'm afraid I don't know anyone by that name."

"He might have joined under an alias, five years ago. Tall, headstrong, prone to getting into fights..."

Finch smirked. "You just described most of my crew."

A small, scruffy girl scrambled down from the rigging and dropped nimbly to the gantry beside him.

"I think she means Gunny Rick," she said.

"Get the photograph, Boom."

The young girl dashed up the gangplank and came back with a framed picture of the crew posing in front of the airship. Finch pointed to a young man squatting in the front row.

"This him?"

Romilda squinted down at the face, her heart racing. "That's my brother! Is he here? I must speak with him."

Finch took the picture back and shook his head. "Gunny left the crew a few months ago, after Captain Murano died."

"Our *real* captain," Boom chimed in. "Half the crew left."

Finch tossed her an acidic look and continued, "He and a few others joined an air-frigate headed up to the pole. Haven't heard anything since. Sorry."

"What was the name of the ship? When did they leave? When do they get back?"

Boom replied, "The *Ophelia*, the fourteenth of June, and the ship never got back."

Romilda stood there, digesting her words. She'd held a wan glimmer of hope that Derrick still lived... that some living aspect of his will tried to reach her, not his shade.

"Has a search party been sent? Another airship?"

Finch grunted a humorless laugh. "The *Ophelia was* a search party. They went looking for the *Talavar,* which vanished back in March."

"The *Talavar* was sent to search for the *Five Angels,* which went missing back in January," Boom added.

"You have an airship," Romilda said. "We could look for him. I can pay."

Finch shook his head. "No, no, no. *Three* ships have disappeared already. 'Tis a fool's journey. We might still have some of his effects onboard, though. Maybe you could bring something back. Boom?"

The young girl beckoned with a toss of her head. "Come aboard, city-girl."

Romilda followed her up the narrow gangplank. The airship's interior reminded her of the crew quarters on her father's yacht: small and functional, no space wasted, lightweight spruce and bamboo fixtures accented with metal structural braces. The only real difference she could note appeared to be an overall sense of grubby utility, and a few pockmarks on the walls that looked like bullet holes.

"This one was Gunny's," Boom said, opening a door barely big enough to pass a grown person.

Romilda crinkled her nose at the distilled smells of an enclosed space that had been repurposed as a junk room. She picked her way through the clutter to examine the narrow bunk with its storage space underneath, run her finger through the dust of a folding table jutting out from one wall, and peered out the tiny porthole. Romilda could spread her arms and touch both walls.

"Cozy," Romilda murmured.

Boom snorted. "You should see where I sleep."

Romilda crouched down and pulled open the storage locker. A meager scattering of papers cluttered the bottom, but nothing of importance.

"Did you know my brother well?"

Boom said, "We were crew," as if that explained everything, then added, "Can I ask you something, city-girl?"

"Please… Romilda."

"Gunny was with us for years. Why're you here now?"

"Father forbade me," Romilda answered, flipping through a notebook at the bottom of the locker. "But in the past month I've seen…"

Maybe I shouldn't tell anyone I'm seeing ghosts.

"Seen what?"

"I've seen… my father's health failing. Mother wants them to reconcile. So here I am." Romilda blew out a frustrated breath. "Families are complicated."

She turned to look at Boom, but the girl was gone. In the awkward silence, Romilda heard the urgent tolling of a distant bell. The airship lurched suddenly, pitching her backward. As her head slammed against the wooden bulkhead, darkness claimed her.

"Romie…"

Romilda heard the whispered voice, as she wavered along the tidemark of consciousness. Only Derrick called her Romie.

"Derrick?"

Romilda opened her eyes and saw a dark silhouette looming over her, peering down. Its eyes reflected an unnatural light, and its substance writhed and iridized like shadows moving through ice.

"Help me…"

"Derrick!"

The figure vanished like smoke sucked back through an opaque screen. Romilda lay on the deck, alone, looking up at the ceiling of Derrick's cabin.

She wobbled to her feet, gingerly holding the back of her head, and stumbled out into the corridor. Loud, but distant, she heard revving engines and gunfire, and the floor lurched under her.

Scrambling from the cabin, she stepped onto the bridge and into a beehive of activity. Finch paced to and fro, barking orders while a very small man stood on a box in front of the ship's wheel and wrestled it to his will. A tall youth wearing thick goggles and missing a hand argued with a dark-skinned woman over a chart, while another crewmember readied a long gun. Shots from below ricocheted off one of the spars, but no one except Romilda flinched. She steadied herself against the hatchway, unnoticed, holding her head.

The gunner shouldered the weapon and sighted out a porthole, murmuring, "Steady now."

A deafening blast and a gust of smoke briefly filled the room. The gunner lurched back with the recoil, then peered out the porthole.

"Steam plume. Got their boiler. They're losing pressure."

Finch said, "Well shot, Mix. Now let's shake these jossers." To the little person at the helm, he said, "Hard to port, Mr. Villiers, we'll lose them in the clouds."

"Aye-yup!" The man whipped the wheel around.

The airship canted sharply, the engines roaring as it climbed. The rest of the crew braced and stood firm, but Romilda bounced off the doorjamb with a startled "Oof!"

The entire crew turned at the sound.

Finch spoke first: "Oh. Just bully."

The dark-skinned woman glared at Romilda with eyes like thrown hatchets.

"Finch, who's this girl?" she demanded, her voice mellifluous, with a French West African accent.

"Claws in, Khady, this is Gunny's sister, Matilda."

"*Romilda*," she corrected him.

Khady scowled. "I mean, what's she doing on our ship?"

"She came looking for Gunny. I told her there might be personal effects in his cabin. Evidently, she was still looking when we scrambled at the raid warning bell."

"The ship jolted," Romilda mumbled. "I hit my head."

Finch said, "First things first. You're not looking too steady there, Miss Gunn. Khady here will escort you to sick bay."

Khady grunted annoyance but took Romilda's arm and beckoned her along with a toss of her braids. "Come along, city-girl, let's get your nut checked."

She hustled Romilda down the narrow access hall to the infirmary.

"Khady," Romilda said, still woozy. "That's a lovely name. What does it mean?"

"It means me. That's how names work." Khady called into the sick room. "Redkin! You sober? Got an injured stowaway. Finch says she's Gunny Rick's sister."

"Gunny had a sister? I thought that boy was raised by wolves."

"Whatever. She's your problem now."

Khady shoved her into the room. Her head woozy, Romilda stumbled into a bear of a man standing with his back to the door. He turned with a grunt, towering over her, breathing a cloud of alcohol fumes.

"All right, girly, strip."

"I beg your pardon?"

"Get those clothes off, let me get a good look at you."

"You will get no such thing!"

The big man blew out an impatient breath and reached for her coat. "C'mon, let's not make this difficult, I *ghgghh-ghhggghh-ggghhhghh…!*"

Redkin convulsed as if in the throes of some violent fit. Romilda stepped aside and watched him fall like a tree, quivering.

She held up a short baton with a forked rod and two metal spheres at the end. A spark crackled between the spheres, and a wisp of smoke drifted up. "I said no."

The impact of his fall alerted the rest of the crew. From behind her, a woman's voice exclaimed, in a sturdy Irish brogue, "Oi! What did ye do to Doc?"

Romilda turned and spied a red-haired woman in the doorway. She wore a mechanic's apron and her fiery hair scooped up into an unkempt bun, her face and arms were spattered with freckles and rimed in soot.

Romilda said, "This drunken lout tried to take off my clothes!"

Redkin groaned from the floor, "I was *trying* to examine you!"

"By undressing me? I hit my *head!*"

"Then tell me that!"

Finch popped up behind the redheaded woman. "What's happening here, Seven?"

She pointed at Romilda. "There's a strange woman on board and she's electrified Doc."

Finch stepped between them. "Bedside manner aside, Miss Gunn, Redkin here is our ship's doctor, and a damned good one. Never lost a horse in his care."

"He's a *horse* doctor?"

"We do with what we have up here, Miss Gunn." Finch held out his hand. "I'll take that device, please. I won't have our guests electrocuting the crew. Plus, a spark near the ammo or fuel would be inadvisable."

Romilda handed him her baton.

"An Equalizer Electro-Wand?" Seven marveled.

Romilda nodded. "The new Mark 3, 1910 model."

Finch passed the device to the red-haired woman.

"Lock this up. And *don't* take it apart."

Seven pouted and left.

Finch helped Redkin to his feet and said to Romilda, "Doc here can be a bit of a gilhooley when he's got a sosh on but sober he's a perfect gentleman."

Redkin nodded. "Apologies, miss. Count on my best behavior henceforward."

Before Romilda could think of forgiving him, the youth with the missing hand poked his head in the door.

"Hey, Finch!"

"*Captain* Finch, Dodger."

"You're gonna wanna come to the radio room. Air Guard, broadcasting on all frequencies." Dodger nodded to Romilda. "And bring the princess."

"Why me?" Romilda asked.

"Because according to the authorities, *señorita,* we kidnapped you."

❧⁓ဢ⁓❧

Dodger took his place in the soundproofed closet that served as the radio room. Finch and Romilda crowded in beside him, with the remaining crew clustered at the door.

Finch told Romilda, "Tell these bulls we didn't know you were aboard. We'll put you down at the first port, and you'll have a grand adventure to tell at your next tea party."

Dodger flipped a switch. The speaker crackled to life.

"Ahoy, *Jack of Hearts.* This is Commander Wells of the United States Air Guard. *Jack of Hearts,* respond."

Finch grabbed the mouthpiece. "We're the *One-Eyed Jack,* Wells, and you know it."

A dry chuckle rasped over the speaker. "Hello, Finch. Been a while."

"I take it those were your hornets who raided the 'Drome and shot up my ship?"

"We weren't the ones abducting an heiress. That's low, even for you. I want to speak to Miss Gunn."

At the sound of the name, Dodger's eyes popped wide. "Gunn? Like, Bouchard and Gunn? The *bank?*"

Romilda nodded demurely as she accepted the mouthpiece. "Hello, commander. This is Romilda Gunn. I am afraid there's been a misunderstanding. I have not been abducted."

Romilda locked eyes with Finch, who looked back more wary than reassured.

"I have hired the *One-Eyed Jack* for an expedition to find the airship *Ophelia.* My brother was aboard when she disappeared. Apologies for the confusion."

Finch groaned, while the crew gasped with a single breath.

There was a crackle of static from the speaker, then a menacing, "Finch…?"

Finch swallowed. "Just like she said, commander."

"All right, we'll stand down. If I may say, Miss Gunn, with your money, you could have hired a real crew, instead of those throwbacks on the *Jack*."

"Opinion noted, commander," Romilda replied.

She stuck her tongue out at the handset and handed it back to Dodger, who snapped off the radio.

"So," she said to the room at large. "Shall we go find my brother?"

∽⤜❦⤛∾

"This is insane!" Khady said, her tone rife with rage. "You just agreed to a suicide mission!"

The crew sat around the map table, while Romilda allowed Redkin to patch her head in the surgery.

"What could I say? The Air Guard were on us like a rash." Finch looked down at his boots. "Besides, that city-girl is right. Gunny was crew. And not just him. Richards, Fang, Suleiman… oughtn't we search for them?"

"They left after the captain died," Khady replied. "We who stayed are crew. We eight."

"Seven-and-a-half, counting Mr. Villiers," Dodger quipped.

Villiers had looped some stay-ropes over the wheel to hold the ship steady. He sat, all four feet of him, on his box, tamping tobacco into an enormous meerschaum pipe.

"It never settled well with me," he mused, "that we didn't go looking for them."

"Nor me," Seven added, twirling a lock of her coppery hair anxiously. "Some of us had friends on the *Five Angels*, too, and the *Talavar*."

Mix stood apart, meticulously cleaning the long gun.

"You're awful quiet, Mix," Finch remarked. "You're part of this crew. You have a say."

Mix blew some residue out of the chamber before replying. "I say better to leave the dead to the dead, than join them."

"But what if they're not dead?" Seven asked, with some heat. "What if they're stranded, or hurt, or been taken by the Quacks?"

Villiers lit his pipe, scoffed. "What Quebec airship could take the *Talavar*? Captain Singh would eat those rebel jossers for breakfast."

"And *we're* supposed to rescue *them*?" Khady said. "Under-crewed, unprepared, and letting some concussed posh stowaway give orders?"

"Legitimate concerns, Miss Khady," Romilda said as she stepped into the room, her head bandaged. "But for clarity, I am a paying passenger, not a stowaway, and I do not give orders, Captain Finch does."

"*Acting* Captain," the crew said in unison.

Finch said, "To be fair to you, Miss Gunn, there is some contention among the crew on whether to proceed with this expedition."

Romilda reached into her coat and pulled out a stack of bank notes. She placed it on the table in front of Finch. He picked it up and riffled through it.

"These are twenty-dollar gold certificates," he said. "There must be…"

"One thousand US dollars," Romilda said.

Dodger blinked. "You walked alone through the 'Drome with a thousand dollars in your coat?"

"And an Equalizer. I didn't think any of your lot would accept a promissory note."

Khady turned her fierce eyes to Romilda. "What's to stop us from keeping the money and throwing you over the side?"

Romilda stared her right back. "Ethical behavior, I should think. Plus, you'd forfeit the remaining payments."

Villier's eyebrows bobbed up. "Remaining payments?"

Romilda nodded. "One thousand now, one thousand when we get back to New York, and a third thousand if we return with my brother."

Finch peeled his eyes from the money and turned to his crew.

"We'll put it to a vote. But either way, we are *not* ditching Miss Gunn. The options are we go find the *Ophelia*; or we turn back, hand her over to the Air Guard, and deal with Wells."

"Some choice," Dodger grumbled.

"That's what it is, Dodger. So, find the *Ophelia*, all in favor?"

Villiers, Seven, and Dodger called out "Aye!"

"Turn back?"

Khady and Redkin called out, "Aye!" Mix nodded.

"Acting captain gets no vote," Khady declared, pointing at Finch.

"Fair. I'll abstain."

"So, a tie?" Seven asked.

Finch looked around. "Where's Boom?"

"Haven't seen her since the raid," Dodger said.

Mix added, "She was up in the rigging when the shooting started."

Everyone's eyes swiveled to the top hatch. Redkin reached up to touch a dark fluid seeping through the seam in the trap door. Blood.

"No," he muttered. "No, no, no, no…!"

Redkin scrambled up the ladder. He flung the hatch open and cursed.

"I need help up here!"

Seven clambered up, and together they gently lowered the limp young girl through the hatch. A red bloom soaked the back of her tunic.

"She's alive, just," Redkin said, as they hustled her to the surgery. "Took a round in the back, got caught in the rigging when she fell."

They laid Boom face down on the table and strapped her in. Redkin tore her shirt open and examined the wound.

"Will she make it?" Finch asked.

"There's a bullet in her spine. It's not good."

"Not the answer I want, Doc. Save her."

"Then let me work."

Finch backed out. Redkin closed the door.

⁜

Redkin emerged an hour later, hands bloody, looking grim.

"She's conscious," he said. "Says she can't feel her legs."

"The bullet?" Finch asked.

Redkin scowled. "Pressing on her spinal cord. If I try to remove it, I could kill her, and if I don't, infection will. She needs a hospital."

"We can't put down now," Khady said.

Romilda spoke up. "Why can't we? That young girl is dying, let's get her to a proper surgeon!"

Villiers said, "We're in contested airspace. If we land, the Geese'll deny us, and the Quacks'll snaffle us."

Romilda searched the sea of grim faces. "I don't understand."

Finch explained: "Quebec — the 'Quacks' — is in rebellion against the Dominion of Canada — the 'Geese'. The United States claims neutrality, but covertly supports the Dominion. Private gasbaggers, like us, can take Quebec airships for plunder, since it helps the Geese."

Romilda blinked. "You're *pirates*?"

"Privateers," Villiers said. "We have letters of marque, signed by President Taft himself."

"To Captain Murano," Khady added. "Since he passed, our status is in question."

Seven scoffed. "What question? The Air Guard hates us, Canada says we don't exist, and them Quack feckers would lynch us on the spot."

Finch spoke slowly: "Except we're *not* pirates. We're a search party, escorting a prominent US citizen."

Khady's dark face went ashen. "You are not serious. Those Quebecois bastards know the *Jack*."

"They know Captain Murano. He's dead. We put down, ask for help, take our chances."

Mix spoke up, "You know what they'll do to me if I'm captured."

Romilda asked, "What would they do, Mister… um, Miss…?"

Mix looked down at her. "That's just it. I'm both."

"Our Mix is a hermaphrodite," Villiers explained.

"And an abomination, according to the French Catholic Inquisitors," Mix added.

"We'll not be trading Boom's life for yours, Mix," Finch said. "You stay on the *Jack* with the others. If things get dippy, dust off and get to Dominion airspace. Redkin and I will take Boom, and we'll bring Miss Gunn, she can vouch for us. Khady, I'll need your French."

"I speak French," Romilda said.

"Of course you do. All right, Khady, stay with the ship. If we get snaffled, you're the new captain."

"*Acting* captain," Khady said. "And we can't crew the *Jack* with four people and no rope-monkey."

"Gunny could do it," Seven remarked. "He was near nimble as Boom. Never thought I'd miss that josser this much."

Romilda looked down at her hands and said, "If I could *wish* Derrick here, I would."

Silence greeted her remark. Romilda looked up to see the shocked faces of the crew looking not at her, but past her. She smelt brine and felt frigid air at her back. Behind her, a familiar voice whispered:

"*Romie…*"

She turned and stared up into Derrick's eyes. He stood solid and lifelike for only a moment, before his face and form dissolved into a silhouette of writhing darkness. Before he vanished like a shadow in the light, he reached out a ghostly arm to Romilda, dropped something hard and heavy into her palm.

Romilda held a bloodstained bullet.

"We all saw that, right?" Dodger quavered.

"Gunny Rick," Finch breathed.

Romilda felt a surge of relief wash over her. "I knew it. He is real."

"You've seen *that* before?" Khady demanded.

"I thought I might be hallucinating, but deep in my heart, I knew otherwise."

Seven made the sign of the cross, quivering. "Why'd you not tell us?"

Villiers picked up his pipe from where it had fallen from his mouth, stomping out the smoldering tobacco. "Because if she had, we'd've thought she was crazy."

"Craz*ier*," Khady amended.

Redkin took the bullet from Romilda's hand.

"Thirty-caliber Springfield. Like the Air Guard uses…"

He turned and ran to sick bay. Chairs slid back with a chorus of scrapes as the crew jumped up and followed.

Boom lay on her stomach, sedated. Redkin lifted the bloodstained dressing and gently felt around the wound.

"No bullet," he said.

"Ow, stop poking me," Boom murmured groggily.

Finch crouched down to see the young girl's face. "How you doing, Boom?"

"Gunny was here. I think he pulled the bullet out of my back. His hands were so cold. Did we find him?"

Finch shook his head. "No. We were voting whether to go look for him or turn back."

Boom said, "I vote we go. Look what I can do now." She wiggled her toes. "Bully, huh?"

"Bully indeed," Finch said, standing. "You heard the tie-breaker. Dodger, Khady, set a course for the *Ophelia's* last known position. Mr. Villiers, man the helm. Let's go find Gunny Rick."

❧⳾❧

Khady and Dodger had estimated the *Ophelia's* last position to within a twelve-mile radius near the northern tip of the Boothia peninsula; technically Dominion land but uninhabited except for occasional nomadic natives. Mr. Villiers guided the *One-Eyed Jack* through a narrow corridor between the Quebec rebels and Canadian airspace.

Boom improved rapidly under Redkin's care and was up and walking the next day. Despite her pestering, Finch kept her off-duty.

They'd given Romilda Gunny's old bunk. She found the food coarse, the accommodations claustrophobic, and the toilet facilities horrific, but abided without complaint.

It was night on the fourth day when Khady announced they would reach the target area by morning. The weather looked to stay clear and calm, and they could start searching at dawn.

"Hopefully we find them before whatever found them first finds us," Khady added grimly.

Romilda asked, "The *Ophelia* disappeared searching for the *Talavar*, which disappeared searching for the *Five Angels*. But why was the *Five Angels* up here in the first place?"

The crew exchanged looks, then Finch said, "They went looking for a star that fell."

Romilda's brow furrowed. "How is that?"

Finch said, "Crews spotted a shooting star over the northern territories that hit the ground somewhere up near the magnetic pole."

"The *Five Angels* headed up that way," Villiers added. "Captain Billings thought they'd take a look. Apart from scientific interest, meteorites are valuable, containing rare and exotic metals. Bringing one back could fetch a fortune."

"Or lead the foolish and greedy to their deaths," Khady said.

"Little ray of feckin' sunshine, aren't ye, Khady?" Seven remarked.

Dodger slid down the ladder from the top hatch, breathless. "Something's not right. I can't determine our position."

Khady scoffed. "It's a clear night, just sight the North Star."

"It's gone."

Finch stood. "What do you mean 'gone'? How did you lose a *star*?"

Dodger beckoned with his head and clambered up the ladder to the crow's nest. Khady and Finch followed, as did Romilda out of curiosity.

The crow's nest was a circular balcony up above the *Jack's* gasbag. Frigid winds buffeted their faces as they looked up into the sea of stars above their head.

"Polaris should be at four degrees azimuth and seventy degrees elevation," Dodger said. "But it's not there."

Romilda thought the sky looked normal enough; beautiful, in fact, in the clear upper air. She knew how to locate the North Star: find the Big Dipper and follow the two pointer stars to Polaris. Except, she couldn't find the Big Dipper.

Khady glared into the sky and grunted in frustration. "Dodger's right. These are not our stars."

Finch pulled a speaking tube out of its sheath and spoke into the funnel, "Mr. Villiers, it appears we are lost. Full stop, descend to two hundred feet, and drop anchor."

"Aye-yup," came Villiers' reply.

Romilda heard the engine slow to idle, the wind abating as they lost velocity. Vents along the fuselage spouted super-heated air in plumes of steam. The *One-Eyed Jack* descended smoothly.

"Look," Romilda said, pointing. "I'm sure that's Jupiter… and it's gone."

Dodger added, "I can see Cassiopeia, fading in and out."

"It's like we're seeing different skies reflected through slow ripples in a pond," Khady mused.

Finch said, "Dodger, keep your eye where Polaris is supposed to be. If it fades in, take sights and lock our position."

"Aye, captain."

Khady opened her mouth to correct him, but Finch silenced her with a gesture. "Just let me have this one, Khady, please?"

Khady relented.

Finch said, "Let's get below. We'll anchor here until daybreak and see what sort of sun rises."

⟋⟍⟋⟍

Day broke with excruciating brightness. They pulled anchor and brought the *Jack* up to four thousand feet. Mix and Seven scanned the area with spyglasses.

"That's the Boothia peninsula dead ahead," Mix reported through the speaking tube. "We're on course."

"Of course we're on course," Khady growled. "I laid it in."

"The binnacle's doing pirouettes," Villiers remarked. "We must be almost on top of the pole."

"We're at the north pole?" Romilda asked.

"North *magnetic* pole," Finch explained. "Compasses are useless here, but that means we must be close."

Seven's excited voice came from the tube. "Smoke!"

Romilda jumped to her feet, her heart pounding.

"I see it," Villiers said, peering out the windscreen with his own enormous spyglass.

Romilda couldn't contain herself. "A signal fire? That must mean they're alive!"

"Could be them, or smugglers, or someone else not so happy to see us," Finch said. "Half ahead, Mr. Villiers. I want everyone else at arms, just in case. Miss Gunn, can you shoot?"

"Well, my Uncle Alistair held shooting parties at his country estate during pheasant season…"

There was a brief pause, then Seven said, "She can help me with the engine."

✦

"I'm getting a signal," Dodger called from the radio room.

Finch slid up beside him as the wireless hissed and sputtered. Dodger twisted dials and flipped switches as an unintelligible voice stuttered through.

Then from the speaker, a woman's voice said, "Ahoy!"

Finch took the handset. "Ahoy, unknown contact, this is the *One-Eyed Jack*, identify yourself."

There was a pause, then the voice from the radio said, "Finch?"

Finch knew that voice. "Fang?"

A stream of agitated Cantonese spewed from the radio, then, "Finch, what are you doing here? Turn back!"

"We came looking for the *Ophelia*. We have Gunny Rick's sister aboard. What's your position?"

"We're grounded, with survivors from four different crews, but you have to turn back!"

"After we rescue you," Finch said.

"Please, please, *please* turn back! It's not safe! It's…"

Finch jumped and Dodger yanked off his headset when the radio suddenly screeched as if some inhuman voice screamed into the transmitter. The sound boomed not just from the radio, but from all around the *Jack*.

Mix's voice shouted from the speaking tube: "Get us out of here *now!*"

"Do it, Mr. Villiers!" Finch said.

Villiers pushed the lever full-ahead, then shoved it forward one more notch to a hand-written setting that read "SLAM IT!"

Back in the engine room, Seven bellowed, "Hang onto something, city-girl!" then she slammed a lever forward as far as it would go. The engine responded with a blast of steam, the propellers whirling to a roar. Romilda grabbed a handhold and hung on as the airship leapt forward, surging ahead as if the Devil himself chased her.

On the bridge, the crew peered out the windscreens in terror and disbelief.

All around the airship, vast inhuman appendages broke through the clouds, reaching for the *One-Eyed Jack*.

"Evasive action!" Finch shouted.

Villiers wrestled the wheel as the ship buffeted through the air in a series of bounces and zigzags; the arms grabbed empty space. Redkin and Boom bounced off of the bulkheads like billiard balls as they ran to the bridge.

"What's happening?" Redkin asked.

"You wouldn't believe me if I told you," Finch said breathlessly. "But we're doing a dash and need someone in the rigging. Boom, you fit?"

"Try to stop me," she said.

"I'll go with her," Redkin said.

"Whatever you do, don't look back at what's after us."

They scrambled up the ladder and through the hatch.

A riot of clawed limbs groped blindly from the sky, reaching for the fleeing airship. A break in the clouds revealed a vast segmented body with eyeless, birdlike heads at either end. Mix watched in horror as the grotesque entity pursued, twisting convulsively through the air, morphing into geometric shapes and back; like watching a writhing centipede through a kaleidoscope.

Then one of the flailing limbs whipped toward the crow's nest. Mix ducked as the hooked claws shattered one of the masts and tore through the gasbag.

The *Jack* lurched and shuddered; falling from the sky.

Back in the boiler room, Romilda and Seven rattled about like pennies in a tin can as the ship shook and dropped.

"What's happening?" Romilda shouted over the noise.

"Sounds like the gasbag's been breached!"

"We're falling?"

"The bag holds separate gas cells," Seven explained. "If enough are undamaged, we can do a soft landing."

"And if not?"

"Then t'was nice knowing ye, city-girl…"

Finch's voice boomed from the speaking-tube: "All aboard: brace, brace, brace!"

The airship cabin hit the ground with a shuddering impact and slid. Windscreens shattered, masts shivered, and the *Jack* slew around until it fetched up in a narrow ravine and crashed to a stop.

"Romie…"

Derrick's voice whispered against a roar of gushing steam and the ringing in her ears.

"Romie, get up…"

Romilda opened her eyes against the thick steam that filled the boiler room, gushing from a ruptured pipe. For a second, she saw Derrick's spectral form pointing to a hole in the fuselage, then dissipating in the steam. She forced herself to her hands and knees, and saw Seven sprawled against the controls and dials, unmoving. Romilda crawled to the red-haired woman. She tried to drag the mechanic out the opening but lacked the strength to move her.

From outside, she heard running footsteps approach.

Romilda found her breath in the scalding steam and called out, "Help us!"

"In here!" someone yelled outside.

Human figures appeared in the hole, dressed in torn and weathered clothing. A slender Asian woman with a bandage covering one eye ran through the breach. She grabbed Romilda by the collar and pulled her out of the wreckage with surprising strength.

Romilda gasped and coughed in the frigid air. She pointed back toward the *Jack*.

"Seven!" she cried.

Another rescuer, a man with a ragged beard, jarred to a stop. "Seven? There are seven more trapped in there?"

"Not what she means," the Asian woman said as she darted back in.

She quickly returned, dragging the unconscious redhead out and away from the wreckage. Seven stirred and coughed.

"Thank you," Romilda said. "Who are you?"

"My name is Fen Geung, but everyone calls me Fang."

On the bridge, Finch quickly checked himself for damage. Apart from some cuts and bruises, he discovered he was still in one piece."

Khady, uninjured, helped him up. "On your feet, Finch."

Villiers sat slumped over the ship's wheel, a stripe of blood running from hairline to chin.

"Not one of my better landings," he groaned.

Finch told him, "We all walked away, wee man. It was your best ever."

Dodger emerged from the radio room; hair tousled, his shirt torn, but unhurt. He pointed out the broken windshield at a small group of people coming around the wreck of the *Jack*.

"We got company."

"Are those the people we came to rescue?" Finch asked.

"Good job, us," Khady said.

"That's Fang," Finch said. "And the one next to her looks like Billings. They have Seven, and Gunny's sister."

Mix emerged from the smashed crow's nest, and the sturdy safety harnesses had served Redkin and Boom well. They extracted themselves from the tangled rigging with help from the newcomers.

Finch and the crew met the ragged group of survivors in front of the wreck of the *One-Eyed Jack*. Fang led the group. She and Finch locked gazes for a long moment, before she ran to him and wound her arms round his neck. They kissed for what felt like forever. The moment finally broke, and she stepped back, slapping him so hard he nearly spun around.

She spewed some rapid-fire Cantonese invective, then said, "Alton Finch, you chuzzlewit! What the hell are you doing here?"

"Looking for you," he replied, rubbing his face.

"We told you to turn back! This place is an airship graveyard!" Fang pointed at the sky. "You've seen Scylla!"

"The thing that chased us? What the hell is it?"

"We don't know, but it smashed up our ships and killed half of us. We call it 'Scylla'."

"From *The Odyssey*," Romilda chimed in. "A monster with many reaching arms."

"We know. That's why we called it that. We think it's attracted to the Artifact."

Finch shook his head. "What artifact?"

Billings, the man with the ragged beard, spoke: "The shooting star, the thing that fell to Earth, was no meteorite. It was something alien. Something dangerous."

"We can't stay in the open for long," Fang said. "Our camp's nearby. Bring what provisions you can carry: we'll tend the wounded and answer your questions then."

They gathered the materials from the wreck of the Jack and made a furtive dash to the survivors' camp. During the trek Seven sidled up next to Romilda and slipped something into her coat pocket. The Equalizer Electro-Wand.

"Just in case," Seven whispered to her. "By the way, I made a few improvements."

"A few *what*?"

�⋅

The survivors' camp comprised a ramshackle cluster of shelters built from parts of the crashed airships, covered over with a stretched canopy of doped canvas sheets cut from wrecked gasbags and camouflaged with sticks and litter to make them invisible from the air.

Romilda looked for Derrick at the camp but could not find him.

Seething with impatience, she cornered Fang. "I came to find my brother. Where is he? Where is Derrick?"

Fang looked back at her blankly. "Who in the Sam Hill is Derrick?"

"Gunny Rick," Boom said from where Redkin restitched her back wound.

The survivors fell silent at Derrick's name.

Romilda looked around in alarm. "What? Where is he?"

Fang forced herself to meet Romilda's eye.

"He's with the Artifact."

"Take me there."

⋅别⋅

None could mistake the location of the impact zone. The falling star had gouged a rut of shattered rock a mile long that ran like an arrow to a fissure punched into the side of a mountain. They made their way carefully over the broken terrain but stopped as someone called out a warning. The group hid under an outcrop as Scylla's shadow passed overhead. Tense minutes passed as they watched the clawed limbs drag across the ground. One of the arms found the outcropping and groped underneath, perilously close to where Romilda and Seven pressed their backs against the rock wall, holding their collective breath. Romilda carefully slid the Equalizer out of her coat pocket. When the clawed appendage reached for her, she jabbed the Electro-Wand into its center. Instead of an angry zap, the device discharged with a blinding flash and a crack like a pistol shot. The acrid scent of ozone filled the air as the reaching arms whipped back and out of sight. Scylla's discordant screech echoed overhead, and the shadow withdrew at speed.

Romilda stared at the still-sparking rod.

She turned to Seven. *"Improvements?"*

Seven grinned and shrugged.

They made it the rest of the way across without incident, stepping into a cave the size of a cathedral. The rock had melted and reformed, lining the interior space, with formations that flowed and changed into odd geometric patterns as Romilda watched. The frigid air smelt of burnt stone, and space and time inside the cavern appeared to ebb and flow like a tide. Glimpses of stars and alien landscapes faded in and out along the rock walls. She found the effect disorienting to the point of nausea.

At the epicenter of the cavern sat an enormous, impossible machine. It looked at first like an irregular crystal, with countless facets and moving parts visible under the translucent surface. Wheels and cogs and pistons moved in a slow ballet of purposeful motion, while indecipherable symbols appeared and faded on circular crystal disks, sometimes floating in the air around the device.

On a platform at the base of the device, Derrick Gunn sat cross-legged, hunched forward and head down, his hands inside the alien machine.

"Derrick!" Romilda cried.

She ran to her brother, but two men intercepted her and held her back.

The burlier of the two said, "Don't, miss, it isn't safe!"

"But that's my brother!"

"You won't help him by putting yourself in danger, my dear," said the other man.

Billings caught up. "This is Dr. Cullens and Professor Byrd," he said. "They're astrophysicists, we brought them on the *Five Angels* to study the meteorite, only we found this instead. If anyone can help your brother, it's them."

Romilda forced her eyes off the sight of her brother to gaze at the machine. "*This* is the Artifact? It looks like a giant clock."

Professor Byrd nodded. "That's our theory. That it is a chronograph of some non-human manufacture, not dissimilar to the ones airships use for navigation."

"Chronograph?" Romilda asked.

Dr. Cullens nodded. "Navigators use the elevation of celestial bodies to determine latitude; for longitude, you can do the same, provided you know the exact time of day of where you started. Every airship has a precise chronograph to navigate longitude."

"That's what we think this is," Byrd said. "Only, instead of just measuring time and space, it bends and shapes them."

"A means of navigating through multiple dimensions," Cullens added. "Only, it's damaged, and out of control, twisting reality into knots. The effect had begun to spread, until your brother intervened."

Byrd said, "We've tried to study it, even to work it somehow, but if anyone gets too close, they get caught in the anomaly and can't escape."

"Then your brother volunteered to run in, and he was able, with our instruction, to slow the spread of the chronostorm, but it only works with his direct intervention."

Byrd said, "This artifact was never meant to be wielded by humans. If he releases his control, the effect could shred time and space itself."

"It's like he's stepped on a land mine, and must keep his foot on it until everyone gets clear," Cullens said. "We can't get him out, and even if we could, who knows what this thing will do?"

"He learned to use it," Romilda said. "This is how he communicated with me. He somehow bent time and space to reach me."

Byrd shook his head. "But we can't reach him."

"I can," Romilda said, and walked into the undulating fractal waves before anyone could stop her.

Romilda felt the increasing flow around her as she reached Derrick's side. His hands tightly gripped what seemed like controls shaped in cryptic, continually morphing geometry.

Romie. You came.

Yes, Derrick, I came.

I used the Artifact, I learned to project myself to find you, to contact you. It worked. I'm here, Derrick, with your old crew.

Romie, I wanted you to bring help, to get the others out, not to get trapped by the Artifact with me.

I've come to take you home, Derrick.

We're stuck here, Romie. I can't shut this thing down. I can't let go.

Derrick, remember Father's old Pope-Toledo motorcar? Sometimes the thing to do with a balky machine is to give it a good kick.

Romilda pulled out her Equalizer Electro-Wand, thumbed the charge to full, and jammed it among the Artifact's clockworks. The device discharged like a bolt of lightning. The Artifact sparked with the surge of power, falling dark and still, but only for a moment. Its mechanisms spun to life again, glowing with an eldritch light, brightening until it reflected a blinding flash from every surface.

For a split second in time, Romilda saw it all: every moment of existence across the universe spread before her in a kaleidoscopic vista, the birth of stars and the deaths of galaxies, individual atoms at the cores of supernovae and vast unending voids of space. She saw the incandescent heart of God, and the lightless, loveless depths of Hell. And she saw herself, an infinitesimal ember of consciousness on a tiny world in an unremarkable reach of space, a single grain of sand on an endless, indifferent beach.

The Artifact stirred. Multidimensional cogs and wheels turned in a precision measured in quantum lengths, damaged but still functional. It grew and morphed into a billion swirling fractal shapes, then vanished as if fallen through a hole in reality itself.

The distortions abated, like a stormy sea falling suddenly to calm.

Derrick and Romilda lay unconscious amid the broken rocks, what was left of the Equalizer melted into slag and Romilda's arm charred to the elbow.

✦

Romilda awoke to the sounds, sights, and smells of great industry around her. She tried to sit up only to find her head light and her body unspeakably heavy. A heavy bandage wrapped her right arm, the damage blissfully numb, but otherwise she felt intact.

She spotted Seven nearby, looking dirtier than usual, bandaging a cut on her palm. The red-haired woman noticed her and turned.

"Well, top o' the morning to ye, city-girl," she said, then called out, "She's awake!"

"What happened?"

"You goosed the Artifact with that gizmo of yours. The damned thing shut down, powered back up, and fecked off." Seven grinned at her. "Now, Miss Gunn, are you ready to go home?"

"How? I thought we were stranded."

"There's a dozen airships lying about, all torn up by that giant floaty fecker," Seven said. "We've gathered the parts and built a new one out of the wrecks."

Romilda blinked, feeling a seedling of hope blossom in her chest. "Why couldn't the survivors do that before?"

Seven scoffed. "They didn't have *me*."

"Or the *Jack's* undamaged boiler," Fang remarked, walking in from outside. "Besides, Scylla would have wrecked anything we built. We've been watching the skies; wherever the Artifact went, it took that monster with it."

"How long was I out?"

Fang said, "Six days."

"And Derrick?"

"According to Doc Redkin, Gunny's stable, but comatose. We wonder if the Artifact still has a piece of him, somewhere in the cosmos."

"Derrick will come back to me," Romilda murmured. "He always does."

Seven bounced up and down with excitement. "Anyhow, can ye walk, city-girl? Y'gotta see this."

Together, Fang and Seven helped Romilda out of the ramshackle infirmary and into the open air.

Dominating the sky was a patchwork gasbag with a tangle of improvised rigging and mismatched stabilizer fins. Beneath, the cabin hung like a hobo's mansion of slapped-together parts, in front of a steam engine that looked, literally, like a train-wreck. Finch stood before it all, directing the finishing touches and admiring the handiwork. He noticed her and turned.

"Ah, Miss Gunn, you're awake." He waved his hand to the improvised airship. "So what do you think?"

"I'm amazed and horrified in turns. What's it called, 'Frankenstein's Balloon'?"

"We took some canvas panels from the *Ophelia* and rearranged the letters. She's called the *hOpe*."

"Says 'hOp,'" Romilda said.

"The 'e' is on the other side. We ran out of space." Finch grinned. "But the important bit is it'll fly. You and Gunny are going home."

"Home," Romilda said wistfully. "After all this, I can't see myself going back to lawn parties and cotillions."

He glanced down at her with mischief in his eye. "I don't know what a 'cotillion' is, but if you're serious, Miss Gunn, would you consider becoming an airship pirate?"

Before Romilda could answer, Khady came up to them.

"Everyone's ready," she said, then added, "Captain."

Finch turned and saw the assembled survivors, standing as straight as they could, watching him expectantly.

Fang spoke: "What are your orders, Captain?"

Romilda nudged him. "Go on, *Captain*."

Finch turned and looked up at the clear blue vault of heaven.

"Let's see where the sky takes us."

The Ring of Hours and Seconds

Jeffrey Lyman

Toten stared at Thierra. His wife sat at the kitchen table, spinning a teacup with her fingers, not meeting his eyes, her mouth pulled down in a light frown. She still wore last night's dress, though it was mid-morning, and she looked exhausted.

"How much did you lose this time?" he asked. His eyes drifted up to the small window behind the sink, looking out at another window into another drab kitchen a few feet away. A bouquet of dead flowers that Thierra had gathered weeks ago sat in a vase near the window. Dried, yellow petals had puddled on the counter beneath it.

For an excellent thief, one of the best, he should have been able to afford a flat significantly higher in the city. But until Thierra stopped gambling, they lived near the mud-choked streets.

"I almost won," she said with a trace of defiance and frustration in her voice. "If that fat old Mr. Sochett hadn't cheated, I'd have cleaned house. I was this close!"

There was movement in the corner of his eye, but Toten didn't look at her. No doubt, she held up her fingers, pinched with the first finger and thumb almost touching. *This close.* It was always this close.

"How much?"

"A hundred thousand," she said sheepishly.

This time he did look at her, his head snapping around, but she was staring into her teacup as if it might reveal the winner of an upcoming horse race, or the next card, or the next roll of the dice.

"A hundred thousand?" He sagged against the counter and tried to swallow, but his throat had suddenly gone dry.

"I was up eighty thousand," she said.

"That doesn't do us any good, does it?"

She leaned back and rubbed her neck. "What are we gonna do?" It was always *we* when she lost.

His breath wheezed in and out as he tried to think. "I got thirty thousand from my share of that last job at the docks. That would have dug us out. There aren't any other big jobs coming up."

She twisted the belt on her skirt. She was twisting hard.

"What?" he said.

"Mr. Beraghar holds the debt. He said we have to pay within the week, and if we don't have the money, he has a job for you."

"You gambled at one of *Beraghar's* houses?" he sputtered, fully facing her now and gripping the back of the empty kitchen chair. Mr. Beraghar should have gone to the guild of Masons and Builders with his request. The guild assigned thieves. That Mr. Beraghar was going through Thierra meant the guild had turned him down. Certain jobs were too dangerous or political for the guild to accept.

"He said it'll clear the books."

Toten turned back to the dirty kitchen window. In the other kitchen, a wife in a housecoat and yellow belt walked past carrying a pot. "It'll clear the books? A hundred thousand just like that? You know that means it's going to be ugly. Probably something against the Baron." *Something that could get Toten killed.*

"I don't know what else to do! We can pay him the thirty thousand, and you can borrow the rest from the guild maybe?"

"I'm already paying off the forty thousand I borrowed for you last month."

She shrank on herself. "I'm sorry," she said. "I wanted to cash out, but I was winning."

"Of course, you were! They let you win, drove up the stakes, and then took you down. It's what they do." He stopped. He'd told her this a hundred times, but sometimes she won big and so he knew she didn't believe the game was rigged. She once won so much she'd bought a proper steam car and a dozen sets of driving clothes and rented a cottage on the far side of the city for six months. The car was long returned to pay debts, and the clothes were packed away for want of a vehicle to drive.

He shrugged into his vest and coat, there was no point in going out if you didn't look proper. "I'll talk to Mr. Beraghar."

She leapt to her feet. "Oh, thank you."

"Don't thank me until we know what the job is."

"I promise I won't gamble again. This time I mean it. I promise."

"I know." Toten kissed her on the cheek, and she hugged him back fiercely, fingers digging into the back of his coat.

Toten walked three blocks to the corner of Grace and Mast where there was a pneumatic lift up to the upper tiers. From there, he could rent an airlift to Mr. Beraghar's lofty apartment at the highest tier in the city of towers. How high could you build? No one knew. The engineers swore they could build higher, but Toten figured the question would only be settled on the day that one of those towers fell. Down here in the depths, the engineers had installed massive steel columns, latticework beams, and arches, often right through the existing shanties and old apartments.

At least they were kind enough not to raze the buildings. They just drove the piles right down through them and let the lower folks live with massive beams running out of their windows. Gotta duck on your way to the toilet. It had happened to one of Toten's childhood friends, who swore he cracked his head on the beam in his living room twice a day. At least he got fresh eggs from the pigeons nesting in the flanges.

Toten crowded onto the lift with dozens of other low-dwellers, all dressed nicely on their way to jobs higher up. Waiters and stewards. The lift had no railing, just a wooden platform on tracks, but Toten figured if he got pushed off, he could leap for a window or a washing line passing by. After a lifetime of thieving, he automatically scanned for escape routes. He knew he did it, but it was second nature.

At the upper tier, he trudged off with other men. The rest continued on to the upper-upper tier. There was an upper-upper-upper tier above that, called the Triple-Ups, and Toten thought the people who named things ought to put more thought into it.

At the balloon-docking station, throat tight and stomach nauseous, he asked for Mr. Beraghar's apartment. "Two hundredth level, St. Aupert's," he said to the old balloon man. St. Aupert's was a private island of tall buildings unconnected to the pneumatics in the rest of the city.

"I can get you to the landing dock at one-seventy-five," the stooped, minimally toothed old man said, pulling on his flatcap. "You'll go through their security from there."

"Of course."

The old man checked a couple of dials on his tanks, unleashed fire, and the balloon lurched up on guidewires. Toten gripped the basket as buildings sped past. Twice, the old driver slowed at a crossing and switched wires, nimbly moving horizontally as well as vertically, passing other balloons of varying sizes. The last crossing, a wire of thousands of feet long between the building cluster at Horitz Street and the cluster at St. Aupert's, was the demarcation between buildings connected to the city system, and St. Aupert's that chose not to be. Thieves didn't steal from St. Aupert's.

"There she is," the old man said, nodding to the soaring arches and carved wood of St. Aupert's highest tower as it approached.

Toten nodded and looked away. He stared instead at the vast city sprawling below and around him, from the docks, to Senate Hill, to the tree-lined, low western suburbs. He knew it all intimately. The sun gleamed off the endless eastern ocean, but Toten had no interest in travel or ships. The city was all the world he needed.

He noted the cluster of black buildings to the southwest. Rumor was that some idiot had released a demon a hundred years ago, turning the old Mukrove towers dark. They said it had never been the same inside since, even with the demon banished—madness and whatnot. Toten didn't believe any of it. Occultists lived there now, quite happy for its notoriety. Thieves didn't generally rob Mukrove either, because of its reputation and because most Occulties didn't have anything worth stealing.

And in between St. Aupert's and Mukrove stood clusters and islands of buildings on a massive scale, two-hundred-plus stories high, basking in clear air and sunny skies. Most of the high buildings had promenades and sundecks where the great people of society lounged in opulence. Thieves were very interested in those buildings, and Toten figured he'd robbed them all at one point or another. He longed to bask up there with them in peace, just once.

The balloon came gently into the landing platform at St. Aupert's on Level 175, and they were met by four gentlemen in long coats with guns holstered at their hips.

"Business?" said the largest of them, a bullnosed man with shaved head who had probably been a low-level cop once given the number of scars on his face.

"I need an audience with Mr. Beraghar," Toten said. "He's asked to see me. Toten Haday."

Bullnose marched to an earpiece on a nearby wall while his three compatriots didn't move away from staring.

"Lovely day, isn't it?" Toten said to them. "You can see for miles." He walked to the railing at the lip of the platform and his neck crawled. It wouldn't be hard for them to heave him over.

It really did smell nice up here without the sewage and coal smoke.

"You're in luck," Bullnose called. "He'll see you. Mr. Gentle will escort you up."

Toten waved at the balloon man, who slipped his moorings and slid away down the wire, then joined the skinny man called Mr. Gentle on a very small lift that pressed them shoulder to shoulder. Toten didn't care for that. At least the curved front was glass, so he could watch the city spread out around him. So many places to rob. Most buildings had different personalities and income levels, but fads came and went. Old stodgy clusters might spring to life again with a new generation of wealth looking to get away from under the eyes of their parents.

"Mr. Beraghar don't normally accept guests," Mr. Gentle said conversationally. "Are you important? Important people don't usually come up the balloons."

"I'm not important. It's about a debt."

"A lot of people owe Mr. Beraghar money. Like I said, he don't normally accept guests."

"I'm as in the dark as you are."

"He's a bit of a slob, he is."

"What?"

"He's a bit of terrible slob. He'll probably meet you in the front room, that's the only one that's presentable. I had to go in once after he and his men had a row with one of the other lords, blood everywhere, I can tell you, and it was a pigsty." Mr. Gentle shook his head, obviously more disturbed by the mess than the blood. "He could buy and sell every cleaning house in the city, but he doesn't let people up very often. Food, plates, teacups, clothes. Everywhere."

Toten grimaced. "Hopefully you won't need to come collect my body."

"See that I don't. Don't want to go in there again."

The lift stopped and Toten stepped off on a private landing platform that fronted a grand, wooden door with iron bands. Three marble steps led up to the door, which was ridiculous as the apartment was on the level and didn't need steps. Was the whole apartment raised up? What was under the floor then? He mulled the possibilities.

"Mind your tongue and see that I don't have to come up," Mr. Gentle reminded as he closed the glass door and dropped from view.

No point in waiting. Toten skipped up the steps and knocked with the ridiculously large and grotesque knocker. A well-dressed manservant answered.

"Wait here," he said, bringing Toten into a vast entry vestibule that towered three stories high and supported many windows. Warm sunlight poured in across elegant portraits of couples in the clothes of different eras. They looked exactly like the portraits on the walls of old families—parents and grandparents and great-grandparents going back nauseatingly far—only Mr. Beraghar was the first wealthy man in his lineage. People from the lower levels didn't have paintings of ancestors.

"Toten Haday, husband of Thierra Haday," boomed a large voice as a large man with a large beard bustled through one of several doors at the rear of the vestibule. His bespoke gray suit looked ridiculously expensive to Toten's practiced eye. A moment later, two bodyguards of even more impressive size followed through the door.

"Mr. Beraghar," he said. "I'm terribly sorry about Thierra last night. She got in over her head and I've come up to offer my sincerest apologies."

"Have you come to pay?"

"I have thirty thousand, and I can get the rest shortly. I'm good for it."

"Thirty thousand is not a hundred thousand."

"Yes, sir. My wife told me there might be a job I could do that would help resolve this problem."

Mr. Beraghar eyed him and stroked his beard. The bodyguards said nothing. "You come well recommended," he said. "I asked around, and it sounds like you could be more successful if you wanted to be. Your wife is holding you back."

"Yes, sir, but what's a man to do?"

"Then you're a sentimental fool. Sooner or later her debts will catch up to her, you know. It's inevitable. Ask my first two wives." He smiled. "Well, it's your choice. If she ends up dead in an alley some night, come talk to me about permanent employment."

"Thank you." Toten replied tightly. He didn't want to think of Thierra dead. It wasn't her fault, she had a compulsion, and he would always steal his way out of her troubles. Love was love. "What can I humbly help you with? My skills only go so far."

"That's not what I hear. Come with me." Mr. Beraghar strode past and exited through the grand front door. One bodyguard followed, and one waited for Toten.

Toten joined Mr. Beraghar at the railing of the landing platform. The bodyguards stood too close and he kept very aware of where they stood.

"That's the mark there. The Mukrove Towers." Mr. Beraghar pointed at the dark towers in the distance.

Toten winced. "Thieves don't go there."

"Of course they don't. It would be silly, right? There's madness and ghosts in those apartments. You're going anyway."

Toten inhaled and exhaled. "What's the job?" What could possibly be worth a hundred thousand in there?"

"There's a necromancer on the 143rd Floor named Nekravé, which I'm certain is a made-up name. I'm not even sure if they're a man or woman due to all the dark robes and theatrics, but they've got something interesting, and I'd like you to steal it."

"What is the object of interest?"

"It's a ring, which Nekravé wears on their middle finger. A clock ring. Nekravé is one of only a few living necromancers to have made one, and I want it."

Toten turned to face the man fully. "You want me to go into the Mukrove Towers, get to the 143rd Floor, break into a necromancer's apartment, and steal a *ring*?"

"Yes."

"Is this a gold ring, studded with jewels?"

"It's an iron ring, studded with gears. It looks uncomfortable."

"How's that worth anything at all?"

"That's my business."

"Well, does it do something? Or shoot something?"

"Again, my business." Mr. Beraghar's voice turned threatening.

"I need to know if it'll hurt me when I pick it up."

"The answer is no."

Toten nodded.

Mr. Beraghar continued. "Nekravé goes out for tea every Wednesday at the Shrop Hanger Restaurant with several other necromancers, and they never wear the ring. I hear it's considered impolite and boastful. That is your opportunity to get into their safe, and you'll have over an hour."

"There'll be necromancer guards on the building."

Mr. Beraghar waved dismissively. "Are you superstitious?"

"I'm not, but necromancer guards are uncannily dangerous. So I've heard."

"You are a master thief. Act like it."

"Fine. But what if I'm caught? What happens to Thierra?"

"Her debt will be forgiven if you succeed and only if you succeed, so don't fail. If you get caught and give up my name, it'll go even worse for her."

Toten grimaced. He did not like Mr. Beraghar, but Thierra had put him in a difficult situation.

Mr. Beraghar threw an arm around his shoulders and squeezed. "What do you think, Mr. Haday? Can you do it?"

"Does the sun rise and set without fail? Does God love this, the greatest city in the world? Of course I can do it. What's your timetable?"

"Two weeks."

"That's too tight."

"Two weeks."

Toten pictured Thierra sitting at the kitchen table. Necromancers terrified her, as did most anything occult, but Mr. Beraghar was a known threat. "Fine."

Mr. Beraghar turned back to the view, arm still around Toten's shoulders. "It is the greatest city in the world, isn't it?"

Toten returned to his same, tired kitchen. This time, he sat at the table with his hands around a teacup while Thierra paced. She was pale, and her sharp eyes were dark. The dried flowers had lost more petals.

"Tell me what Mr. Beraghar wants you to do."

"No."

"Tell me!"

"It doesn't matter. He wants something, he's going to get it."

"Is it dangerous?"

"I don't know yet."

She stopped pacing and hugged herself, looking small. "This is all my fault."

"Come here." He slid his chair back and she sat on his lap, wrapping herself around him, burying her face in his neck. He felt the dampness of her tears against his throat. "They wanted me for a job, so they set you up. Mr. Beraghar has people who do that." He rubbed her back gently. "We'll get through this."

"But what if something happens to you?"

"I'm the best there is. You believe that, don't you?"

She nodded.

"Then we'll get through this."

"Just tell me the job."

"I can't. I know you won't tell, but the walls have ears. Now jump off." She slipped off his lap and he stood. "I have to plan, and that means I'm going to be late for the next bunch of nights. I don't want you gambling. Right? No gambling…"

"I don't have any money."

"Let me hear you say it."

"I won't gamble. Happy?"

"Of course I'm happy. I'm always happy with you."

She pulled him in for another tight hug and kissed him. "I can't sit around doing nothing," she said. "I'll go back to my job at Marta's."

"That's good. They need help."

Sometime later, he stood on the third-floor balcony of a shuttered restaurant, looking across at the start of the Mukrove city block. Several shops were boarded up, but most were doing fine. Mukrove itself seemed a lively enough place, and people came and went in a continuous trickle, so the dark rumors weren't keeping people away.

There were five towers in the complex, all the color of old ash, but only two of them soared to great heights. Who sunned themselves on the topmost decks? A number of midsized and lesser buildings filled the spaces in between, and a park meandered around them all. The park had been let grow wild, with vines and creepers coating the trees and lampposts and the lower stories of the buildings in an explosion of growth. It seemed almost planned for ambiance.

He looked toward the front door of the target tower. He'd want to get to know the cleaning staff and maintenance men. Maybe apply for a job. He'd watch Nekravé and get to know their patterns and personality.

Should he rent a balloon and drift across the buildings to get a higher view? As dangerous as necromancers were, they were still human with the usual failings, weaknesses, and vanities. He'd be fine. Thierra would be fine.

Two weeks was tight for a difficult job, though.

Mr. Beraghar must want the ring quickly for a reason. Toten would also have to scout out his new employer. There was no point in succeeding and then getting stabbed from behind after the job was done. He needed to know what the ring was for.

⌑

Two weeks later, just after three-thirty in the afternoon on Wednesday, Toten stumbled from a street-trolley into his favorite steak house, a long way from the Mukrove Towers. The iron clock ring lay cradled in his pocket, jabbing him with an edge.

Clouds of steam billowed from the kitchen, and the place smelled deliciously of cooking meat, but he was cold and couldn't concentrate. Today, the smell and the sizzling, the calling cooks and waiters, had no impact.

He wiped sweat from his forehead. How could people live in those towers? There was truth to the madness that people whispered about. It hung thick. The walls and air were tainted with it, smelling of old lilacs. How did they stand it? He'd spent two weeks working there and he would never go back.

He'd get this ring to Mr. Beraghar and be done with it. He didn't want a celebratory steak, he wanted a scalding bath, but steak was what he did every time. It was his good-luck habit.

An impeccably dressed waiter with a festive, yellow handkerchief in his breast pocket brought a rare steak and a potato. Toten began sawing at them with little attention. Then the sound and atmosphere in the room shifted. He'd spent his life listening to ambiance, and he looked up as a familiar, dark robed figure swung around him and pulled out the empty chair at his table. He backed away quickly as people openly stared. Nekravé's hood swung loose and low, preventing him from getting a look at their face above a strong chin, vanishingly pale lips, and a hint of shiny copper.

He'd watched them long enough to recognize their limp.

"You've taken something important and made me cross this whole forsaken city chasing you," Nekravé said in an obviously fake, obviously annoyed, sepulchral accent.

"I don't know what you're talking about," Toten said firmly, preparing to bolt for the door.

Nekravé peered down at Toten's plate. "How can you eat that?" they said. "It looks revolting. I'm a vegetarian."

Before he could reply, Nekravé raised a closed fist, opened it, and blew powder at his face.

Toten coughed violently, and his vision dimmed.

⁓ঞ৹৹⁓

He awoke, slumped, strapped to a chair in a stuffy, dimly lit room. It took a few minutes to gather his thoughts. How much time had passed? The room held an unsettled atmosphere that he recognized like an itch at the back of his throat, and he shuddered at the smell of lilacs.

He finally shook off the drugs, and his eyes fastened on a collection of brass and wooden instruments hanging on a disturbingly red wall to his right. Sexual implements? Each hand-held device, with its leather bindings, clamps, pistons, and coiled, braided steam-hoses, had been lovingly polished and displayed to prominent effect. He jerked his eyes away in terror, looking around, but the small room held nothing else except his chair, the table before him, and two sputtering gas-lamps on the wall. Their uneven hiss the only sound.

He yanked at the straps that bound his arms, but they were too tight to reach the buckles. No worry—he'd be a poor thief if he couldn't escape a binding. He had to hurry. Nekravé would return soon, that was certain.

With a twist of his hand, a small blade on a spring leapt through the fabric of his sleeve cuff. He began sawing at the thick strap, making quick progress, breathing rhythmically to keep from panicking. Got to keep control, or he was lost. That was a motto and a lifestyle. In moments, the strap was through, and he tugged at the buckle on his opposite wrist. Then to the shin-straps.

It may have only been thirty seconds, but that was too long. Got to go. He leapt to his feet and dodged around the table. Hesitating at the door, he listened, then pulled it open. Of course, Nekravé stood right there in the corridor, black-robed, reaching for the doorknob. Without hesitation, Toten charged into them, knocking them back, sprinting down the corridor for the stairs. Nekravé did not shout or say a word, but he felt them following. How close? How fast could a limping necromancer realistically run in robes?

He'd memorized the layout of the building, and each floor was the same. A corridor in a loop around the core, apartments outside the loop and elevators and stairs inside. The same burgundy patterned carpet lay on every floor, worn into tracks after so many years, and wall sconces cast flickering light from small gas flames. Time to take the stairs.

If Nekravé was smart, they'd take the elevator and try to catch him at the bottom of the building, so he'd run up instead.

He burst into the stairs, noting the floor number in tile on the wall — "143" — and ran up, keeping the slap of his shoes on the stair treads to a minimum. He had energy, he had breath, he could run a long distance. He didn't hear the door of the stairwell crash open beneath him, so Nekravé must have chosen the elevator. Good. Now where to get off? He'd scouted the underused landing platform at 154 last week.

A short time later, his lungs heaving, he came to a stop on the landing at 154. His headache was worse, not better, but he tried to listen over his own gasping. There were no voices calling beyond the door, no one obviously waiting. If he could get to the cables that the balloons used, he could initiate a daring and stupid escape.

How had Nekravé followed him? Could they do it again?

He'd have to lay low for a while and find another way to appease Mr. Beraghar. He'd check in with the Thieves' Guild and let them know about this whole cock-up. Nekravé might lodge a complaint.

He took the smooth, bronze doorknob out to the landing platform and pulled. Nekravé stood there outside, hand extended, and threw powder into his face.

⁘

Toten awoke, strapped to a chair in a brightly lit, stuffy room. His head was slumped forward, and he had a terrible headache. He didn't recognize anything, but he felt like he'd been here before. What had happened?

His eyes fastened on the brass devices displayed on a disturbingly red wall to his right. Sexual implements? He had to get out of here! He jerked his eyes away and looked around, assessing, but the small room held nothing else but his chair, a table, and four sputtering gas-lamps.

He yanked at the straps that bound his arms, then twisted his wrist. Nothing happened. What? Looking down, he saw a fresh hole in his sleeve, but the blade was not there. Fear settled in his heart.

The door opened as he was unsuccessfully trying to get his hip-blade to flip out. Nekravé entered carrying a straight-backed, wooden chair. They placed it across from him and sank onto it while Toten made his expression deliberately calm.

As before, Nekravé's face was only visible from the tip of their nose down to their chin.

"Please stop cutting through my leather," they said in that same oddly fake sepulchral voice. "It's expensive to replace."

"What are you talking about? I haven't cut anything."

They shrugged lightly and held up their slender, pale hand, revealing the black, iron clock-ring with all its gears and angles on their middle finger. "This is the third time we've done this dance, though you won't remember the first two. In both of those prior times you revealed a cleverly hidden blade and cut through my straps. I've relieved you of both of those blades. Please stop."

"You drugged me and took my memory?"

"No drugs, except for the sleeping dust. This clock-ring has many attributes, one of which is to reverse time. You escaped, I knocked you out and reversed time, and here we begin again. Only I can remember this reversal, as I am the ring-holder. For you, this is the first time you've been here except that you're lighter a pair of blades."

Toten stared at the ring in consternation. Magic wasn't real. He assumed Nekravé was lying, and she'd drugged him. "No wonder people want that ring," he said half-jokingly. "Reversing time? The things a thief could do with that."

"Yes, they could, I suppose. That's not its purpose."

Toten leaned back, feeling around for his ankle knife as fear began to set in. He looked at the array of devices hanging on the wall, then back into the impenetrable cowl. "What happens next?"

Nekravé started shaking slightly, and it took a moment for Toten to realize they were laughing. "Those aren't for you, silly. Those are mine, and I hang them there for remembrance."

"Yours?"

"We could take them down to play, if you like."

"No."

They reached up gently and lifted their cowl from their face to reveal horrific damage. Half of Nekravé's face was metal. Toten twitched, then stilled his expression again.

Nekravé was a woman, at least he thought she was, thin to gauntness. Nearly the entire side of her head and face had been replaced with sculpted copper. Her hairline stopped abruptly above her right eyebrow, and half of that eyebrow was gone. Her temple, ear, and cheek had been replaced with polished metal; her right eye was a bronze artifice, turning in its socket, mechanical pupil dilating and adjusting; her neck tendons were delicate pistons that disappeared down into her black robes where the shoulder seemed to be artifice too. The flesh of her forehead and cheek were raw where they met metal.

"Do you like it?" she said, tilting her head.

"Whoever did the work is amazing," he said, refusing to turn away. "Best I've seen."

"I was an artist at the highest levels before the accident. People paid great sums to watch me perform, so I could afford the best artificers."

Toten squinted, looking at her, and then at the wall of toys, comprehension dawning. "You were a courtesan?"

"I was an artist!" She half rose and then sat again. "I was an artist, until a steam cannister exploded. The damage was significant to my body and my brain. Wealth can only repair so much, but I survived. I can no longer perform, but I've acquired an alternate viewpoint on life and its excesses in the highest towers."

"That's when you became a necromancer?"

She nodded, the pistons in her neck extending and retracting noiselessly. There was gold inlay to complete her truncated eyebrow, and delicate filigree to recreate the look of a jawbone.

"I'm forever trapped between life and death," she said, "so why not worship at its altar?"

Toten shifted, uncomfortable with her blasphemy. "What do you want of me?" First Mr. Beraghar, now this mad necromancer. He was not used to being blackmailed, but he would listen to her demands.

"I could kill you," she said. Her fake accent had dropped, and she had a typical educated woman's accent of the north quadrant. "The guild won't protect you. You stole outside of sanction, and worse—you got caught."

"Or?" Toten prompted, waiting.

"I want you to explore a new piece of the necromantic realm while I sit here in safety."

"Necromantic realm?"

"You've never heard of it?"

"I make a point of not prying into necromancer business."

"Until now, that is? At its simplest, it is a parallel world of darkness and shadows. There are places of great value in it, at least to necromancers. There are libraries left by the ancient ones, tombs of powerful demons, and creatures made of darkness."

"Sounds lovely." It sounded like a bad hallucination. "So I just scout out the place, and then I can go?"

"Of course. I'll have no more need of you. You've already told me Mr. Beraghar is your employer."

Toten jerked forward. "I never told you that."

"In one of the other two times you were here, when I was torturing you on this table, you sang like a bird."

"I don't believe you."

"I don't care."

Toten looked around for any chance of escape. The gas lamps hissed, the tools on the wall looked even more frightening now, and the atmosphere of the room weighed on him. He didn't want to be drugged and at her mercy.

"What do I have to do if I say yes?"

"Oh good," she said, half smiling with the human side of her face. "I knew you'd be reasonable."

"What do I do?"

"I've developed a new door into the necromantic realm, one that leads much higher up in the scale if I'm right."

"What does that mean?"

"It doesn't matter, I just need you to go in and come back and tell me what you saw. I think you'll be dizzyingly high, far away from all existing doors. A new place entirely. A new zone on the map." She clasped her hands together excitedly. "I could win an award at the annual banquet."

"Just go in, come back, and tell you what I saw?" He'd play along and pretend he saw something. The explosion had obviously damaged her brain.

"Yes."

"And what are the odds of my head getting bitten off by one of those beasts you mentioned?"

"High. But the odds of you screaming to death on this table are also high."

"So, I don't have a choice."

"Of course you have a choice. And if you go in, whether you survive or not, I'll make sure your wife's debt is settled. Is that fair?"

Despite his fear of what was about to happen, Toten felt a flush of relief. "Fair. Where's this door then? What do I need to smoke or inhale? Is there prep work?"

"Not like that." She held up the clock-ring again. "This is the door, and it's far more complex than the older, existing rings, I can tell you that. I'm quite proud."

"That's a door?" he said doubtfully. Maybe she'd already introduced some sort of gas into the room to make him hallucinate. Was it already too late?

Nekravé nodded eagerly. "We have dozens of rings like this—simple and more limited in their function, and they're all doors." She pointed to the largest gear poking out from the side, its fine teeth curving back into the black face of the ring. "This is the wheel of hours. It was how I reversed time to catch you. Below it are additional gears and wheels—minutes and seconds, obviously. In between those are smaller and smaller wheels. They allow you to slip between minutes, cut between seconds. The spaces that get forgotten. You know about those spaces, don't you? You live in those spaces. Places where no one sees or hears. A lot of people live in those spaces and the city forgets them. That's as true for your world as it is for mine."

"There are hiding spaces between seconds?" He wasn't following her logic.

"This ring is special because of the quantity and quality of the gears. I can cut the seconds finer, slipping into smaller spaces. I will go places no one has ever gone."

"You mean I'll go."

"It's a noble sacrifice. There are necromancers whom we call Lamplighters. They find safe paths through the darkness. I would be a Lamplighter to my people, but it doesn't do anyone any good if I'm killed while doing it. So, it's a time-honored practice to use proxies for our explorations. Others have gone before you, others will follow—some are successful, and some are not.

"Now what do you say?" She rustled her robes and looked expectant. "Are you going to do this, or do I begin dissecting you? I need a willing participant."

"Are you a monster?"

"I'm an artist."

He stared into her human eye for a long moment, and she didn't blink. She was so utterly convinced of this that he began to get nervous. "Where will I be when I go through the door? I won't go without some idea of what to expect." If he was going to make up visions for her, he needed to know what she expected him to see.

"I'll describe it in terms you can understand but know that it isn't like this at all. These are approximations. You'll see darkness at first, and the air will be hot and dry. You'll be standing on gritty soil, with vague impressions of bushes and trees around you." Nekravé closed her human eye. Her open, bronze eye continued to turn in its mechanical socket. "It's night with no moon, and the stars are not our constellations. Your eyes will adjust enough to see the ruins of houses scattered around you. That seems to be typical for the city."

She was taking this seriously. He had an itch between his shoulder blades. "How big are the houses? How close together?"

She opened her eye. "One or two stories, wood-framed, spaced apart. It doesn't matter, you can't explore them. There are eyes on you from every window. Not long after, the dogs will come." Her gaze was far away. "They're not dogs, of course, but how else do you describe the indescribable except with familiar names."

Toten fought laughter at her naivete and gullibility. "Am I looking for anything specific?"

"Light. You're looking for one of the rare houses that are lit brilliantly. There are a few in town, and the town is vast. They're library houses. You can't avoid the dogs, but they don't like the light. If you can get to one of those houses, you'll be safe." She waved her hand with the iron ring. "Successful rings open doors close to those houses and give us safe access, unsuccessful ones lead to darkness and therefore death."

"I hope your ring works."

"It will." She kissed the ring and held it up. "There's a mountain—you can see it by the hollow lack of stars and a couple of bright houses scattered across it. There's a single beacon at its peak. That is the house we're aiming for." She shivered.

"Has anyone gone up there before?"

"How could they? They don't have my ring." She stood. "Time to go."

"Now?" He jerked against the straps.

She came around the table, tugged off the ring, and slid it onto his finger. She leaned over and began twisting wheels and gears. "Have you ever left the city before?"

"No, why would I?"

"You're in for a treat. I've put thirty seconds on the timer." She stood, and he noticed that the arm on her damaged side seemed shorter. "That's this button here." She pointed to a tiny button on the ring's edge.

"Thirty seconds isn't much time."

"It's too much time in there. Remember, you're cutting through the seconds, elongating them. The dogs will come, so start running immediately. Zig and zag, don't run in a straight line. I hope you return."

He stared at the rotating gears in the ring, transfixed. He could hear it ticking, counting the seconds. Three…four…five…

"Don't steal anything," she called, stepping to the wall. "Also, ignore the voices and don't read the books. Both can drive you mad if you don't know what you're doing."

"Voices?"

The room suddenly began to tremble with a nauseating hum, and the gas lamps dimmed. …Seven…eight…nine… Toten yanked at the straps again, hurting himself.

"Thirty seconds — but the seconds are bigger there. Good luck."

The room vanished.

Toten snapped open his eyes and it was, as described, very dark. He was standing, no longer bound, and the air was thick, hot, and prickly, and it stank of mildew. Where was he? He spun, disoriented, his boots scraping on sand. The bushes she'd spoken of moved unnaturally in his peripheral vision. Some were as big as trees, restlessly contorting. He couldn't focus his eyes on them. A half-collapsed house loomed beyond them in the darkness and an intense feeling of being watched grew. There were voices at the edge of hearing. This couldn't be real. He was hallucinating. Turning his head, he found the double-gabled mansion that Nekravé wanted, the only source of light in this place. It was up a steep hill. It was not close.

Fear clawed at him, but he had to do this for Thierra. Damn Nekravé.

He heard a noise and dove and rolled without hesitation and came up running at a sprint, boots chewing into the sandy ground. He dodged right and curved back left, terror driving his legs as hard as they'd ever gone.

Darkness leapt at him, and he felt searing pain across his back. He stumbled but kept running. Light meant safety! Nekravé had said so.

How far uphill? A hundred and fifty feet? They were right on him, the dogs with snapping jaws, when he burst across the last gap, hurtling up the steps onto the front porch, slamming into the front wall of the house between a window and the door. He spun to face them, but there was nothing there—just barren soil sloping steeply away. He hesitantly returned to the top of the steps, panting and sweating in the heat. The light only reached so far, and he saw great bodies of darkness pacing beyond the circle of light, glaring with wolfish eyes.

His presence was resented.

"This isn't real," he said, begging himself to believe it. "Come on, hold yourself together. She drugged me. Wait it out, it'll end soon." The whispering voices swelled and fell, the susurrus of a crowd, and if he listened hard, he could almost understand them.

He gingerly pulled his coat off and stuck his hand through the slashes in the back then tossed it over the porch railing. Next, he peeled off his vest. It was damp with blood. Probing with his fingers, he didn't think the cuts were that deep. He'd survived worse. He put the vest back on and buttoned it, wincing.

"You're too slow," he yelled out, but his voice fell feebly in the heavy air. "I'm not a paunchy necromancer in flouncy robes." He felt their surge of anger and a deep growl arose from the darkness farther down the hill. A hundred throats took it up, and the furious rumble moved slowly from left to right.

Trembling, he lifted the clock-ring to the light, inhaling a shaky breath. Was it ticking? It wasn't ticking, and he felt cold panic despite the heat. Suddenly, it clicked, the gear moving once, and then it stopped again. He shook it next to his ear. What had she said about seconds lasting longer? Damn her. How long was a second? He counted almost to seventy before the clock ticked again. It was still moving, and he felt a rush of relief.

He stared out at the pacing, growling dogs. It was real. It felt *too* real. Necromancers were fools to come here.

He lowered the ring and took his bearings, struggling to ignore the noise and smell that were burrowing into his head. The porch was limned in warped and peeling boards, once white, but it was otherwise empty of rocking chairs and potted plants. It disappeared around the far corner of the house into darkness.

She said he shouldn't steal here. Screw that. There were libraries in these houses, but was there anything actually worth taking?

Glancing out one last time, he couldn't help himself, he noted the pinpricks of light far below him. The other beacon houses down on the plain. The strange constellations above and the lights below might have been beautiful in another place.

He felt blood on his back, hot on his spine.

Turning, he pushed through the front door into an oddly barren foyer. Dark wainscotting wrapped the lower walls, and plaster peeled above in disturbing patterns. Everything blazed with light, like the porch. It came from everywhere and nowhere.

He closed the front door, muting the relentless growling, but now he heard scratching in the walls instead. Mice?

There were three closed doors across the foyer from him and a narrow stair going up. Something wet and nasty had been dragged down the stairs, leaving a thick, rancid smear. Toten tore his eyes away.

Keep moving. Keep moving.

The clock-ring ticked again.

The doorknobs of the three interior doors were plain brass, and he gripped one gingerly with his fingertips, heart thumping. The door opened into a brightly lit, front drawing room with blackened windows out to darkness.

The air in the room was hot to breathe, and he could feel the rising and falling growl through the walls, but nothing moved here. He stepped across the threshold.

There were bookshelves, packed with huge leather tomes with no titles on their spines, but what captured his attention were two tables, about six feet to a side. Each supported an elaborate model of a village. Bright lanterns on tracks hung from the crumbling, blue ceiling above each.

He edged slowly up to the first table. It held amazing detail at such a tiny scale. There was a cluster of maybe fifty wattle-and-daub huts, each about as tall as his first knuckle, all slightly different, gathered around the banks of a muddy river. He'd seen drawings of places like these in grade school. There were gardens in miniature behind each hut, and broader fields beyond. It looked so realistic that the river could have been flowing. It even looked like there were smudges of smoke rising above the huts. He leaned forward. Were the people and animals moving? He gasped and reared back, then leaned forward again. They were! But at such a tiny scale that they were moving incredibly slowly. The animatronics must have been assembled with a jeweler's loop; they were only half as big as his pinky nail.

Why were they built, and why here?

He turned to the second table, which held a town on the low slopes of a fake, rocky mountain, whose sheer rise ended abruptly about three feet above the table. There was a crystal blue lake in front of the village, and vibrant, green meadows. Squinting, he could see the tiny animatronic people and animals and carts moving here too. Circling the table, he studied the wooden struts and plaster that held up the back of the hollow mountain. From the front, the illusion was complete. Beneath the table, there was a small lamp on tracks. The moon? Looking up, he realized that the brighter sun-lantern was moving slowly along the ceiling track.

There was nothing worth stealing here, and the stifling heat was getting to him. The scratching in the walls seemed louder and his back throbbed. The ring ticked.

Wiping his face with a handkerchief, he hurried back to the foyer and hesitantly opened the second door. A dim, narrow hallway led down to the rear of the house. There had been pictures on the stained wallpaper once, he could see the pale squares where they had hung, and there was a yellow ball on the floor, halfway down.

He traversed the corridor as quickly and as quietly as he could, neck crawling. An empty kitchen with blackened windows lay on the right. There were smeared stains across every countertop and an empty dog crate on the floor. He wasn't about to open the cabinets or larder. The other room off the corridor had probably been a dining room. Three tables with models took up the space where the dining table would have stood. The wooden buildings in the models were taller here and built much closer together. These were large towns, with narrow lanes and tenement buildings, and a few grandiose governmental buildings at the center. One had a bustling market wrapped around a fountain, with hundreds of tiny people shopping. Another had progressed beyond donkey carts into steam cars and trolleys.

He shook his head. It made no sense.

The corridor was just as oppressive and nerve-racking the second time, so that he practically ran back to the foyer.

The third door off the foyer led to the other front room. Here, there were five smaller tables crammed together. An island village dotted with strange trees caught his attention. He'd read about tropical islands. Boards had been nailed around the edges of the table to hold water, and when he dabbed in his finger, it came away wet. A fan powered by some unknown mechanism sat on a nearby stool and blew rippling waves across the tiny ocean.

Scanning across the ever-present bookshelves and black windows, he thought he saw movement beyond the glass, so he returned to the foyer again and confronted the stairs. Did he really want to go up? The stairs felt different somehow, like a threshold he shouldn't cross. The ring had ticked another three or four times, he could just wait it out here, right? The scratching in the walls grew louder, following him.

But he'd never backed down before, so using all his skill to keep silent on the creaky steps, he climbed and kept his feet clear of the awful smear. That same red-brown stain continued down the corridor above and turned into the rear bedroom. He wouldn't follow it further.

The front bedroom on his right held another model, he could see it from where he stood, but it didn't look like any city he'd ever seen. Soaring buildings of metal and glass stretched nearly to the ceiling. Before he could investigate, he froze at the sound of snoring in the front bedroom on the left.

Peeking in, he saw with shock an old man, beard long and gray and draped down his chest, sleeping in a chair. Someone lived in this terrible place? He wore workman's coveralls and was coated in sawdust. A table stood beside him, piled with knives and tools, bags of plaster, wood, wire, and jars of paint. There were other, larger tools hanging on the wall. A huge city was under construction to his right, and Toten was startled by its size. The table took up most of the room, with buildings rising six feet high and more. These towers rivaled the bedroom opposite, but they were made up of tiny bits of wood and iron rather than smooth metal.

His eyes alighted on boots with fat, gold buckles near the man's feet. *Finally! Here was something to steal.* He wouldn't think or ask himself why or how or even what this man was until later.

Sliding forward, breathing in shallow, smooth breaths, he listened to the snoring with his whole body. The scratching was above his head now, probably in the attic.

Under the harsh, overhead lamp, the old man's face was as pale and hard as marble, heavily lined. His eyebrows rose like wild spiders, delicately sprinkled with sawdust.

Toten crouched to take the boots, and looked up at the city's towers. He froze at this new perspective, recognizing everything. The Bayat Towers, the Frist Towers, the Huyagalla Towers. There was St. Aupert's where Mr. Beraghar lived, modelled in elaborate detail. There was his private landing platform. Toten located the Mukrove Towers, painted darker gray with splotches of black. Tiny hydraulic lifts with people on them rose from the depths to the heights. Little balloons moved on suspended wires.

Why was this man building a copy of his city? Toten stood in wonder and leaned over the model-in-progress. He knew the city, and he knew the model just as intimately. Every avenue, alley, and restaurant was here in detail. The longer he looked, the more un-canny it became until he couldn't deny that this actually *was* his city. How? He felt faint. Tiny crowds crossed at street corners while trams came and went. Cars filled the boulevards. An aeroplane cir-cled then swooped down for a landing on the strip at the city's edge, while commuter trains trundled back and forth on elevated tracks.

He suddenly realized the snoring had stopped and he spun around. The old man's eyes were open, and Toten trembled. They were black from edge to edge, deep and swirling with stars. Eyes capable of swallowing worlds. A furrow grew along his stony forehead.

"Ha'baktha a La?" The man said in a low growl, sitting up, fury transforming his face. "Agakta lue olak!"

Toten snatched the first knife his hand came to on the table and held it forward. It was covered in glue and paint. He backed up. "Are you God? Are we toys?" Those eyes threatened to devour him. "The other cities and the island? Are they real too?"

"Bak," the old man rumbled, standing and yanking a massive carving blade off a hook on the wall.

Toten glanced once at the boots with gold buckles, then bolted, hurtling down the stairs, still avoiding every creaky board by instinct. The old man followed with a roar, careening off walls, bellowing unintelligibly.

Toten fumbled with the front door, yanked it open barely in time, and threw himself across the porch, almost tripping down the stairs. The growling of the dogs swelled into a howl when he emerged, and he slid to a stop on the dead, sandy soil, still holding the useless knife out in front of him. The old man crashed through the front door behind him and stopped on the porch, carving blade in his clenched hand.

The clock-ring ticked again —Toten felt it.

"Arraghava," the old man shouted into the night, looking over Toten's head, and the dogs roared back, driven to a frenzy. Just beyond the light, darkness roiled.

Toten dropped into a crouch against the noise, barely able to fight the urge to run … run … run anywhere. He gripped the knife so hard his hand cramped.

The old man shouted again, loud above the cacophony, and light flared from his eyes, billowing out from the house, licking the underside of sparse clouds like flame. The dogs, horrid mockeries of skinless beasts, fled before it, scrambling downhill and squirming under the porches of derelict houses. Vanishing. The voices paused.

Toten stood in awe, knees popping. He could see all now. The abandoned and haunted town sprawled down the mountain below him and across the plains like a shapeless stain with no end. But that wasn't what grabbed his attention. Giant monsters walked out there.

God-Beasts a thousand feet tall, as tall as the mountain, ambled ponderously on four legs or six. Their indifferent steps crushed houses in swaths hundreds of feet long. They were hairless, the color of livid pus, and their nightmare-faces, level with the ground where he stood, were part-human and part-insect. Heads swung back and forth slowly, half lidded eyes searching. Mandibles chewed. Below them, the lanes and alleys of the town rippled and churned with the motion of—for lack of a better word -dogs.

The old man closed his eyes and darkness dropped, leaving Toten in his small ring of light, blinking. He remained still, hoping his insignificance would save him as the susurrus of voices rose again. The old man strode back inside and slammed the door.

The gear of seconds ticked.

Trembling, he lifted the clock-ring and gently clicked the gear of hours back four ticks with his fingernail.

∽∾ᘐᘐᘗᘗ∾∽

Toten took a seat at his favorite steak house, a fresh bandage on his back. Clouds of steam billowed from the kitchen, and the place smelled wonderful. He felt cold and his hands still shook.

The clock-ring was nestled in his vest pocket where he'd shoved it when he returned, and the knife was wrapped in a newspaper at his hip. His coat was lost, still draped over the railing of the porch back at that house, so he was underdressed for the room. If he'd calculated correctly when turning the hour gear, he had taken himself back to just after his original theft.

A waiter with a red pocket handkerchief in his breast pocket brought steak and a potato, and Toten began sawing at the steak, waiting. The sudden shift in atmosphere announced that Nekravé had arrived. He looked up as the dark robed figure pulled out the empty chair at his table, noting the slight hesitation of her copper and bronze parts.

"You've taken something important from me and made me cross this whole forsaken city chasing you," Nekravé said in her fake, sepulchral accent, just like before.

People were staring, and Toten didn't care.

He pulled a clunky iron ring out of his pants pocket, a replica he'd made a week ago, and held it up between his thumb and finger. "You told me that if this didn't work, it was useless. Well, it didn't put me at the house so it must be useless. It's mine now. I'm keeping it."

Nekravé's arrogance evaporated, and she shoved back the hood from her face. Her flesh eye was wide, the bronze eye was fixed on the ring. "What?" she said in a strong northeast quadrant, lower-class accent.

"The house was too far away. I barely outran the dogs."

"You went?" she said excitedly. "You did, I see it in your eyes, and then you shifted hours back to meet me here. Of course you did. How did you outrun the dogs?"

"A lifetime of outrunning things that mean me harm." He shivered and looked at the chatting lunch-goers. Were they all automatons? Nekravé was, by her own choice, but now that his eyes were opened, he could see the artifice binding everyone together. Rubber bands and stuffing and pistons for beating hearts. Toys of a monstrous god.

"What's inside the bright houses?" he said.

"Libraries. Books. Some we can read, some we don't dare."

"What else?"

"Nothing, why?"

So there weren't models of worlds in every house? Was this the only such house? "What does 'Arraghava' mean?"

She looked at him quizzically. "It means 'Not yet'. Where did you read that."

He shrugged.

"Oh, you have some stories to tell, don't you? Give me the ring."

"It didn't work."

"I'm not going to allow it out among you thieves, turning back hours. Give it back and tell me everything you saw. I'll let you live."

Toten drew the paint-spattered knife out of the newspaper, set the fake ring on the table, and slammed the butt of the knife down on it. It cracked and gears tumbled out. He hadn't expected it to be that easy. "There." He returned the knife to its newspaper. "It's yours."

Nekravé looked down at it in horror. "You broke it," she said in a small voice, and Toten knew that she couldn't make another. She'd intended to modify it to try again.

She jerked her closed fist up from beneath the table. He was ready. When she opened her hand and prepared to blow powder in his face, he was already blowing back. She looked startled as the blue dust hit her.

"We did this before, didn't we?" she slurred with the working half of her mouth. Her bronze eye in its mechanical socket dropped down with a click. Her shoulder slumped. She toppled forward onto the table.

He drew a handkerchief out of his breast pocket and swept the pieces of the ring into it. Two waiters hurried over.

"She'll be fine," he said. "Sleeping powder. She'll be up again in no time."

He tossed a generous sum of money on the table beside his uneaten meal and left the restaurant. The true ring was still hidden in his vest pocket.

Up above, the sun shone. He squinted, raising his hand to shield his eyes, and saw the wires and the track of the lantern crossing the sky. Turning his head, he could see the glue and bits of cut balsam that made up the buildings. He felt like he'd always seen this, only he hadn't noticed.

Nothing was real. This city was a model on a table, at the whim of an old Maker in a world of absolute nightmares.

Did the necromancers know? No, he didn't think so. Nekravé seemed to only care about the books, she knew nothing of what moved about her in the darkness.

He took the knife from the newspaper as he approached a trash can and tossed it in. To his surprise, it speared cleanly through and out the other side of the can like it was paper and stuck in the brick walkway almost to the hilt.

Staring at it, then looking around to see if anyone was watching, he snatched it up by the paint-spattered handle and gently folded the knife back into his newspaper. The Maker's knife could cut through the world.

∾⊰⊱∾

He waited on Mr. Beraghar's lofty landing platform, holding his newspaper, looking out. He felt like he could see forever. How far did the model go? People lived out there on the edges of the city, so what did they see when they looked out?

He'd hidden weapons around the platform a week ago in anticipation of this moment, but now he didn't care. They were props in a play.

"Toten," Mr. Beraghar called, trotting down the faux front steps with his security guards in tow. "Did it go well? Did you see any ghosts?"

"It went fine," he replied in a flat voice, still staring out. Wind blew across his face from some giant fan on a nearby table.

"And the necromancer? You didn't tell my name, did you?"

"Nekravé is face down in a restaurant right now and will undoubtedly be coming after me as soon as she wakes."

"I can hide you."

"You can't." Toten turned to face the jovial, bearded man. "Tell me something, have you ever left the city?"

"There's no need to." He threw his hands wide. "Everything's here. Why?"

"I don't know anyone who's left the city. Not a single person. What if we can't?"

"What's this about?" Mr. Beraghar said, his smile fading.

"I'd like to go far away."

"Hah, travel, eh? Avoid the necromancers? Can't say as I'll join you. I've always thought of foreigners as barbaric and uncivilized."

Toten laughed sadly. "That's what I always thought too."

"The ring." Mr. Beraghar held out his hand.

Toten placed the handkerchief in his palm, barely making eye contact.

"What's this."

"It was damaged."

"Damaged?!" Mr. Beraghar clawed open the handkerchief and poured the pieces into his hand. His face slowly twisted in anger. "What happened?"

"Necromancer magic."

"You don't believe in magic!"

"Yet it's the truth."

"Your wife's debt is not canceled." He turned to his security guards. "Hang him from the railing and find me another thief. We'll get another ring."

They approached. Toten gently lifted the knife from its newspaper sheath, careful of the blade's edge. They glanced at it and smirked, but he'd already done this twice today, going back in time with the ring to do it again. Do it better.

The man on the right lunged, surprisingly quick. Toten could see the powerful pistons in his legs and arms working in unison. He sidestepped and slashed. Stuffing split along the man's midsection, cut wires spilled out, and he coughed a small waterfall of gears. Toten knew that wasn't what everyone else saw.

The second man, despite his partner's swift fall, was already stepping in to attack, swinging a metal bar. Toten blocked with the knife, and the man's expression turned to surprise as the blade passed through the bar like butter, sending most of it tumbling away. Toten continued his motion and stabbed into the little gearbox at the center of the man's chest.

Mr. Beraghar stood frozen for a moment, then turned and fled into his house. Toten followed up the steps and tugged at the massive door. It was heavy and it was locked, so he cut a new door through it with the knife and walked inside.

⚜

Toten returned home, exhausted. It was getting on toward dinner time, and Thierra was cooking. Waiting for him. She turned as he opened the door, all her whirring parts now visible to his eyes now, and ran and threw herself into his arms.

"You did it?" she cried, hugging him tightly.

"I did it."

"And Mr. Beraghar has forgiven the debt?"

"We talked for a while, and Mr. Beraghar was most gracious. He forgives everything but he says you're not to gamble in his halls anymore." Toten was glad that Mr. Beraghar was a coward as heart. He hadn't had to hurt him.

Thierra pulled back, looking at him. He could see her, the old her, if he didn't look too hard.

"What was the job?" she asked. "Tell me. Are we in danger from the Baron?"

He stepped around her and pulled a bottle of expensive liqueur from a high shelf. His pour was generous. She waited.

Leaning back against the counter, he smiled at her. "It has nothing to do with the Baron, but I can't tell you anything else. I probably never can."

She looked frustrated, but he was firm. He'd have to deal with Nekravé and the Necromancer's Guild eventually, but that wouldn't be much of a problem. He'd buy them off with stories of the necromantic realm.

It didn't matter. Nothing really mattered, did it? He had the clock-ring and the knife, and he could steal anything, anywhere, at any time.

He pulled her into another hug and closed his eyes against his new vision. Tears gathered. Love was what mattered.

Something scratched inside the walls.

Saving Time

Jody Lynn Nye

I remember to the moment when my fate was set in motion. It was my tenth birthday, 4:58 in the afternoon of December the tenth, Eighteen-Hundred and Eighty-Six. I was surrounded by friends and relatives. I had just blown out the candles on my strawberry layer cake. My grandfather gave me his watch.

"It's been mine since when *I* was a boy," he said, unfastening the chain from his waistcoat pocket. "So, I don't think it's too large for you."

He placed the round gold case into my palm and fastened the heavy chain through the middle buttonhole of my shirt. The gold gleamed against the brown of my hand like a jewel in a setting. First, I felt the cold metal touch my skin, then a buzzing surged through my entire body. It grew until I felt I might vibrate through the floor; then it softened, but didn't completely die away. It felt like people were looking at me from every direction, even though I couldn't see them. He watched me with knowing eyes and nodded.

"Did you feel it, Nick?" he whispered.

I met his gaze, open-eyed.

"What is it?"

"The Universe," he said, and gave me a smile. I felt the gears inside the watch turn, and I felt tiny as an ant.

"It's too big for me," I protested, trying to hand it back.

"It's too big for everyone," Gramps said. He took the watch from my hand and tucked it into the pocket of my linen jacket. I could still feel the ticking through layers of cloth. It made my whole body twitch. Gramps smiled at me. "But you'll do good with it. I know it."

My mother brushed off the moment as though it didn't matter. Did she know? She must have. She clapped her hands. "Sit down, Dad. Who wants cake?"

My grandfather laughed and pulled up one of the carved wooden dining room chairs to watch the fun. I always felt that he *observed* harder than anybody else in the world. His eyes, darker even than his skin, took in everything.

Although I had every kind of toy and book that any child could wish for, that pocket watch felt more important than anything else. My lessons and family duties took up a lot of the time when I wasn't playing with friends out in the streets of Harlem. I had a new velocipede in which I took immense pride and polished the frame until it gleamed. But the watch told me what to do, or so it seemed.

It had to be wound about once a week. The gold stud on the side of the shining case clicked and popped out a fraction of an inch when the gears inside ran down. I always stopped whatever I was doing when it did and twisted the stem until I felt it stiffen. Uncanny things happened if I didn't.

There was the time I saw a strange motorcar hurtling across the sky, right around twilight, a boxy vehicle with an enclosed roof and four thick tires. Nobody believed a twelve-year-old Black boy when I told them. It zipped overhead through the orange-tinged clouds, dipped slightly, and kept going, out into the stars that were just peeking out in the west, just like a meteor. I thought I could see two White people inside with their mouths open in screams, but it was gone as fast as it came. It was like a nightmare.

My best friend, Terry, told me I should have told a newspaper reporter about it. "Think of the fame!" he said, chuckling. Even he didn't really believe me. The sight haunted me. And all that time, the watch kept nudging me, reminding me I hadn't wound it. Hastily, I turned the stem until the gold timepiece calmed down. Nothing else bad happened after that, as long as I was careful. I felt as though eyes were spying on me all the time, and only the watch could keep them at bay.

Ten years passed before I forgot again, and I'll never forgive myself for that one. The watch kept banging away at my ribs, even though the timepiece itself was in my waistcoat on the sidelines of the Harvard University tennis court. I ignored it because I was in the middle of a match versus a formidable opponent, Stevens, a compactly-built white man with slicked-back blond hair who ran like a greyhound. He had a backward spin that sent the ball on an arc that would veer off right before it hit my racket. For once, I had him on the run, chasing after lobs I put into the corners of the court. He had always been scornful of anyone not from his fancy school or his side of town. I was determined to show him that we were just as good sportsmen as he was, even if I was of the working classes and sponsored to the college by my church

This one match meant nothing in the broad scheme of things. No prizes or fame hung on my success or failure; I was just focused, seeing his strategy and racking up points for my side, but the watch pinged away at me like someone poking me in the shoulder. I thought gears would pop out of my ribs.

When I finally finished with the set (I lost, in case you wanted to know), I saw a young woman from the bursar's office standing at the sidelines. She waved a handful of papers at me. Her sympathetic expression got me worried. I hurried to take the slips from her and read them.

It was bad news. I had received a dozen calls from my mother. My grandfather had had a heart attack. He had been calling for me from his hospital bed. His condition was worsening steadily.

The last one was the hardest for me to read, which I did through tears. He hadn't made it. The watch had been trying to tell me, and I ignored it. My heart felt as if it fell right out of my body, leaving me hollow.

I was devastated. He had been my friend and guide all my life, teaching me, listening to me when no one else did, and watching me as if he knew something about me that I didn't. And the watch had stopped because I neglected it.

"Turn it back."

A voice murmured in my ear. It sounded like Gramps.

"I...."

"Turn it back, son. *Now*."

The stud on the side of the watch popped out, and I felt that stinging sensation, like an electrical shock. It wanted me to wind it. Obediently, I went to turn the tiny dial, but it would not move forward, only backward. Curious, I twisted it.

All around me, people started running backward, like one of Edison's motion pictures shown in reverse. I saw myself running backward out of the college gymnasium with my five teammates. We looked dapper in white flannels, our hair freshly cut and brilliantined, like the champions we knew we were. I was seeing the past. I wanted to shout at myself not to fall into the trap the white player set, but my mouth wouldn't open.

One by one, the messages in my hands disappeared. The young woman came running to courtside. I went to meet her. The watch's stud popped back in against the edge of the case. The young woman handed me a single slip of paper.

"It's your mother, Nick," the girl said, her big brown eyes wide with sympathy.

I read the note.

Your grandfather has had a bad heart attack. He is at Bellevue Hospital. He wants to see you. Please hurry. It was signed by my mother. I crushed the white page in my fist.

"You should go," the young woman said.

"But, I…." I started to say that I had a match. Then I give myself a hard kick. I couldn't miss the chance to talk to him one last time.

I never felt so helpless in my life, but I turned to leave the gymnasium, turning away from my friends. Tom, our leader, a darker-skinned man a good six inches taller than me, and I'm tall, grabbed my arm and gave me a weird look.

"Where are you going? The match's gonna start in five minutes!"

"My grandfather." I held up the message, as if that explained everything. "He had a heart attack. I gotta go."

Tom let loose of my arm. "Sympathy, my friend." He looked at the others. "We'll get it done."

I hesitated for a moment, then decided it couldn't do any harm. "Don't fall for Stevens's feints. He'll send in those spinners and you'll miss the return volleys. He's not much of a runner. He gets out of breath easy. You can beat him."

"What? He can't run? But he's beaten us every match this season!"

"Trust me," I said, knowing how strange it sounded. "I… I had a dream."

They scoffed at me, but I was already running out the door.

The watch kept poking me in the ribs as I signed in at the hospital, four hours later, after the most harrowing train journey of my life. A nurse in a starched blue uniform dress under a long white apron directed me to the fifth-floor ward. Mom met me at the door of Room 513. Her face was drawn and smeared with tears.

"He's very weak," she said. "He wants to see you."

I felt as if I was floating away from my body as I approached the bedside. The man in it didn't even look like my grandfather. There hardly seemed to be much left of him but a lanky doll of brown parchment wrapped in a shroud of white linen. His eyes were sunk into waves of brown wrinkles, but they remained watchful. I'd never felt so helpless. My universe was breaking apart.

"Nick." He put out a hand and felt for my waistcoat pocket and tapped the watch. "I'm sorry to do that to you. It happened too suddenly. I thought I'd have more time to explain it to you."

"It's all right, Gramps," I said. His head moved from side to side a fraction of an inch.

"No, it's not. I put a big responsibility on you because I knew you could take it. I just meant to explain before the burden fell to you."

I felt like crying, but a sharp look from those dark eyes dried up the tears. "You've never been a burden, Gramps."

"You stop that right now. I don't have a lot of time in this body." His wrinkled fingers felt along my arm until his hand covered the watch. "That twist back you took to get to me in time. It's going to cost you."

"Anything, Gramps!" I protested.

He gathered strength from somewhere, and glared at me like he was fifty again and I was a little kid. "Don't you dare say that. Don't you dare, boy!" I fell silent. "I'm trying to tell you the most important thing in your life. Listen to me. I don't want you to wind back time again unless you absolutely have got to."

I leaned forward. "Tell me what happened, Gramps," I pleaded. "What does the watch do?"

His eyes grew bright. "It holds you in place while it turns the world back. Not just the world, the whole Universe! You see ghosts of yourself back to the point when you stop. But it's not a miracle. No, it's a curse. Because you pay for it. I did." For a moment, his lips pursed tightly. "I'm gonna be paying a long time. For every minute you turn it back, you pay a year. Not now, but after you die. When your body stops working, you become part of it. *I'll* become part of it, real soon now."

"How do you know all that?" I asked.

"Because it told me. *They* told me." He tapped the watch again.

I looked at the gold timepiece with horror. "There are people in there?"

"Dozens of them, maybe hundreds. This isn't the only one in existence, God knows I've looked for others like me. I asked them not to talk to you yet, so you could grow up a little. I hoped I'd have more time." He barked out a sharp, rueful laugh, which ended in a cough. "I'll have all the time in the world, but it won't be my own." He grasped my wrist even more tightly. "You can wind time back, even stop it cold. Don't use it unless you can't help it. Some of the people who had it were greedy, used the power over and over again. Now they're in the clock forever, or close enough not to matter. Don't make that mistake. Don't set a rod to your own back. Go, live your life and be a good steward."

"But why me?" I asked. I felt even more overwhelmed.

"Because I know you won't misuse it. They know. They tell me the same. You'll be a good guardian."

"You can hear them even though I've got the watch?"

Gramps smiled. "Once it touches you, it's always with you. Now, go get your mother. It's time."

∽ঞৣৡন৵

Gramps had been right. The moment the old man's eyes closed I felt the buzz in the pocket watch again. My mother collapsed, wailing, over his body, but I knew he wasn't really gone. This time I could hear the others, a whole crowd of voices, men and women, a few high-pitched children, even growls and chirrups that weren't human at all. I knew all of a sudden that they had been there, dating back before there were clocks, before there was time. And I heard Gramps.

"Take her home," his voice said. It sounded strange, almost tinny.

"C'mon, Mama," I said, drawing her up with an arm around her shoulder. "Let's go."

She raised tear-filled eyes to me. "I'm not ready to say goodbye!"

"No one ever is," Gramps and I said at the same time, though she only heard my voice.

She looked up, like she was seeing me for the first time. "You remind me of him," she said.

I glanced back at the empty husk on the bed as the orderlies moved in, gently wrapping and concealing it in compassionate draperies. "I'd be proud if that was true."

∽ঞৣৡন৵

I couldn't help but feel like an old-time prophet or something, carrying the responsibility of the ages around in my pocket. I listened to the voices sometimes, hearing them argue about whether or not something could, or should, be undone. But I kept the year-per-minute equation in the top of my mind all the time. By going back hours to be able to sit with my grandfather for the last time, I had accumulated at least two hundred sixty years that I'd have to be imprisoned in the watch, on the chain of someone else who maybe wasn't like me. It did sound like a magical power, but as far as I was concerned, nothing was worth spending eternity stuck in a circle of gold, glass, and gears. I realized I already knew what forever felt like.

I got to know a lot of the personalities who were in there. One of them didn't speak. I only felt his — its? — emotions. It had been there a really long time because it had kindly feelings toward other beings. Most of them were pretty nice and had wisdom to share, like Gramps. Some of them, I learned to tune out, because they complained all the time.

One who spoke in a high-and-mighty way kept trying to make me use the watch. It was like he wanted me to be stuck in it longer and longer. Once when I was walking back from a free concert in Central Park, I saw a motor car collide with a small, open-topped carriage in the middle of an intersection. The crash made me cringe, but I joined the throng of people who rushed into the street to pull people out of the wrecks. Other cars and carriages shrieked to a stop as their drivers hauled on the brakes to avoid the accident.

"See there, youth!" the voice exclaimed. "Turn it back and save lives! Three could perish there! And more will be drawn into the chaos!"

"It's the first driver's fault," a dry voice with a nasal accent said. "That rat didn't care where he was going. He'll do it again. You stop him, and he'll kill someone for sure next time."

I ignored the escalating argument. By then, I was already beside a big, brown-skinned man in coveralls. He was trying to pull open the small carriage's door. "C'mon, *hijo*, help me," he called.

I wrapped the hem of my jacket around the frame which had twisted into sharp tines of broken metal. I nodded to the man, and we hauled it open. A very small woman with a thick black braid and long, almond-shaped eyes hung sideways in the crushed seat

"Help me," she begged. "Please, get me out of here! My daughter! I can't see her."

"We'll get her, lady," the big man assured her.

I heard sirens behind me. Someone had summoned the police.

In what felt like a minute, we were pushed away from the wrecks. A crowd of people rushed in to gawk. The little woman and her daughter sat on the back of a horse-drawn ambulance, wrapped in blankets, being seen to by resident doctors from Bellevue Hospital. The automobile driver, a middle-aged white man with slicked-back hair was bundled into the back of a police wagon, yelling the whole time. A uniformed police officer who looked like my Uncle Darrell took a statement from me.

"Those cuts bother you?" he asked, pointing his pencil at my hands. "The doctors can bandage you up."

I looked down, seeing for the first time that my palms were leaking blood. "I'm okay."

"Go home, hero," the officer said, with a wry grin. "Try not to do any more good deeds on the way, okay?"

"Got it," I said.

I felt pretty good, even if my hands did sting. I had to listen to the argument all the way back to my dorm.

"See?" my grandfather said to the others. "He didn't need it this time."

The upper-class voice grumbled.

But there were times when I did. After my return to Cambridge, I saw a young black woman in a tight-fitting, bustled dress chasing her toddler, then heard the squeal of brakes from a truck that was barreling up the street. They weren't going to make it. I ran toward them, but I knew it was too late. I closed my eyes so I didn't see the truck hit them. But I heard it, the whole thing. I thought I was going to throw up. That time, I twisted the stem backward until I heard the mother calling for her child to stop and come back. I opened my eyes and jumped onto the curb in front of the little boy.

I swooped him up in my arms and handed him to the woman. No blood, no broken bones. He did kick me in the ribs.

"Thank you, thank you!" she kept saying.

"No problem," I said. But I glanced at the watch. Two minutes gone. Two more years in the watch. I felt like I was being punished for trying to help. But I wouldn't have done anything else. I couldn't have.

By the time I met Ginene, I'd racked up a hundred and twenty years more. I first saw her in World History class, and found an excuse to introduce myself. I ignored the guffaws from the watch's voices as she smiled at me. She had light brown skin and surprising green eyes, and her curves, encased in a corset that made her waist an hourglass, setting every nerve in my body tingling. Her curly black hair was swept up in a pumpkin-shaped hairdo, the most fashionable of styles of the moment. I couldn't help but stare in admiration. Her major was Archaeology, a topic that fascinated me. She was even interested in tennis, and was the captain of the women's team.

With some harsh lessons about the value of time, I treasured every minute we had together. We liked the same things, the same music, the same authors. Her greatest fault was that she was lax about getting to places early. I found myself waiting again and again, feeling every minute pass with dread, feeling the universe around me twisting and writhing as if it was in pain. Her lateness caused the only real argument we ever had, when I was disqualified from being in a tennis tournament because I didn't get there on time to add my name to the roster.

"Why are you so driven by punctuality?" Ginene asked, after she watched me storm up and back in front of the shut doors of the arena. "I don't need a lecture from you every time we go out."

"Pull back, boy," Gramps said in my ear. I stopped short before I almost let loose the words that were on my tongue. Instead, my breath gusted out.

"I'm sorry," I said. I couldn't tell her about the sensations I was feeling. "I'm upset about missing this tournament. I guess I do care about time."

"Maybe too much," Ginene said. She smiled. "I know I'm bad. I promise I'll do better. But you have to do better, too. You'll be in the next one. And so will I," she added with a mischievous smile.

I wouldn't have bet against her.

❧❦❧

"You heard about this?" Two days later, Tom, our team captain, spread out a newspaper on the table in our club room.

The rest of us, Ginene included, leaned forward in our chairs to stare. In a photograph that took up most of the front page, I saw a city set on a bright ocean front filled with stone buildings. In the middle of the street was a crevasse that seemed to swallow sunlight. The newspaper photographer had managed to catch cars and carriages hanging halfway over the black gap. The ones behind had them skidded to a halt. The crack in the ground reached to the buildings on either side, lightning bolt-shaped scars climbing up stone and brick structures. The buildings had fallen apart, littering the ground with chunks of façade bigger than a trolley car. People lay on the ground with doctors attending them. Nothing had ever struck such fear into me as viewing that photograph.

"What the hell is that?" asked Diego, one of our players.

Tom looked grave. "It's Charlotte, North Carolina. It happened this morning. This came in over the photo-telegraph. The ground just started tearing itself apart. About eight hundred people died."

"What caused it?" I asked, aghast. The voices started shouting in my mind, and I felt the universe closing in.

"Nobody knows," Tom said. "This is the fourth sudden subsidence that's happened in like two days, all of them in places that have never had earthquakes. Certainly nothing like this."

"Charlotte is where the national college tennis championship is taking place," Ginene said, her emerald eyes wide with horror.

"That's right," Tom said. "Just wanted to let you know that we're not going in as players—the tournament's been cancelled—but I have volunteered to help out with disaster relief. My dad's a fireman, you know. A large part of the NYFD is going down to help. Maybe some of you can come with me."

I felt the watch thumping in my pocket. I suddenly felt like I had to wind it really tightly, like it was working hard to hold back some cosmic force. Was this something I was supposed to do? What could I do? I was just one man, a kid really. I twisted the stem until the milling in the edges sanded skin off the end of my finger and thumb.

"I'll come," I said, although I had no idea how I could help.

"Oh, no, you won't," my mother said, when I phoned from the bursar's office to ask her for permission. Tom's dad said anyone under twenty-one had to get a waiver from parents or legal guardians.

"But, Mom!" I pleaded.

"No. Don't you ask me again." Her voice was as hard as rock. "I lost my parents. I lost your father. I am not going to lose you. You stay there where you'll be safe."

I felt as if I was letting the world down. I couldn't change her mind when she sounded like that.

"All right, Mom. I won't go."

"You better not!" I heard her choke back a sob. "I don't know what's happening to the world. I love you."

"I love you, too," I said, and ended the call.

I wasn't the only one who had to turn Tom down. Ginene's parents told her no, too. So did Diego's. We felt horrible we couldn't help, but Tom didn't blame us.

I could hardly wait until I was alone in my dormitory room. I needed to talk to the voices, to Gramps.

"What's happening out there?" I asked, making sure that I kept my voice low. "Is this something that I am supposed to do?"

"No!" Gramps said, almost deafening me from the inside of my head, overpowering the protests of the others. "This is coming from far outside. Earth's gotten in the way of a force it's never experienced before. It's trying to balance itself against the chaos. You've felt it, I know you have. All you can do is stay safe."

"I'll try," I promised. I felt like a little kid facing a whole army of invaders, like in a story by Mr. H.G. Wells.

"Just essay what you find within your capabilities," the upper-class man said. "No one could ask you to do more."

That didn't help me at all.

❧

Just because she couldn't aid in the relief effort for Charlotte with Tom didn't mean Ginene was going to sit on her hands. With a group of her friends from church, she started a local drive for donations. With no games and classes suspended in sympathy for the people affected by the disaster, she roped the rest of us into helping her. I found myself driving Diego's beat-up speedster back and forth across town to pick up blankets and food. We were supposed to drop them off at the fire station for transport to North Carolina.

"She's a keeper, son," Gramps always said. I completely agreed with him.

The watch insisted that I wind it more often than ever. The voices harangued me less than usual. That worried me even more than having them in my ears all the time.

I still hadn't told Ginene about any of this. If it wasn't going to hold back a planet-threatening disaster, I thought it was better that she not know anything. I hated keeping secrets from her. She was a lot more level-headed than I was, but what if she didn't understand?

Less than a week later, another gash appeared in the earth, right in the middle of Switzerland, worse than any of the previous events. A nature photographer was lucky enough to have his tripod set up on the slope of an alp when the disaster began, and sent it worldwide by photo-telegraph. Whole mountains fell into the ravines, taking towns and cities with them. Thousands died. It would take months, if not years, to discover the names of all the dead.

People were finding it harder and harder to cope with each new disaster. I had the same sensation they did of being trapped with no way out, since nobody could tell when or if it would happen again. Classes at the college were cancelled. Concerts and sports events across the city were postponed indefinitely. I wished desperately for the distraction of those occupations to keep my mind from being haunted by the cloud that seemed to surround the Earth.

People in the city were torn between "It can't happen here" and "It's going to happen here." I wish the latter group would have been wrong.

I was supposed to meet Ginene that afternoon to take her rowing on the Charles River. The weather was nice, and we just wanted to enjoy the sunshine. We needed to calm our minds and relax. Ginene had just about turned herself inside out to help with the relief effort. It was her way of coping. I did everything I could to help, but dread weighed me down. She was the only bright part of my world, a world that felt more and more fragile.

I waited for her near the boat launch. She was late, as usual. Instead of getting upset about it, I listened to the usual argument among the voices in my head. The elegant-sounding lady was going on and on about eternity, when I heard a shout from a distance.

"Hello, Nick!"

I looked up to see Ginene coming toward me through a crowd of children and parents. Dressed in a white flannel dress and jacket with a broad brimmed hat pinned on her hair, she had a long-strapped bag over her shoulder with the top of a wine bottle sticking out. I grinned. She was the most thoughtful, beautiful, intelligent, and compassionate woman on Earth, and I was proud that she let me be her boyfriend. Once I graduated and found a good-paying job, I would ask her to be my wife.

I waved. She waved.

Then, the watch stabbed me in the gut. Gears cut into my midsection, drawing blood right through my waistcoat. I felt a bolt of lightning stab through my body like nothing I had ever felt before. And the world fell apart before my eyes.

Just like it had in Charlotte, the ground split into a dark chasm. Screams erupted from the crowd. I started to run toward Ginene, but the stretch of land on the other side just dropped out of sight. She fell, flailing at the air. I dashed to the ravine and threw myself down with my arms out, trying to catch her. Tons and tons of dirt, rocks, and grass tumbled like a whirlpool made of earth. I saw hands and faces as they were dragged down into the rubble. For one horrible second, I saw Ginene's face. Then, she disappeared. Hundreds of people had just died, but Ginene—! I couldn't stop screaming.

"Turn it back!" Gramps shouted. "Stop bellowing, boy! Turn it back!"

The pocket watch!

I pulled away from the precipice and twisted the tiny knob backward. My hands were shaking, but the watch stopped me turning it too far. The broken land threw itself up again, shooting everyone back to where they had been just moments ago.

"Hey, Nick!" Ginene cried. It was happening all over again. I couldn't save them all, but there was time to save one…

"Run!" I bellowed. "Hurry, run! Right now!"

Ginene must have seen the terror on my face. She didn't hesitate. She came sprinting toward me. I grabbed her wrist and pulled her to safety just as the ground disappeared under her feet. The crowds disappeared into the bloodstained soil and their cries died away. But she was safe. I lay on the ground with her on top of me, panting.

"What was that?" she demanded.

"Another event," I said.

She stood up and looked down into the hellscape at our feet. "Oh, my God. They're all dead! That could have been me!"

"You're alive," I said, in between pants.

She stared at me. "How did you know to tell me to run?" she asked.

"I… I just knew." But her face told me she knew I was lying.

"You've been spooky ever since all this started. Did you foresee it? Do you have second sight?"

"Not exactly," I said. She wasn't satisfied with that answer. I wouldn't have been, either.

"Tell her," Gramps said.

"Trust in her." "No!" "Yes!" The voices were all over the place with their opinions.

"What else are we here for?" Gramps demanded.

For that, no one, including me, had an answer.

I tracked the second hand tracing its way around the face of the watch. I took both of Ginene's hands in mine, and I explained the whole thing: the watch, the price, and the Universe.

Ginene kept her eyes on mine the whole time, never even looking at the timepiece. I felt the moments ticking away like they were stealing my life. Because I knew. I knew what she was going to say.

"You have to save them," she said. When I started to protest, she placed her hand on my shoulder. "I don't want to hear it! Tom would do it. Diego would. Even I would! It won't kill you. Yes, it's easy for me to say, because I wouldn't have to pay the price. But it's all those lives! Look at that!" She pointed to the bloodstained earth below us. "All those people. Children! They are all innocent. It'll cost you time, but it's life long after death. Who gets a gift like that and doesn't use it?" She cupped my hands around the watch.

At that moment, I knew it wasn't just Ginene begging me to help. It was the Universe. I felt it through the watch. I heard it through the voices in my head. Whatever was attacking the Earth, I could avert it.

Around us, horse-drawn emergency vehicles gathered, and firefighters in rescue gear strung ropes from trees to let themselves down into the ruin. I felt the earth starting to move. It would swallow them up. I could protect them. I could do the right thing. I had to.

I twisted the watch stem.

Unlike all the other times I'd helped someone out, dialed back a little to rescue one or two people from an accident, I felt the presence of hundreds, even thousands of lives buried in the bloodstained dirt. I hoped my strength would be enough to pull them back to life.

The rescue teams ran backward. Ginene stared at them.

"Is this what you saw?" she asked. She swallowed. "Did I...? Was I...?"

I nodded, my teeth gritted together, unable to form words. Something fought me, something stronger than anything I had ever felt. Molten ice filled my veins, trying to stop me from turning the stem.

The watch erupted with electrical shocks, digging its gears into my palm. We were becoming one, fighting the menace. This was the biggest battle of my life.

The rescue vehicles rolled away backward, the horses tossing their heads. The ground before me began to churn. People fell upward out of it. One at a time, then in handfuls and hundreds.

I dropped to my knees. Under my feet, the world vibrated like it would shake apart. I thought my bones would break. Ginene clung to me, encouraging me. The watch chain unbuckled itself. I had to grab for the gold case before it fell. Ginene gave me a nervous smile and refastened it as I kept turning, turning, turning time backward. The watch was secure in my hand, and I had control.

At last, the vibration stopped. The dark chasm had filled in. The buildings and trees were all back. The children ran among their parents, laughing. Ginene and I ran into their midst and persuaded them to run to the safe side of the park. Some of them resisted, refused to listen to us, a couple of Black students, but others responded to our desperate pleas.

When I felt the rumbling start again, we hadn't saved them all. We retreated and watched the chasm open. When the maelstrom stopped, we tried again, and again, until we got everyone away from the crack in the earth before it opened. The crowd stood on the edge of the abyss, staring down into the darkness, hugging their children tightly, wide-eyed but safe.

The menace wasn't gone, but it had been driven back. For now. The Universe would exact its cost later, but I was too tired to care.

I took a deep breath and sat on the ground. Ginene slumped beside me.

"Good boy," Gramps said. "I knew you were the right choice."

"I didn't do it alone," I said.

"The voices?" Ginene asked. I nodded. "Tell them… tell them to let me join you. For," she grabbed my wrist and looked at the gold face and counting the minutes, "a hundred and four years. And however long it took you to save me. And any more time you'll owe, I will owe it, too. It's worth it."

"What?" I asked, staring at her. "You don't have to pay this price. It's mine. I took on the responsibility."

"You don't have to do it alone. Does he?" she asked the watch.

Gramps clicked his tongue. "She's a keeper, son."

"A time-keeper," I said. I took her hands and looked into those beautiful green eyes. They were watchful, like Gramps's had been. I felt the massive weight of the Universe pitted against my puny strength and the power of the watch. It was such an unequal battle. "We won't be able to save everyone."

Ginene kissed me, and my heart filled with hope. "We can try."

Reimagining the Mechanism:
An Exposition on the Nature of Time

Bernie Mojzes

In the face of the myriad epistemological difficulties surrounding any investigation of the so-called "Chaos Clock," it might be tempting to consign its existence to the realm of myth. Fiction. Fantasy and fabrication. How, in fact, could one hope to detect the alleged influence of such an object, a device purported to possess effects so pernicious as to affect the very flow of time itself?

Should this lecture simply enumerate and describe that which is objectively known about the Chaos Clock, I fear I should have had to stop before I began. In contrast, the acts and attributes spuriously ascribed to this elusive object have grown at a rate so prolific that any attempt to inventory them would be rendered obsolete before the next speaker rises to stand at this podium.

No, we cannot address the question of the Chaos Clock directly. We must, instead, speak *around* the object of our interest, in hopes that we may catch a glimpse of it from the corner of our eye, so to speak, or of our mind.

The science of timekeeping has seen a great many advances since Christiaan Huygens introduced the pendulum as a measure to affix to time once and for all the nature of discrete, uniform units, and, in the process, profoundly reordering the entirety of Human existence. Under the dictates of Industry, Science, and Capital (or *Kapital*, as our dear friend Herr Marx would say), Time has been transformed from a qualitative element to a quantitative one: discrete, precise, uniform, measurable, exact, inexorable, and absolute—the concept of time as the medium through which we experience our lives has been supplanted with the concept of time as a unit of measurement. Where once we looked to the heavens to understand our position in the world and the tasks needed to survive within it, we now look to clocks: Mr. Harrison's marine chronometer has enabled global shipping and transport on a vast scale, whilst the aforementioned Herr Marx correctly notes the decoupling of Time and History, and the wholesale subordination of society to the rigours of the factory floor time clock.

Needless to say, any processes that modify, modulate, lengthen, shorten, omit or insert, loop, or otherwise interfere with the natural flow of time would be undetectable from within the structure of Time Itself, which is to say, the Universe. Likewise, the very machines tasked with the meticulous keeping of time — yes, like your pocket watch, Mr. Danville, please put it away; this lecture is unlikely to be shortened by your incessant consultation of said device — these very machines are singularly incapable of detecting any variation in the flow of time.

Paradoxically, the objective view of the time clock is by its nature subject to the effects of the Chaos Clock and is thus subjective. Logically, then, it is only by resorting to purely subjective means that we might triangulate upon an objective view.

What do I mean by this? Surely, any child who has endured Sunday services can tell you:

Time is not linear.

The incoherent droning of the pastor is interminable.

Sunday

              will never

                           end.

Of course, it eventually does, which demonstrates the power of the human imagination to create its own chronomatological gravity.

One must endeavor, in this case, to undertake a phenomenological investigation of l'artefact qui nous intéresse — the artifact of interest — to observe and analyze through subjective experience that which cannot be objectively scrutinized.

How, though? How does one experience something that is fundamentally unexperienceable?

Here is where I must beg your indulgence as I depart from the traditional format of the scientific lecture and expand upon my own unquantifiable experiences.

Rather than seek the Chaos Clock itself, I would experience the world from the *perspective* of that obscure object. What I needed to do was experience all times simultaneously. A hopeless task, you have surely already told yourself, even as the words left my lips, but not so: There are precisely two places upon this Earth where one might make a claim to all times, or to be outside time itself — at least in some limited sense.

The choice of north or south pole was no choice at all — after Captain James Cook's sighting of an ancient city sleeping, *perchance to dream*, in the depths of the South Pacific, what choice could there be? For what is dream but to be free of the strictures of time? Can it be a coincidence that the ancient city of R'lyeh lies so close to one of the poles?

The challenge remained, of course, as to how to reach the South Pole itself, a feat no man had hitherto accomplished. Men no less accomplished than James Clark Ross and Dumont d'Urville had failed in their efforts, and an overland expedition will not succeed until 1911, some two decades hence. It is incontrovertible that the body you see before you is hardly a fit specimen to be chosen to accompany such arduous ventures, and the intervening twenty years would undoubtedly do little to improve my physique. Should I wish to conquer the southernmost frontier, I would need to find an alternate means of travel.

No, I had no intention of trudging across the ice pack to a nearly certain death. Indeed, a more comfortable means of transport was available to a man of sufficient imagination, and sufficient means. I found my salvation in the genius of the late Dr. Solomon Andrews, and the generous access to his notes and records afforded by his daughter, Harriet Cornelia Hilton, and, of course, in my beloved Annabelle's family estate, which paid for the research necessary to expand upon Dr. Andrews' inventions, and to transport the resulting airship to the edge of the Antarctic ice pack.

My darling wife raised no objections regarding my purchase of the assets of Andrews' bankrupt Aerial Navigation Company, deeming it a harmless past-time that would distract me from what Annabelle contemptuously called my "l'obsession petite." Little did she know that my interests in uncovering the undiscoverable truths of the Chaos Clock were hardly *petite*, both preceding and exceeding my interests in her, and that my *every* move was made in service to said "obsession."

Utilizing fluctuations in buoyancy to generate forward momentum, Mr. Andrews' *Aereon* was itself an ingenious invention for its time, but it would not suffice for the journey I envisioned. However, the value of powerless propulsion was undeniable for a trip of indeterminate duration. Used in combination with steam-powered propellers, it would increase our speed, extend our range, and reduce the weight of our coal stores.

Annabelle believed my aerial ventures to be of a practical—by which she meant "commercial"—nature, though likely misguided, and was delighted to humor her eccentric husband. Several iterations demonstrated the promise of the technology, but the *Aereon V* was to be the airship finally worthy of reaching the South Pole. Nearly five times the length of Mr. Andrews' original flying machine, its five hydrogen-filled balloons supported an enclosed gondola capable of carrying a crew of five and a score of passengers from London to Paris in half a day, at an extraordinary cost. Perhaps a viable business might have been made of it, had I the inclination.

A most infuriating woman, my Annabelle. Stunningly brilliant, she had a head for both science and letters, and business acumen sufficient to maintain her family's fortune despite my excesses. However, while her hunger for knowledge took her to any lecture hall willing to seat a woman, whatever the subject, she had no patience for the most important question of the age.

No. No, when the woman discovered that I used the money she had provided to build berthing towers across Europe to instead purchase and refit the *Patria*, a whaling vessel originally of Belgium, capable of withstanding the harsh southern seas, and large enough to carry the disassembled airship in her hold, both her suspicions and her ire were aroused.

Once those unpleasantries were agreeably resolved, we departed Antwerp in March of 1890 with the intention of reaching the Antarctic circle in the dead of winter, which even the dimmest amongst you understand, in the southern hemisphere, is the height of the summer months. Due to circumstances beyond my control, we did not arrive until March the following year. I shall not bore you with the tedium that is life upon a sea-bound vessel. There were hardly enough books to consume a month, much less a year, and no useful improvements could be made to the airship at this point. Even Annabelle had ceased to provide amusement. She had grown sullen and uncommunicative, locked in her cabin, while the ship's crew paradoxically considered her very presence aboard ship unlucky yet made every attempt to put themselves in her company. I was obliged to shoot Mr. Henry, the boatswain, who thought to avail himself of her attentions after prying open her cabin door.

Idiot. She might have escaped.

How, then, could I have proved to her the reality of the Chaos Clock? I could not have revealed to her its hidden truths, as I shall shortly — Ahem. Miss Harcourt, whilst I am certain the contents of your glowing tablet are *far* more interesting than your professor's incoherent ramblings, our discussions here are of greater import than the images of cats currently dancing upon your tablet and reflected in your spectacles, or any of the *other* images you may have been previously perusing. Please, return to your seat and restrain your invective. There is nowhere else to go. It doesn't matter what class you *thought* you were attending, or even what college. You are here now.

Whatever "now" means anymore.

All of you. Sit, and be quiet. None of you are here because you are *good students* — you are all far too clever for that — and I should know better than to expect a well-behaved lecture hall; nevertheless, please take this opportunity to shut up and listen. Take notes on whatever it is you have at hand, pen and ink, pencil, quill and parchment, stylus and clay tablet, or glass tablet, like Miss Harcourt's. It matters not the medium; what matters is that you reinforce the memory of *this* time. Of *this* event. That is how we ensure it remains real.

Where was I? Ah yes.

At last we had reached the limits of the *Patria*'s usefulness. Over the next three weeks, we laboriously unloaded the *Patria*'s hold onto the ice and assembled the airship. One by one, the four-hundred-foot long balloons took form, their cigar-shaped bodies lashed one to another and fitted with the cables that would reshape the gas-bags to shift the buoyancy forward and aft to generate forward motion. Though the *Aereon V* could be piloted by a single person for a short time, I would take a crew of three with me, and, of course, Annabelle.

Do I need to tell you of the bitter cold that frosted our beards and encrusted our gloves and boots? Of the frigid wind that cut through our coats, piercing us to the bone? No need, I think, if your misted breath is any indication. Rub some warmth into your fingers and let us continue.

I cannot adequately describe the feeling when the ropes are released, and one is lifted aloft, free of the Earth and the Earth's grip. The motto of the Aerial Navigation Company, penned by Mr. Andrews himself, seemed most apt: *Tempus Fugit; Tempore Fugit Homo.* Time flies; Now man flies. As if he understood the true purpose of his life's work. As if he understood the *essential equivalency of time and consciousness.* Perhaps some of you have known what it means to fly, the illusion of freedom those first few moments as the world drops away. The stomach-dropping elation, lingering timeless and immortal in memory, before the cold, and the wind, and the tedium set in.

How long we travelled I cannot say. I knew better than to trust any timepiece in our possession and cast all of them over the side shortly after we set out. They would do nothing for us but lie. The days grew short, and the sun abandoned us entirely. We had filled our hold with fuel and food and flew low enough that we could lower buckets at the nadir of our trajectory to scoop up snow to feed the boiler and wet our lips.

Despite the engineers' best efforts to insulate the gondola, the cold crept in; ice frosted the windows and encroached along the outer walls, and any warmth provided by the engines was lost whenever anyone ventured to restock our water supply.

There were storms in which we were tossed mercilessly until we were able to rise above the clouds, or once, when we were driven down into the snow. The expedition was almost lost, then. We vented as much hydrogen as we dared to reduce the internal pressure of the balloons and minimize the likelihood of them rupturing, knowing that if we lost too much, we would never have sufficient lift to become airborne again. We lost only one of the balloons that day, irreparably torn on a jagged outcropping of ice, and when the storm eased, we were forced to reconfigure the craft to rebalance with only four balloons.

Even so, our buoyancy was so degraded, our airworthiness would have been in doubt had something hidden in the barren ice—drawn perhaps to the heat of the fire we had built of our supply crates—not eaten Ellsworth and Jones, thus reducing our ballast by a couple hundred kilograms. We took to the air once again with some haste, Mr. Donovan and I taking turns manning the billows and piloting the ship and hacking with axes at the limbs that clutched at the hull. Nubilous as frozen milk, the massive, rope-like appendages assailed us, dragging us earthward. Even Annabelle roused herself from her catatonia to assault the pythonic beast, and at last, we wrested free of the leviathan's cnidarian appendages and lurched into the sky.

The severed limbs continued to twitch, so we threw them overboard, all but for one, that Annabelle wished to study; however, in the relative heat of the cabin, it quickly grew fruiting bodies, and we hastily disposed of it before it could disperse spores.

Released from the insensibility of her earlier melancholy, Annabelle wasted no time working her charms upon the hapless Mr. Donovan, who, having survived an assault by an unutterably foul eldritch creature, fell victim to something far more dangerous: my wife. Had I not already known the depths of her infidelity — even one so disinterested as I could not but be scandalized by the variety of women drawn into her bedchambers — I would have been more surprised. Her customary loquaciousness returned, she implored the man to join with her to turn the ship away from what she called "this madman's errand" and "certain death," and return to "safe harbor." Sadly, her words found purchase, and we were forced to continue without Mr. Donovan's further assistance.

Never mind, it only hastened the inevitable. These men were strong and capable, certainly, with invaluable and indispensable skills necessary to get us this far, but nevertheless remained unimaginative dullards. I had no intention of allowing their perspectives any influence on what I was certain we would discover.

Unfortunately, I could not count on dear Annabelle's assistance in piloting the craft, nor trust that her promises not to interfere were made in good faith. Even in her apparent catatonia, she had been carefully watching the crew as they worked and was easily as clever and capable as all of them combined. I had no doubt that given liberty, she could handily manage the airship on her own, at least for a short time. I bound her into the co-pilot's chair, where I could keep her in clear sight as we proceeded southward toward our final destination.

Our progress was hampered by certain practicalities. Unwilling to trust Annabelle, I was now solely responsible for piloting the craft, maintaining the engines, shoveling the coal, and fetching snow to feed into the boiler, and I dared not take more than a few moments of sleep at a time, lest the furnace die down, and the pipes freeze — a more significant risk than I had anticipated, especially after the monster's attack broke many of the windows. Even with doors closed to unused cabins and cracked windows boarded over as best we could with whatever little scraps remained of our supply crates, icy drafts cut to the bone, and froze any water that leaked from the pipes before it could reach the floor.

With Mr. Donovan gone, another task fell to me — to periodically climb outside the gondola and, with a pickaxe and my mittened hands, clear the steam engine's exhaust of ice. Perilous and harrowing, I was amazed I survived the first time, and came to have an appreciation for the former crew's arguments over this duty. I returned from these forays stiff with cold and nearly unable to move until I had thawed by the furnace for a time.

As at last our destination was nearly in sight, a violent storm arose, the fierce wind driving northward against us. I topped the boiler — I needed only to gather the snow that accumulated on the gondola — and filled the furnace with as much coal as it would hold, but our headway failed, and we were driven backward.

No, we were too close to our goal to retreat now. Ignoring Annabelle's cries, I vented the balloons and dropped us into the snow.

Until this point, Annabelle had held some hope that we could, in the end, return to the *Patria* and, ultimately, home. Disabused of this fallacy, she raged at me for some time, but when her fury eased, her natural inquisitiveness re-emerged.

"If my bones are destined to adorn this horrid winter world for all time," she said, "let them not say I fell short."

No, you are correct, Miss Harcourt. Her actual words were less composed, but there is no call to repeat such vulgarity in polite company, nor in your own, Miss Harcourt. Regardless, the true offense was not her language, but her intention to take my achievement for her own, clearly impossible, since she still loudly proclaimed the Chaos Clock a hoax. Laughably, my darling wife appeared to believe that being the first to reach the South Pole was a laudable goal in itself. Never mind. As long as it got her there.

When the storm passed, we equipped ourselves as best we could — Mr. Ellsworth's spare coat required the fewest alterations to fit Annabelle's frame — and set out on foot. Or rather, on snowshoe. Annabelle had to teach me how to walk with the things. Most humiliating.

But she has always been the smartest person I've known — with the glaring exception of her refusal to take the Chaos Clock seriously — and the most capable. Surely when the evidence was laid before her, she would accept the truth, and turn that beautiful, brilliant mind to the intractable problem of the Chaos Clock.

I believe I would not have achieved the South Pole without Annabelle's assistance. When my hands and feet had gone numb and the frigid air burned my lungs, when my eyes froze shut and I fell to my knees in surrender, it was Annabelle who brought me back to my feet.

"You don't get to give up," she said. "I want you to witness me reach your goal before you."

Of course, that would not do. I lumbered to my feet and stumbled after her.

You may wonder how we knew where the South Pole was. I cannot tell you. We did not use instruments or measurements. We could not study the path of the sun, for there was no sun. We did not bother with the stars, for they had ceased making any rational sense, unfamiliar and ever-changing constellations that moved haphazardly across the sky. Some force tugged at our feet, drawing us onward, inexorably. We simply knew, and neither of us questioned it.

For a time we pushed through the snow together, supporting each other against the numbing cold and the biting wind, picking each other up when we fell, closer now, here, at the literal ends of the Earth, at the ends of Time, than ever through the course of our courtship and marriage. I had always found her an admirable creature and was happy to allow her to use the sham of our marriage to further her place in the world and shield her from the scandals that would have otherwise driven her from polite society, to be the person who created the conditions to realize her dreams, just as she provided the means for me to bring my own goals to fruition. Something warm stirred in me, in my stomach and in my heart, and when next we stumbled into each other's arms, my heart skipped, and my face flushed. Was this love? Was this how it felt?

Ah, Annabelle, could you not feel it as well?

We were close. Fifty meters, perhaps. Annabelle broke away from me, pushing forward across the snow.

I called to her, but she ignored me. Perhaps the wind whipped my words away.

She could not reach the South Pole before me. It would ruin everything. I called again.

I could not feel the pistol in my frozen hand, finding my grip by sight alone. When I pulled the trigger, the pain was like fire driven from the palm of my hand up into my shoulder.

The winds raised swirls of snow around her silhouette as she continued moving away from me.

I picked the gun up from where it had fallen and fired again.

If the nature of clock time is contiguous and discrete, a tyranny of uninterrupted series of infinitely divisible, identical increments, it must be understood that the Chaos Clock maintains much of this conceit: that of time as discrete, infinitely divisible increments. Where it differs is that the increments are both non-contiguous and non-identical.

Was this what made my heart skip a beat?

Is a world in which we can never know endurable?

Can the tyranny of the clock be overcome?

Imagine, if you will, time experienced in the absence of the clock, of time experienced not as an increment, divisible, but as a *duration*, a continuous motion — yes, Mr. Filbertson, qualitative rather than quantitative, continuously interpenetrating itself. You have read the works of Henri Bergson. No? Deleuze? I am not familiar, but perhaps he has not been born yet.

My interest is piqued, Mr. Filbertson, but it grows darker, and the cold is seeping in. Let us press on.

Ah, Miss Harcourt, if only you could have heard my dear wife, whose vocabulary far surpasses your own, as I dragged her through the snow. The bullet that shattered her hip did little to incapacitate her tongue, which she turned against me most unfairly. Did she still not understand? I needed to be the first at the pole. Alone in the entire world, only I had the singular will and unrelenting fortitude — l'obsession énorme — to find the Chaos Clock in this barren place and *hold it here long enough* for other, more robust and imaginative minds to intercede.

No, I shall not repeat her words, but you can hear them yourselves, I think, if you listen carefully to the wind.

For she is still here, with me, with us, so much stronger than I, even as her blood stains the snow. Strong enough to imagine all of you here with us — you dreamers and doodlers, you who scribble in the margins, you who do not march to a different drummer but flutter to a distant piccolo. You who could have been straight A students if only you would apply yourselves.

So that together, you can imagine for us, and for all the world, a means to subvert the tyranny of the clock. So that you can imagine for us all a world that is finally free.

Sky Rivers of Gray

Will McDermott

I remember clearly the day of my trip into the countryside to visit my childhood chum, Shawn. A crisp December breeze stung my eyes as I drove my newly completed steam carriage through freshly fallen snow that cleansed the world overnight and left a crystallized sheen on the hedgerows.

It felt good to leave the dank, grimy air of London behind and enjoy the cold winter sun on my face as I weaved my steam-powered carriage through quaint villages wrapped in the cozy embrace of winter's blanket.

My best mate and colleague, Harold Pierce, a fellow in the school of engineering, had designed the steam engine and helped me build the carriage over the previous year. The final piece, a machined boiler coupling, had just arrived during break, and I had not yet had a chance to put the Iron Camel—as Pierce had named it in honor of the "hump" of the mid-carriage boiler—on the road.

Thus, when the dean of archeology asked me to check on Professor Shawn Ludlow, whom I had known since childhood, I jumped at the chance. I wanted to see how fast the Iron Camel could go with a full head of steam, and had not visited Shawn's family manor since we traipsed the grounds as lads between terms.

It was somewhere beyond Stevenage when I had my first inkling that something was amiss. The crisp winter breeze that had stung my eyes and filled my lungs with fresh, clean air began to turn acrid.

It reminded me of the smoke-tinged skies surrounding the mills of Manchester. But the midlands had no industry, so from where could this putrid smell emanate? That puzzle quickly solved itself but presented even more questions when I noticed rivers of smoke flowing through the air as I drove through the rolling countryside. The black haze radiated from a central point like the waning rays of the sun at dusk—if its beautiful reds and oranges were instead an inky black and purple miasma.

As I continued north, driving toward the nexus of the dank clouds, I wrapped my scarf about my face, not to keep the cold at bay but to save my lungs from the tar-like substance that hung thick in the air.

At that point, I noticed something even stranger. The very landscape had changed. The land beneath the streams of black mist had turned gray. The entire snow-covered landscape had lost its hue.

No more did the green hedgerows twinkle from a shimmering snow cover. The hedges and snow remained, but both appeared an ashen gray. They were not covered in soot, though. It was as if the color had drained away, leaving only a dirty, drab silhouette behind.

And yet, in the distance, where the sun still shone between the rivers of smog, the colors of the world remained vibrant, their bright, shining hues taunting the gray lands to either side.

As the road twisted and turned through the low hills toward Shawn's family manor, my steam carriage alternately passed from color to gray and back again. I was amazed to find the air fresh, clear, and full of life in the vibrant sections, but dead and ashen in the gray sections.

My mood, too, changed back and forth, moving from lightness and joy to darkness and despair as my car breached the intersections between the two, separate worlds.

I soon realized these miasmic rivers of death emanated from the Ludlow Manor. And, as I drew into the lane leading to my friend's family home, the deathly twilight became almost ever present with mere slivers of life and light between the thick, dark rays.

Then I saw the manor, which despite the peculiarities I had already witnessed, stole my breath in an instant. Large chunks of the manor had been removed, leaving huge gaps in the walls. Stray bits of stone and masonry teetered along the edges of the gaps, threatening to fall at any moment. And yet, no debris lay on the ground around the foundations. The wall sections had simply vanished.

From every gap in the manor, thick, black fumes belched forth, staining the edges of the walls the color of burnt charcoal. I had found the origin of the Rivers of Gray in the sky!

I brought my steam carriage chugging to a stop and ran to the door, not daring to enter through one of the charcoal holes. I burst through into the foyer and shouted for Shawn.

At first, I heard no response. The air was still, fetid, and oppressive inside. I found it hard to breathe and rewrapped my scarf around my mouth and nose after yelling my friend's name.

Then I heard a scrabbling sound, barely more audible than a rat in a wall. The sound emanated from the parlor, which I could see from the vestibule was ashen gray throughout despite the giant hole in the wall that should have permitted sunlight to penetrate the gloom.

"Shawn?" I yelled again as I moved toward the edge of the gray parlor.

The scrabbling sound responded again. This time I could tell it was the rasping of a voice too hoarse to rise above a whisper.

"Is… that… you, David?" the weak voice called out. Having been to many a rugby match with Shawn over the years, I could discern his voice even when it sounded hoarse from screaming non-stop for eighty minutes.

And yet, I tarried at the edge of the gray line just inside the parlor, both unwilling to bear the blackness of despair I knew awaited me inside, but also worried that perhaps long exposure to the dank air was what had robbed Shawn of his voice.

From my vantage point outside the gray parlor, I bore witness to several sights that eventually forced me to overcome the overbearing dread and fear I felt.

An enormous, Egyptian sarcophagus, the top of which had been pried off and lay half-overturned against an overstuffed sofa, dominated the center of the parlor. Scads of darkened and shredded linen wraps seemed to have erupted from the ornate-inlaid casket and lay draped across nearly every surface in the room.

Five ashen-faced bodies lay strewn around the sarcophagus as well, half-wrapped in the cloth straps, their gray blood staining the dark cloth. I recognized the faces of several of the corpses, including that of my mate, Harold Pierce, the engineer.

The general gray tone of their dead faces, as well as their hands and even clothes was not the strangest sight of these dead bodies (of which I had seen enough during my time in the military). It was the expressions on their faces that gave me pause. I had seen fear in death before. I had even seen dread and surprise, as well as calm acceptance of death's embrace.

But here I saw abject horror captured on each face, as their wide-open eyes competed with their gaping mouths to see which could yawn the farthest open.

More than that, however, each face looked like a monstrous caricature of the person I had once known, with every feature exaggerated to ridiculous proportions, as if they had frozen at the moment of death in the most gruesome expression imaginable.

I was no stranger to the many faces of death, but these expressions made me wish to flee the manor and never return. I might have done so if Shawn's moaning had not stayed my feet.

I tore my gaze from the bodies, lingering for a mournful moment on Harold's twisted visage—which nearly ripped my heart in twain—to seek my childhood friend, whose rasping moans continued to beckon me forward.

I found him draped across a wooden chair that seemed to have been carved from iron, so steely gray was its color. The chair sat before a gray desk upon which stood an elaborate, metal mechanism that looked part clock, part automaton, and part puzzle box. I had never seen its like and pray I never will again.

The clockwork mechanism stood at least four-foot high and almost as wide and deep. The center-front of the mechanism contained a face not unlike that of a clock with thirteen hands rotating in a complex pattern around no less than five points.

Two sets of mechanical arms extended from the sides of the mechanism, one each near the top and another set extending from the base. As the clock hands revolved around one another on the face, the arms on the side performed an intricate dance with one another, as if trying to find purchase on some unseen object or objects in the air.

Inside the device, innumerable gears, pulleys, ratchets, suspensions, bezels, pendulums, and springs all noisily clicked away in a convoluted and complex rhythm of oscillating and pulsating movements.

I knew not from where this clockwork monstrosity hailed or what connection it could possibly have to an Egyptian sarcophagus. I shall probably never learn the entire truth about the awful machine, but I will swear until my deathbed that the machine's movements did not obey the natural laws of physics.

"Stop the clock!" Shawn rasped, his ashen gray arm reaching toward the mechanism from where he lay atop the chair. "End the chaos!"

With that, my friend slumped, his torso folding over the chair's thick wooden arm before slipping off and dropping to the floor. I could hear his rasping breath, so knew my friend still lived, but I could tell he had spent much of his remaining energy to prompt my action.

With that, I made the decision to enter the room. But I was unprepared for the current of despair that flowed through me as I pushed my way into the River of Gray. Every step required more exertion than the last as the current lashed at me and tried to force me downstream, away from the chaos emanating from the clockwork.

As I moved, the gray whipped at me so strongly it felt like my skin was being shredded by a riptide of knives. I pressed forward despite this death of a thousand cuts, only to reach a second stage of agony when the River of Gray attacked my mind with the fiery flames of doubt and remorse.

If only I hadn't dawdled at the college to await the final piece of the Iron Camel. Why hadn't I been here with my friend all along to protect him from his unbridled desire for knowledge? How could I continue now knowing how utterly I had failed him…failed everyone? All these deaths lay on my conscience.

With renewed resolve, I vowed to push through the mental torture. I could not alter the past. I had to focus on the present. And yet every step brought waves of despair that ate away at my will. I gritted my teeth to squelch a bleating wail, tensed my leg muscles, and pressed forward as I had done a thousand times before in the middle of a rugby scrum.

The final steps through the gray were the worst, however. Nothing up to that point had prepared me for what lay in wait, hanging in the air like the specter of death above a corpse.

As I got within a step of the mechanism, the River of Gray became a thick mist as black as charcoal. Within that inky blackness, a swirling vortex of dark purple appeared between me and the mechanism. The return of color to my gray and dreary world startled me and I almost faltered.

Faced with falling into the swirling black and purple nexus gaping before me, I might have quailed had Shawn not stirred anew. I could no longer see him. My world had been reduced to the fog, the vortex, and the silhouette of the chaos clock beyond. But from my feet, the voice of my childhood friend reached me. It was faint and almost dreamlike, as if it had ridden the winds from leagues away.

"You can do it," Shawn called, his voice little more than a whisper. "I… I believe in you!"

Perhaps I only imagined it. Perhaps at that moment, standing at the edge of an otherworldly nexus, I truly was leagues away. Whatever the case, my friend's belief steeled my resolve, and I pushed my way past the nexus to reach the giant mechanism on the desk.

Not knowing how to halt the intricate clockwork machinations that whirred and whizzed inside the giant machine—or even whether my fingers would survive being jammed into the midst of the spinning ratchets and gears—I settled on the final option left to all men who fail to understand the ways of this modern world. I grabbed the entire metal apparatus by a corner and dashed it to the floor.

The moment the clockwork mechanism impacted the hardwood will be indelibly etched into the very fabric of my memory forever. I would never divulge this to anyone with the power to consign me to a sanatorium, but I would swear on a stack of Anglican Bibles that the giant mechanical apparatus screamed in pain as it crashed and sprayed metal parts across the parlor.

I have heard the anguished squeal made by a wild boar as its skull was crushed beneath the butt of a rifle. I have heard the screams of villagers on the subcontinent burned alive and the angry screams of soldiers faced with a firing squad for their war crimes. Nothing will haunt my days more than the death wail of that apparatus as it echoed throughout the manor.

In the aftermath of that rumbling howl came a deathly silence that had been absent while the machine ticked and clicked and whirred. The pressure upon my brain also began to ease as the ever-present current from the River of Gray abated. The monochrome maelstrom that had beckoned me into its embrace swirled away to nothingness, leaving only the parlor, still tinged in gray, before my eyes.

I'm not sure what I expected upon destroying the massive clockwork apparatus, but I was surprised color did not immediately return to the world. In fact, if I am truthful with myself, the gray darkened somewhat in the aftermath, as if the sediment of the Sky River began to settle around me.

In that moment, I almost despaired of ever seeing the bright colors of day. I worried the gray would rule my life henceforth. I could hardly bring to mind any other hues. The greens and reds of the berried hedgerows I had driven past that morning no longer lived in my brain. Neither did the blues, whites, and yellows of the sky. I knew intellectually these colors still existed, yet for the life of me I could not summon them to my mind.

Shawn's moans once again pulled me from my dark reveries and snapped me back to the serious concerns of the present. I grabbed my childhood friend by the shoulders and dragged him toward the entryway, which I was gladdened to see remained in full color, even if that color was the deep, dark brown of stained wood.

Once we passed the parlor's threshold and left the River of Gray behind us, I pulled Shawn to his feet and attempted to seat him upon a bench, but my friend balked at the placement.

"Sun," he whispered, his hoarse voice regaining some strength. "Take me into the sun!"

And so I gathered Shawn's arm over my shoulder and helped him out to my steam carriage, where I settled him into the seat behind the boiler. I must admit the sun did my demeanor a world of good as well and I was glad for my friend's suggestion.

I felt I could never again enter the manor of my lifelong chum—a house that had been filled with happy memories of playful childhood summers and misspent adolescent holidays. But the sharp and painful thoughts of the gray would forever pierce all those gay times with irreparable incisions, like a scalpel through a photo.

Beside me, Shawn begged for water and pointed to a pump at the corner of the manor. I ran to the pump where I found a bucket and ladle. Upon spooning some cool water into my friend's mouth, he regained a modicum of strength. He even sat up in the Iron Camel and grabbed the ladle to splash water on his face.

"So, what the hell happened here?" I asked as Shawn wiped his damp face with the tattered remains of his right sleeve.

"How long has it been?" Shawn asked, answering my question with one of his own. "What time is it? What day?"

I must admit I was dumbfounded by these questions. In an age where one can wear a clock on a chain, where automatic horns call men to factories in the mornings and send them home at night, how does one not know the day of the week or the time?

"Why it is Wednesday, the eleventh day of December in the year of our lord eighteen-hundred and ninety-five," I replied. Shawn looked at me expectantly as I pulled the pocket watch from my vest. "It is currently one-and-three-quarters hours past noon."

I watched as my friend calculated some interval on the fingers of both hands, not understanding yet what issue he had with the date and time.

"Twenty hours, give or take," he muttered. "I doubt I would have made it twenty-four."

That's when it dawned on me. My friend had lain in the River of Gray since dinnertime the night before. He had been trapped for most of a day inside that monochromatic nightmare. I had spent less than ten minutes in the gray parlor and knew for a certainty the vision of that unholy maelstrom would haunt my dreams forever. I could not imagine what that horror had done to Shawn's mind after twenty hours, but I doubted he would ever be a whole, functioning person again.

I decided to not force any additional information from the wretched creature before me, but after he took another long draught of water, the story began to pour forth from Shawn as if the only way to rid himself of the experience was to share it in the full light of day.

"I arrived home after the end of the Fall Term a week ago," he began. "I was giddy with expectation, for I had gotten word that my crate had arrived from Egypt the previous weekend."

"That sarcophagus?" I asked, incredulous at the breach of university protocol. "Why send it here instead of the college?"

"I wasn't certain of its provenance," Shawn replied, as if that ex-plained everything. I stared at him hard, willing him with my stern countenance to explain, which he did, although it seemed with some — quite warranted — trepidation.

"The college elders knew nothing about this," he said a bit sheepishly. "I made the purchase privately through a dealer I had met during my trip to Giza over the summer."

"A black-market dealer?" I asked.

Shawn nodded before taking another sip of water while awaiting the coming storm of my condemnation.

"What were you thinking?" I demanded, aghast at my friend's cavalier attitude toward protocol, not to mention the scientific method. "Nothing can ever be proved without proper provenance."

"I thought this was too important a find to leave to the glacial machinations of the college elders," he said. "If I could but prove its worth and unearth its provenance, I hoped to donate the sarcophagus to the school."

Shawn looked so small and withdrawn sitting behind the giant boiler of my steam carriage. The man had lived inside a literal hellscape for nearly a day. Perhaps I should find it within my heart to withhold my academic reprimands for now. But then I recalled the bodies still lying within the Gray inside the manor.

"What of Shelly, Pierce, Wells, and the others?" I asked. "How did they become involved in all this?"

A deep sadness descended upon Shawn, draining the newly regained color from his cheeks, and weighing his eyes down to the point where he stared at his own feet.

"It's all my fault," Shawn whispered, his voice faltering again. "I should never have included them in my fool's errand."

I reached out to lay a hand on my friend's shoulder to console him as he folded in on himself in the seat and began to sob.

"It's okay," I said, hardly believing my own words. "It will be, eventually."

I wanted to add that life would go on, but I knew that it wouldn't. Not for Harold Pierce, nor for Shelly, Wells, or the two students I barely knew. And not, truly, for Shawn, whom I knew would be haunted by his decisions and the horrors he had witnessed until he passed from this mortal coil.

After a while Shawn began again and told me how the dealer had reached out with an irresistible offer of a mummy encased in a gold-inlaid sarcophagus that had been liberated from a heretofore unknown set of catacombs beneath an isthmus near Alexandria.

The mummy, it seemed, was pristine. But more than that, the chamber where it had been located—which had been buried beneath another chamber and so never robbed—contained some great dis-assembled machine strewn inside a large, granite box alongside the sarcophagus. In addition, the dealer informed Shawn that the interior of the sarcophagus contained a message etched in some language or code never seen at other sites.

"I had heard whispers of rudimentary clockwork machines in the time of the pharaohs," Shawn said, some of his vitality returning as his mind revisited the excitement of the search. "But no one had yet discovered anything more than pictograms; nothing to prove that the ancients had mastered the art of advanced engineering.

"If we could reconstruct the device and decode the message, there was no telling what this sarcophagus could tell us about the world of the ancient Egyptians," Shawn exclaimed. "Perhaps it could even prove the theory that great machines were used in the construction of the pyramids. It would have been the greatest discovery of the modern age."

"Or a complete hoax," I prodded. "That was no rudimentary clockwork mechanism. I'm not sure even Harold Pierce could have designed such a device, and he is—was—a master of steam and clockwork."

"Thus the secrecy," Shawn said, calmer now after his earlier outburst. "And, yes, as the machine took shape, I too doubted it could have been buried in a tomb thousands of years ago. Perhaps the dealer was an agent of chaos and sold me this devilish modern contraption to further the goals of some foreign cult. Perhaps the device itself had been created by the god-like being it awakened. I do not know. That was why I summoned the greatest minds I knew in engineering, mathematics, and cryptography. We hoped to unravel this mystery and publish our results."

Shawn explained that they broke into two groups with Harold Pierce working with a doctoral candidate on the machine, while Wells, the master of cryptography worked with Shawn and another student on the code. Shelly, the mathematics professor, leant her expertise to both teams as needed.

Hours turned to days as both teams worked feverishly, around the clock. One team or the other would take breaks to raid the pantry for bread, cheese, and leathery hunks of dried meats, or to nap on a sofa. Shawn had sent the staff on holiday to avoid prying eyes and his parents had long passed beyond the veil. The five academics were all alone in the huge house—alone with their respective puzzles.

Pierce's team made the first breakthrough some 40 hours into the process, but only after Shelly noted with some surprise that the pieces of the contraption could never fit together inside three-dimensional space.

"What do you mean by that?" Pierce had asked.

"A new theory by Charles Howard Hinton predicts a fourth dimension we cannot see while trapped inside our three-dimensional space," Shelly had replied. "Perhaps this contraption was built in four-dimensional space."

"If I cannot see this fourth dimension, how do I rebuild the device?" Pierce had demanded.

"Hinton's diagrams suggested what a four-dimensional cube would look like in three dimensions," Shelly had said. "It was two cubes, one nested inside the other with vertices connecting the corners. In four-dimensional space, these vertices would form 90-degree angles, but in a three-dimensional representation, they were half that. He called it a 'Tessaract.'"

"So, perhaps we can visualize the fourth dimension within our three dimensions by nesting the objects," Pierce had whispered, his face beaming with ideas.

Shawn told me he had overheard that conversation, which gave him an idea for the cypher as well. Perhaps it too had an additional dimension he hadn't considered.

The two teams redoubled their efforts after the tessaract discussion, making good progress as they toiled through the next night without any breaks at all.

As the device began to take shape on the desk behind him, Shawn decoded a single word near the end of the message. The word was "Iteru," the ancient Egyptian word for "River." Sadly, Shawn, told me, this sent him down the wrong path as he searched for hours for a word in the cypher that would translate to "Hapy" the Egyptian name for the Nile.

It was Wells who came to the rescue. As Shawn complained about his plight with the missing "Nile," the cryptographer realized that a message inside a coffin was more likely to speak about the river of the dead than any river found amongst the living.

"You should search for 'Duat,'" Wells had urged, "the land of the dead in the Egyptian mythos. Funeral barges followed the path of Ra along the West Bank to the Duat."

Shawn was too excited to ask Wells how he knew so much about Egyptian funeral rites. He was even too excited—and too caught up in the hysteria that had gripped them all—to notice the dark circles under the cryptographer's eyes.

Looking back on the events in his mind as he retold them, Shawn now understood that all of them had become enraptured in their work, trapped inside a trancelike state as they drove onward toward the answers to their respective enigmas. No one had eaten or slept in nearly two days since the tessaract discussion, and the only liquid they had taken in that time came from bottles of liquor in the parlor.

"We were the walking dead already," Shawn told me as he took another long swig of water. "We just didn't know it yet. The only thing that mattered was completing our tasks. We no longer had any other choice."

I realized then how gaunt my friend looked. His face had sunken in on his cheekbones and the hollows surrounding his eyes made him look more skeleton than man. I fished a few scraps of bread and cheese I had packed for the trip from my satchel, which Shawn greedily devoured before continuing his tale.

"Within a few more hours," he began anew, "both teams neared completion."

He faltered for a moment, and I thought it was to take another bite of the Stilton, but I looked down to see Shawn staring at the manor, the gray streams of the Sky River stagnant in the air above.

"I honestly cannot remember who finished first," he said at last. "Looking back, I believe we all walked through a shared delusion, marching from one dreamscape to another, leading each other through the various demesnes of our communal visions."

I had no reply to this statement, and once again feared for the sanity of my friend. Eventually, Shawn continued. From his description, the clockwork team must have completed their task first, for Shawn remembered hearing a loud ticking sound as he turned to the group to share the completed message with them:

> *"Whosoever possesses my tomb shall lay claim to all that dwells beneath the sky should they acquire the key to the clock of chaos ere they cross the River of Death."*

Shawn recalled the ticking of the clockwork mechanism seemed to grow louder as he recited the message, and that it changed in cadence to match the rhythm of his speech. Upon completing the message, all thirteen clock hands spun to vertical positions and began rotating in unison, clicking through the seconds simultaneously with acute precision.

What happened next, I will attempt to reproduce in Shawn's own words as exactly as I can to avoid losing anything to translation.

"We, all of us in attendance, were so transfixed by the simultaneous operation of the hands that none of us had eyes for what transpired behind us at that moment," Shawn told me.

"When the clock hands all reached the vertical again, the automaton arms became active, further transfixing our gazes. The hands weaved a complex pattern in the air more intricate than the forms displayed by any Eastern dancer I'd seen in a Turkish bazaar.

"I felt as if I had just deduced the pattern when a gray mist began to form at their various mechanical fingertips. The sight drew me closer, which ultimately saved my life. Even though I entered the River of Gray first, I was farthest from the sarcophagus when the mummy rose and shed its wrappings in an explosion behind us.

"Shelly's screams broke my revery and I turned to see the entity that had once lay in state standing ten feet tall above the tomb, its arms raised to the ceiling as if holding it in place. I did not recognize the being from any pictographs of the Egyptian pantheon, but there was no doubt this was a god.

"I was so taken by the gruesome beauty of the creature that it took a moment to realize that Shelly lay crumpled beneath it. The god's skin was covered in scales that reflected the colors of the sea as it turned and twisted in the lamplight.

"But it was its face that commanded my attention. The creature's skull was translucent. It had a multitude of eyes encircling the top and nearly invisible tentacles trailing off beneath its head that writhed about its shoulders.

"As I stared into its many eyes, the god waved about a sinewy limb, which held a golden key. It then reared back and lashed this limb forward and impaled Wells with the key, dropping him to the ground.

"I turned, hoping to stop the clock, for I knew in my heart the mechanism and the god were connected through the key. But I also knew that the entity possessed both the key and the tomb, so it owned everything under the sky, including all of us. As I pushed toward the clock, I heard the screams of my colleagues as they perished one after another. Each died with an unearthly squelch as that scaly, tentacled limb lashed at them.

"The current from the River of Gray held me back. After days of not eating or sleeping, I had no strength to wade against the swift current of the Gray. When I saw the monochrome maelstrom inside the River,

I knew instantly this was the home from which the nameless god hailed, a place where tessaracts existed in full, four-dimensional space.

"I made one last valiant attempt to reach the chaos clock, lunging with all my might in a vain attempt to cover the last two feet. I did not make it, but my leap saved my life. At that moment, the nameless one lashed at me with its key.

"Instead of impaling me through the heart, however, the key sliced through my clavicle, sending me sprawling across the chair. I lay there, barely breathing and half dead with a seeping wound in my shoulder.

"Before my eyes closed, I saw the scaly tentacle push the key into the clockface and twist. At that moment, floodgates opened within the device, spewing the Gray into the air in all directions with such velocity that I could no longer move."

At this point in the story, Shawn nodded off, his head lolling to one side against the seat. I glanced at the house, and part of me did wonder if the key was still inserted into the chaos clock inside the Parlor. For the briefest moment, I imagined what it might be like to claim all that lay beneath the sky.

But I knew that path led only to madness. I also knew that once my friend awoke from his slumber it would be too late to do what must be done.

When Shawn finally awoke, upon hearing the Iron Camel roar down the lane, I asked him where the old god had gone.

"Gone," he said. "I know not where but I fear I may have doomed us all."

I nodded silently. I could only hope my actions had limited the old god's influence somewhat. I glanced back at the house, which blazed in the light of the fires I had set.

As flames licked at the multiple rooflines, the Sky Rivers of Gray began to burn as well. Fire spread across the sky, consuming the gray streams and turning the rivers to ash. The ash fell to the ground, slowly, like a snow shower. But, instead of covering the ground in a pristine white sheen, everything the ash touched crumbled, as if it had been consumed by the fire as well. The Gray was gone, but death remained.

"You can rebuild," I said as my friend stared at the conflagration consuming his manor.

"No, I don't think I will," he replied. "This chapter of my life should remain buried beneath the mountain of death I wrought."

The Reclaiming of New York City

Marc L. Abbott

Roosevelt Smithers glanced up at the massive envelope of the hot-air balloon that carried him over the East River from Manhattan to Brooklyn. Designed and constructed by industrialist William Tyner, the balloon was a feat of ingenuity. It featured a large clock face embedded in its panels and a gondola designed to mimic an actual boat but with steel decks. A modified burner pushed steam, not hot air, into the envelope, allowing the balloon to carry greater weight.

As the science reporter for the *New York Times*, Smithers found Tyner's work fascinating and ingenious. Seeing it up close was exhilarating. He retrieved from his pocket the invitation that Tyner had sent him and read it while wondering what marvels the man intended to reveal this evening. As he placed it back in his waistcoat, he glanced down the gondola and spotted New York City Mayor Miles standing by the railing staring perplexed at the smokestack.

"I'll be damned," Roosevelt whispered to himself as he approached him. "It's steam."

Mayor Miles was startled. "I beg your pardon?"

"The white smoke is steam. The ship is powered by water. Tyner built a device that allows the ship to suck in moisture from the air then convert it to steam power. He's a real man of the environment."

"Interesting." He pointed at Roosevelt. "Do I know you?"

"Roosevelt Smithers, reporter for the *Times*." He extended his hand. "Honor to meet you Mister Mayor."

"William didn't tell me there were reporters invited to this meeting."

"I report mostly on the science-based industrial work Tyner does."

"Ah. You're the one who did the article about his designs for submersibles to cross the East River. I recognize your name now." Mayor Miles' gaze narrowed. "I took particular interest in how you thought we should pay for it by cutting *my* salary."

"Only my opinion, Mister Mayor."

"Some things are best kept to oneself."

There was a moment of uncomfortable silence between them. Roosevelt smirked as the mayor stared into his eyes as if daring him to respond to his comment.

"I'm looking forward to seeing what Tyner is presenting tonight," Roosevelt said, breaking the silence. "Apparently, he's discovered a way to help combat the city's hunger problem. Beyond the soup kitchens, of course."

"Hm," the mayor folded his arms. "That explains why he didn't tell me anything."

"Touchy subject, Mister Mayor?"

"Not at all. Tyner likes to make a bigger deal about that than it is. If those people simply pick themselves up and get to a good job that wouldn't be a problem," Mayor Miles said. "Uh, and that's off the record."

"Of course." The gondola jerked and the balloon started to descend, the boat-shaped gondola settling into the water. "See you at the event."

Roosevelt headed forward, leaving Mayor Miles to ponder what Tyner wanted to show them.

⁕

The gondola docked at a private pier. As Roosevelt, Mayor Miles, and his security detail, Patrick and Anderson—two Pinkerton detectives dressed in long coats—exited, they spotted a specialized trolley waiting for them. The windows were covered with velvet curtains so no one could see inside, but clearly it was Tyner's, bearing the inventor's signature style. Built completely of copper and steel, it too ran on steam rather than the electrical cables, as the city trolleys did. Such a trolley could go anywhere in the city and not be affixed to the tracks.

Upon their approach, the back door of the trolley opened and a portly man in a red waistcoat stepped out. Roosevelt recognized William Tyner from the photographs they'd run in the *Times*. His slick handlebar moustache was more impressive in person.

"Gentlemen," Tyner beamed. "So happy you could make it. Welcome to Brooklyn. Come on aboard. We have a big night ahead of us. Refreshments are inside."

"William," Mayor Tyner said, "My time is limited. You have one hour."

"I understand, my old friend. An hour is enough." He shook their hands, starting with the mayor's. "Roosevelt, a pleasure. Let's go."

Once everyone was aboard, Tyner ordered the driver to take them to the special site. Roosevelt barely heard him, marveling as he examined the interior, so elegantly appointed, clearly for Tyner's own comfort. His attention, however, was quickly caught by a table that ran the length of the trolley. It held an impressive array of fruit.

"Where did you get all of this?" Roosevelt said in astonishment.

"You'll see soon enough. Please, enjoy. Try some grapes. And there is pineapple over there."

Mayor Miles eyes widened as he moved in the direction Tyner was pointing. "Pineapple? This must have cost a fortune. Even by your standards."

"There is more where this came from."

As he picked up a fragrant bunch of grapes Roosevelt noticed three crates full of fruits off to the side. Before he could inquire about them, the trolley slowed to a stop. Tyner opened the door, picked up one of the crates, then left the trolley. He was gone only seconds before he got back on empty handed. The trolley started up again as soon as he shut the door. They stopped two more times before they reached their destination.

"What were those stops for?" Roosevelt asked.

"Just spreading my good fortune with the less fortunate," William said.

Everyone filed out of the trolley and found themselves in front of a tall fence. Beyond that stood a skyscraper. The façade was done but Roosevelt saw through a window the inside was still incomplete. Tyner led them to an open gate where a guard stood watch.

"Why are we here at night?" Roosevelt asked.

"I didn't want any publicity if someone saw the mayor, and it's better to do this while the workers are away. Watch your step," Tyner pointed. "We're going into the foundation over here. Then we go up."

A touch nervous, Roosevelt kept his eyes on the wood planks they crossed. Once across he looked up at the dimly lit skyscraper before them. Tyner led them to an open-air elevator that ascended along the side of the building. Once they all entered, Tyner pulled a lever to his right.

"Everyone, stand close. Don't want anyone to fall out."

The elevator ascended, giving them a look of the rooftops of lower Brooklyn with the lights of Manhattan twinkling in the distance. Ferries crossed the East River slowly, smoke drifting out of their stacks.

"We finished the facade last month. There's still internal work to be done but the tower is complete. That's where we're headed," William said. "Beautiful city, isn't she? She can be the crown jewel of this country after I show you what I discovered."

"You want to tell us what this is about?" Mayor Miles asked.

The elevator suddenly stopped with a jerk. Tyner excused himself and stepped off the platform onto the floor. He then approached an iron door with three keyholes in it. Reaching inside his waistcoat pocket, the industrialist removed a ring with three keys and proceeded to unlock the door. Roosevelt noticed he used his weight to push it open. Dim light filtered through the doorway and somewhere inside, something ticked loudly. Tyner waved them all forward then pulled a lever connected to a power source and illuminated the room. Roosevelt gasped in astonishment at the largest clockface he had ever seen.

It sat up off the floor on a long iron base with two clamps at the ends to keep it straight. The body of the clock was made of polished copper and the hour numbers shone in beautiful brass. The dials, made of cast iron and bolted together, were enormous. Roosevelt could see the main and escape wheels behind the open face. The construct took up one entire side of the room leaving only a few inches of clearance between it and the ceiling.

"This, gentlemen, is going to be the beacon seen atop this building. It already keeps perfect time. I plan to have three more made, exactly like the clock tower in London. Did you know the dials on that clock are twenty-two-and-a-half feet? Mine are nineteen. Didn't want to overshadow the one over there." He chuckled. "This building will have a clock that faces all four points of the city. And this one… oh, this one will be the centerpiece."

"You brought us here to see a *clock*, William?" Mayor Miles said.

"This is no ordinary clock." Tyner walked to the far side of the room and retrieved a medium-sized metal ball adorned with gears on the side. Numbered and lettered typewriter keys mounted atop thin, three-inch-long rods clustered above the ball.

"Is that a Hansen writing ball?" Roosevelt asked, excitedly.

"It was. I made special modifications to it. Let me show you."

He pressed seven of the keys. The gears started to whirr and spin. The ball shook in his hand as the top half with the keys turned counterclockwise. Tyner pressed down on a center key and the top split from its lower half. Removing the top half, he placed it on the floor then turned it so they could see the inside.

A series of wires and small tubes snaked together around a copper ring a half-inch thick. In the center of the ring sat a piece of black, metallic stone held in place by two tiny tuning forks.

"That's graphite, isn't it?" Roosevelt asked.

"Yes, that's exactly what that is. It stores the energy then serves as a battery. You see this?" Tyner pointed to a small black button on the copper ring above the tuning fork. "That's what starts the reaction process."

Roosevelt moved closer for a better look. "What's this for?"

Tyner motioned for them to follow him behind the clock. Roosevelt was fixated on what Tyner was about to do. He approached the pendulum, which was moving back and forth at a steady pace. Standing before it, he pressed the button on the device, then, as the pendulum passed him, he attached the device to it. Then he shooed them back around to the face of the clock, where he removed his pocket watch, opened it, and slid his finger clockwise on the inner cover.

A humming sound started out soft then progressively grew louder. Electrical sparks crawled and danced over the large clock's face and numbers. The dials began to turn in opposite directions. Tyner held the watch up higher. An electric spark shot out from the bolt holding the dials and seized the watch. He let it go and watched it levitate through the air and into the center of the bolt.

"Back up!" he said.

As they did so, a horizontal energy wave blasted out and passed through all of them. It stopped, turned vertical, and then moved back to the clock. When it struck, the clockface burned bright white. After the light dissipated, the face was gone. Like a painting in a frame, a different world sat before them where it had been.

Roosevelt marveled at the sun shining in a crystal blue sky when above him stars twinkled. And at the green pasture, adorned with fruit and nut trees as far as he could see. He saw no sign of animal life or any other people. But he could smell the clean air wafting through.

"What the hell?" Mayor Miles said.

"Is that real?" Roosevelt said.

"As real as we are. Come."

Roosevelt followed Tyner to the edge of the clock. He motioned for him to wait then he stepped over the frame and into the world beyond. Approaching one of the trees, he reached up and plucked two apples. He walked back out, handed one to Roosevelt and to Mayor Miles.

"Is this safe?" Mayor Miles asked.

"I wouldn't give it to you if it wasn't," Tyner said.

Mayor Miles bit into it and chewed. His eyes widened as a smile grew on his face.

"Tastes as good as the one you fed us on the trolley."

"It came from the same place." Tyner pointed to the clock. "There are thousands of trees on that side waiting to be picked. I planted some of the seeds myself. Since time works differently on that side, what would take years to grow here took only days. There's enough food that we could feed all of New York City ten times a day and still have more."

"How did you… I mean, this place you found…" Roosevelt said.

"That machine I built creates a high resonating sound that when attached to the pendulum creates a temporal rift within the clock. At least, that's what I believe it's doing. So far it has opened portals to two different worlds. This one here has an endless supply of food. I have been bringing things back and giving it to the workers to take home to their families. Those stops we made tonight; those were for the soup kitchens.

"The other world provides me with building materials. Steel, iron, and bricks. As much of it as I can use, which has been a godsend with all the projects that I have around the city. The beings of that world have been extremely friendly because I bring them food as well. Much like the poor souls of our city, they're suffering from hunger and… well, hold on, let me show you."

Mayor Miles held his hand up. "I'm sorry, did you say beings?" he looked at Roosevelt. "Did he say beings?"

"He did," Roosevelt answered without looking back.

Tyner opened his watch again, placed his finger on the face, and rubbed a circle around the edge.

The picturesque world before them dissolved and what appeared next made Roosevelt cringe.

A dreary landscape appeared before them. A light rain fell over an industrial city. Tall smokestacks in the distance billowed thick, black smoke into an already overcast sky. A flash of lightning revealed four large creatures that resembled whales coasting in the sky, their flippers moving up and down slowly propelling them through the air. As one of them got closer to the portal, Roosevelt saw their bodies were outfitted with metal plating. Porthole windows embedded in their sides glowed with light.

Among the buildings, set atop tall trestles, were rails where a train moved slowly then stopped. At first it looked like it was about to derail as it listed to one side. But then it righted itself and started to lift off the track backward. What Roosevelt had thought were wheels bent outward and took on the shape of claws. The rear "wheels" clamped down on the track as the locomotive stood up. Its back was a train, but the underside was an organic creature that let out a half-scream/half-whistle as it looked in their direction.

"What madness is this?" Roosevelt whispered.

From in front of them came a croaking sound, followed by clicks and wheezes. Roosevelt's gaze fell on a single street, slick from rain and shimmering in the lamp light. A humanoid creature, no taller than him, walked toward them, hunched over. As it neared, Roosevelt could see that it was wearing armor over one of its hands. The other hand was a fleshy claw, but it had only three long fingers protruding from a stump. The wheezes and clicks came from the covered hand, where piston-like rods moved up and down from the elbow to the stump. It lumbered closer, its webbed feet slapping against the stone street as it walked.

Roosevelt recoiled in horror as its face came into view. A single eye sat dead center where a nose should have been. Below that sat a gaping hole—a mouth, he supposed—with teeth on the top and bottom. Two protrusions sat atop its head... ears, or devil horns? Thick, fleshy tendrils covered its head and went down to the middle of its back.

Tyner smiled and moved to a crate against the wall, selecting an apple and moving toward the portal. The creature croaked again but higher pitched and it hurried to greet Tyner as he stepped through the clock frame. The creature hugged him, then stepped back, turning its hand over and waiting for Tyner to give it the fruit. Once he did, the apple disappeared into the gaping hole. Roosevelt quickly looked away from the oscillating mastication.

"Ellis, my friend, how are you? Where is your brother?" Tyner asked.

Ellis croaked loudly and a second creature lumbered out of the dark to greet Tyner.

"Roosevelt, toss me your apple." Roosevelt tossed it through the portal. Tyner caught it and handed it to the second creature. "Here you go, Tobias."

Tobias ate the apple and began to undulate up and down with apparent joy. It then ran away down the street and disappeared around a corner. A grinding, scraping sound rose from that direction, and after a moment, Tobias returned dragging a massive water pipe. It passed Tyner, stepped past Roosevelt into the clock room, and set the pipe down. The Pinkertons scrambled to cover the mayor, but Tobias ignored their presence. It returned through the portal and hugged Tyner.

"Thank you, my friends. These men here are also friends, and I wanted them to meet you."

Ellis and Tobias looked at Roosevelt, Mayor Miles, and the Pinkertons, then waved with their metal hands. Only Roosevelt waved back.

A crack of thunder shook the foundation. All eyes looked to the sky. It turned from its dark dreary tone to an aubergine as the clouds started to part. A creature resembling a giant jellyfish floated above them. Its tentacles—long, thick, and covered in spikes—seemed to dance as it moved.

"Oh, dear," Tyner said. "Roosevelt, quickly, get the entire crate."

"What in God's name is that?" Mayor Miles yelled as he pointed.

"Nothing you should be concerned about." Tyner held out his hands. "The crate."

Roosevelt picked up the crate and rushed it to the portal.

"Hurry, step in," Tyner said.

"What?"

"Cross over and give it to me. It's okay, you're safe."

Fighting trepidation, Roosevelt stepped through the portal. He kept his eyes on the floater. His hands trembled.

"Here," he said.

"This is my friend, Roosevelt," Tyner said as the creature moaned, then tilted on its dome and continued to float. "He is a good one. You see, he brought the crate."

Tyner took the crate, showed it to the creature, then handed it to Tobias who took it and ran off.

"We can go," Tyner said. "Ellis, I will return soon. More food."

Tyner and Roosevelt stepped back through the portal and it closed behind them.

"Was that creature a god?" Roosevelt asked.

"Not sure. I know that the creatures there have a relationship with it," Tyner said. "These beings look up to it and it allows me to feed them as a form of trade."

"This is iron," Mayor Miles said as he looked at the pipe. "Real iron."

"That one piece of pipe will be taken to Gowanus and get cut and fashioned into everything from tools to rivets for the bridge you want to build." Tyner smiled. "Think about all we can accomplish, and it will barely cost us pennies to obtain the raw materials."

"Lower manufacturing costs means more money in our pockets," Mayor Miles said grinning from ear to ear. "I see where you're going with this, William."

"I don't think you do. You see, the less we spend on manufacturing, the more money the city has for the people," Tyner said. "We could give the hard-working men and women of this city the kind of money that will help them thrive. They'll be able to afford houses, own businesses, be more productive."

Mayor Miles' smile fell. A confused look took its place. "You mean you're thinking of making everyone in this city *wealthy*?"

"Well, that's impossible to do. You can, however, make them comfortable. Think about the brick mason who comes to these sites everyday getting paid enough to live in one of the homes he's built," Tyner said. "Wouldn't that be great?"

"You think the wealthy families in this city want a brick mason living next to them on Park Avenue?"

"Why not?" Roosevelt said as he joined the conversation. "You're always saying that this is a city of opportunity. That people deserve a chance."

"I meant through hard work, not charity," Mayor Miles said.

"This isn't charity," Tyner added. "They will work, it's just that the money…"

"Since when did you care so much about the common man? You're practically swimming in money from city real estate and your investments," Mayor Miles said.

Tyner's gleeful look turned to sadness. "Since that horrible fire at the warehouses in Red Hook. Those poor workers who died there. Burned beyond recognition. Families lost. That area suffered from unemployment and homelessness because of that. Those people deserved better. With this I can make amends by providing food and jobs."

"William, I told you a hundred times to let this go. We did everything we could for those people. It's not our responsibility to give handouts." Mayor Miles raised a finger. "You're not to mention this to anyone else or give out any more food until I say so."

Tyner shook his head. "I would have thought you would be on board with this. After what you…"

"Shut the hell up, *Tyner*." There was fury in the mayor's eyes. "The people of this city, the *proper* people, entrusted me to keep New York strong and unwavering. I will not let it fall into the hands of the lazy and the poor. You will not go over my head, is that understood?"

"I thought my contributions were enough to earn that right since I put you where you are," Tyner said. Mayor Miles looked shocked. "So, all that talk about wanting to save this city was balderdash?"

"I *am* the city. You want to change that, you'll have to take my place and you don't have what it takes. Finish your building, have your ribbon cutting, and know your place. I forbid you to continue to use this device." He held out his hand. "In fact, give me the unit you use to open this."

Tyner shook his head. "Absolutely not. This stays with me."

"Patrick," the mayor called over his shoulder. The Pinkerton on the right drew a firearm from inside his coat. A modified break-action Colt Navy Percussion revolver with a thin telescopic sight attached to the top. The cylinder turned on its own and locked into place.

"You heard the mayor, hand it over," Patrick demanded.

"Miles," Tyner said. "You would kill me over this?"

"I refuse to be made a villain. I won't let that happen, so hand over the device." Mayor Miles held out his hand. When Tyner didn't comply, he dropped his hand and sighed. "Okay then, have it your way." The mayor looked at Patrick. "Do it."

Patrick took aim but then changed his mind and holstered his weapon.

"What are you doing?" the mayor asked.

"Gun would be too messy," he said. He reached behind his back and produced a hunting knife. "I'll make this up close and personal."

He advanced quicky. Tyner staggered back. Patrick grabbed the device, moved in close, brought the knife around behind Tyner and stabbed him in the upper spine. He removed the knife and stabbed him again lower then again in the kidney. Tyner gasped and started to fall to the floor, letting go of the device.

"No!" Roosevelt screamed. He rushed toward Patrick who spun around and slashed at him, cutting him across his upper arm. Roosevelt stepped back, looked at the knife, and went for it. "Give me that!"

They struggled. Patrick tried to break free of Roosevelt's grip but when he couldn't he struck him in the head with the device, sending him to the floor. While Roosevelt rolled back and forth holding his head Patrick moved to the mayor.

"It's time to go, Mister Mayor." He handed over the device then turned to Anderson who had been silently watching. "Get him out of here. I'll finish these two."

"I'm sorry it had to come to this, Tyner," the mayor said as Anderson escorted him briskly back to the elevator.

Patrick turned his attention to Roosevelt. He knelt next to him, held him still with one hand, and raised the knife with the other. Roosevelt attempted to fight back but Patrick slapped his hand away and stabbed him in the shoulder. Roosevelt cried out. As Patrick raised the knife again, the portal flashed. He turned to see a creature, five feet tall with an elongated head, no mouth, long oily skinned arms with tendrils for hands and a single eye near the top of it head, step out. It looked at Tyner, made a sad cooing sound then looked at him.

"Holy Mary Mother of God," Patrick said with a look of horror. He scrambled to his feet as the creature let out a horrible cry.

Patrick tossed the knife and drew his Colt. Firing twice without aiming, he missed. The creature advanced. Panicking, he fired four more times, missing twice more but scoring two hits. The creature paused, looked at the wounds on its arm, then growled and advanced quicker. Patrick pulled the trigger in rapid succession but was out of shots. He ran for the elevator but tripped over the water pipe the other creature had dragged in. As he hit the floor, his gun went sliding out of reach. Looking over his shoulder, Patrick tried to scramble to his feet as the creature turned its eye toward him. A horizontal slit formed in the middle of its face, parting to expose rows of sharp teeth. Patrick's scream blended with the creature's roar as it whipped out its tendrils, wrapped them around his throat, and dragged him over to its mouth. Patrick tried to struggle but something about the tendrils paralyzed him. In the end, all he managed was to let out a faint scream as it began to chew his face off.

Roosevelt ignored the sound of muffled screams and gnashing teeth as he rolled onto his belly and crawled on his good arm.

"Tyner?" Roosevelt reached over and turned him onto his back. The industrialist cried out his upper body stiffening, while the lower lay limp.

"Roosevelt, I-I can't feel my legs."

"I'm going to go for help. Hang on."

"D-Do you know why I asked you to come tonight?" Tyner's eyes turned to look at him. "Because of all the people I know, I respect your intelligence and integrity. The heart you have for this city. I knew you would understand what I was trying to do."

"Tyner, the mayor will pay for this, I promise you."

"I think you've earned the right to call me William, don't you?" He closed his eyes and took a deep breath. "So much for my grand idea to help the city."

Roosevelt looked over and saw the creature stand. It took hold of Patrick's right ankle and dragged him to the portal. With a powerful shift of its arm, it tossed his limp body into the other realm. Roosevelt cried out but quickly covered his mouth with a trembling hand. The creature then lumbered toward where Tyner and he lay. Roosevelt dropped his hand stared at the creature with a mix of shock and fear.

Tyner opened his eyes and looked at Roosevelt. "Roosevelt, don't fear it. They are my friends, those creatures."

The creature reached down and scooped William up in it arms, cradling his body as though he weighed nothing at all. Then it turned and walked quickly back to the portal.

"William!" Roosevelt cried with his hand outstretched as if to grab him.

William didn't respond. As he and the creature disappeared into the other realm, the portal shut.

For a long time, Roosevelt stared at the gateway in disbelief. When he finally snapped out of his daze, he crawled as far from the clock as he could and perched himself against the wall in a sitting position. With some effort, he got his shirt off and made a sling for his arm.

While struggling to get to his feet, the portal opened again. Roosevelt pressed his back against the wall bracing for the creature's return. But William came through the portal, dressed in a brown long coat, with hooks instead of buttons holding it closed.

"I hoped you would still be here," he said. Smiling and limping, he approached. A hiss accompanied each step, and Roosevelt saw peculiar movement under the coat.

As William drew closer, Roosevelt's eyes widened in shock and disbelief. Embedded in the right side of the man's face was what looked like a giant starfish with a bulbous eye in the center of its body.

"What the hell is that on your face?"

"The Charybdis—that's the name of those creatures—use this to help me heal. Time moves differently beyond the portal. I've been there for several weeks their time. I learned how to calculate time in a place where it doesn't exist." He chuckled. "They showed me how to use the portal from their side so I could return at this point. Miles neglected to take the piece off the back of the clock, so I was able to home in on the gateway here. Anyway, onto the business at hand." He reached into his pocket and removed a letter. "Leave this for the foreman of this site, Cosgrave Paerdegat. Put it under the door of his shed downstairs." He slid it into Roosevelt's pocket. "Now, this is for you." He reached under his right sleeve and removed what looked like a wristwatch, though there were no numbers on it, just a dial and a green flashing light.

"What is it?"

"You're part of my inner circle now. Show this to Paerdegat when you're ready to see me again."

"You're going back? What about the mayor?"

"Paerdegat will handle him. Incidentally, when you go to the hospital, tell them that you were mugged. They'll believe that more than the truth." He handed him the wristwatch. "Remember, show it to Paerdegat. See you soon." William turned and walked back through the portal.

Roosevelt felt a twinge of fear when what appeared to be a single eye watched him from the back collar of William's coat.

Several weeks after the incident, Cosgrave Paerdegat called a press conference to address the progress of the building. Roosevelt attended. To his surprise, Mayor Miles showed up as well, along with Anderson. While Paerdegat spoke, Roosevelt and the mayor made eye contact. Miles looked nervous until Roosevelt turned his attention back to the press conference and ignored his presence.

"I'm in charge while Mister Tyner is away. I am excited to announce the tower will be ready in two weeks." Paerdegat stretched his arm back, presenting the building to those assembled. As he gestured, his sleeve pulled back from his wrist, baring a wristwatch like the one William had given Roosevelt.

"Mister Paerdegat, Richard Madison, *Chelsea News*. Many Tyner properties have been getting overhauls around the city. The Mercantile on the west side of Manhattan, the commerce bank in Queens, and the Galviston Center of Art in The Bronx are all being refitted with ornate rooftops."

"I fail to hear a question."

"Why are these additions being made from brass? There is rumor going around that Mister Tyner is doing this as an experiment with power. Is he trying to circumvent the New York Gas Light Company's regulations?"

Paerdegat stared at the reporter for a moment, then his pointed gaze moved over to Mayor Miles, who watched him with interest. The foreman cracked a smile then turned his attention back to the reporter.

"It is an experiment. Brass is a great conductor of electricity, as you know, and being that the buildings you mentioned are some of the tallest in the city, Mister Tyner believes that if we can harness electricity directly from the atmosphere it could provide a new way to power the buildings. It would reduce electrical costs and put money back into the pockets of the people of this great city."

"Ladies and gentlemen of the press," Mayor Miles put his hand up. The press focused their attention on him. "What Mister Paerdegat hasn't noted is that Mister Tyner's experiment must still go under review. He's been a bit impatient about things which is why…"

"If you all will excuse me," Paerdegat interrupted. "Thank you for coming."

With a nod, the foreman departed. The press called after him, but he ignored them.

Roosevelt followwed at a slight distance as the foreman moved toward the building. When Paerdegat reached the door, he stopped and turned abruptly.

"Stop following me. I'm done talking to the press," he said.

Roosevelt pulled up his sleeve and bared his own wristwatch.

Paerdegat's eyes widened. "Are you Roosevelt?"

"I am."

Paerdegat's gaze softened. "Sorry about that. William told me all about you. How's the arm?"

"Healing."

"That's good. That SOB mayor got something coming to him."

"You have been in contact with Mister Tyner? How is he?"

"Come with me. William said you might stop by."

Paerdegat led him to the elevator, and they boarded it, riding in silence to the tower. When they reached the tower, the doors opened, and they stepped out into the area of the clock.

It looked very different from weeks ago.

The concrete walls had been covered by galvanized steel panels held together with rivets. Brass panels covered the floor. Before the clock stood a huge arch with gears that turned counterclockwise within its metal surface. At the top, on either side of it, exhaust holes poured out steam. Heat and moisture permeated the air, making it uncomfortable to breathe.

"This is all in preparation for his final return," Paerdegat said. "He's been back a few times with his friends from the other realm. They've been supplying us with materials to finish this building and the enhancements around the city."

"You know about the creatures?"

"I spent time in that world among them," Paerdegat said. Roosevelt gave him a shocked look. "I was once one of the city's poor souls you see William trying to help. He gave me a job on the Mercantile. I helped reconstruct it after discovering a flaw in the design. He was so impressed he insisted I help design this tower. After discovering the portal, I volunteered to go through, broker the deal for materials and built a stable relationship with them." Paerdegat rolled up his sleeve, exposing the wristwatch. "I'm supposed to let him know you're here. Give me a moment." He turned the dial and the portal arch started to light up. "Be warned, William isn't the same man you knew."

When the portal opened, Paerdegat walked before it and waved. "He's here, William."

William stepped through the portal using a brass cane, his hand resting atop a glowing blue orb. Small, writhing tentacles extending from it wrapped around his wrist. He was dressed in the same brown coat as before only this time it was open, exposing gill slits on either side of his stomach. The right side of his face was covered with tiny boils that upon closer inspection opened to reveal eyes. The hiss of a piston accompanied the movement of his right leg. Roosevelt looked down and saw that from the knee down had been replaced by a bronze metal appendage with injection pistons and rods embedded in the flesh of his thigh. The sight caused Roosevelt to retch.

William stared at him for a moment then turned to Paerdegat. "How did it go?"

"The one from the Chelsea paper took the bait. Asked about the rooftops around the city. I told him exactly what I told you I'd say, and the mayor jumped right in and took control of the press conference," Paerdegat said. "The last conduit will be in place by the end of the week."

"Excellent." William's left eye watched Paerdegat but the other eyes stayed on Roosevelt. "Don't look mortified. The Charybdis did this so that I could live among them. I assure you, I've never felt better. Or wiser."

Roosevelt took a step back. "What have you become?"

"One who has seen the error of his ways. I've made a deal to save *my* city from the evils of men. This world must go to bring about a new one. A new chance at life for the poor. Wait until you see what I have in store." William stepped closer. "You will be a part of it too."

Roosevelt scrambled away despite the weakness in his legs. He ran for the door to the elevator room, his heart thudding rapidly like an overwound watch. He was almost there when he was tackled to the ground. Paerdegat rolled off him then brought him to his feet.

"W-What are you going to do to me?" Roosevelt asked.

"Take care of him," he heard the thing that used to be Tyner say. "The salvation of New York City is at hand."

Paerdegat reared his hand back and slapped Roosevelt so hard, he blacked out.

The heat woke him. He felt as though he were floating. Wherever he was, machine gears ground around him. To his right large pistons and gears pumped and turned. On his left, wet tendrils of ooze dripped down the walls. When he lifted his head to look forward, he discovered he lay on a moving gurney, which stopped abruptly. A Charybdis stepped up, spread its tentacled hand, and spewed black ink from the center into his eyes.

Roosevelt fell into a state of euphoria as strange images appeared before him. He saw mountains of metal and rock where creatures collected large chunks of materials and brought them to factories. Smokestacks billowed plumes of black smoke, turning the sky to ash.

At the rumble of thunder Roosevelt expected a storm. Instead, structures rose from the ground. They looked like buildings attached to one another, varying in height. While they shifted and turned, he saw stairs and windows. He recognized the shape of Brooklyn's iconic brownstone, glowing from lines within the rock.

Huge creatures made of rock ascended into the sky; their backs arching as they carried the buildings on them. Their heads billowed fire and smoke from open mouths. Four more rose in the distance.

The world around him melted away like a watercolor painting in the rain. He found himself on the bridge of an airship strapped to a chair by his wrists and ankles. The entire room, including the floor, was thick glass. He looked down and saw one of the floating, living islands. Miles of streets lined with brownstones, townhouses, schools, and supermarkets, even a few high-rise towers that looked like office buildings. An amusement park and regular parks, as well. A whole city except there were no people. No life moved among the streets.

"You've come out of the vision," Tyner said as he stepped into view.

"What did I just see?"

"Exactly what you see before you. Each one of these islands is a fully contained, self-sustaining neighborhood. All the energy comes from within the giant *Mitsukurina owstoni*, whose backs they're built on. In a few hours they will be filled with those New Yorkers our illustrious mayor and city council have abandoned. The downtrodden will want for nothing. They won't have to work hard to have the best."

"In return you will turn people into something like you?"

Tyner put on a smile. "Only those who stay behind and live in the old city face that fate." He reached over and undid Roosevelt's bindings. "Let me show you."

Roosevelt cautiously rose from the chair and turned around. A large machine, resembling an engine, sat in the center of the bridge. In the middle of the machine, in a glass cylinder filled halfway with a lavender fluid, floated Mayor Miles, naked and terrified.

"What did you do to him?" Roosevelt said.

Mayor Miles glared at them. "You let me out of here this instant!"

"I'm afraid not." Tyner approached a table before the engine. A map of New York City lay opened on it. Atop that was the city charter. "I would like to thank you for getting this document amended for me. Believe me, you made a great deal." Tyner rolled up the document, then looked at the map before him. X's marked various locations. "Come see this, Roosevelt."

Roosevelt drew closer. "What are all the X's?"

"Those are the buildings I and Paerdegat have prepared with the Charybdis's help. They are the conduits that will transport New York City into the outer realm."

Roosevelt froze. "I'm sorry, did you say *transport* it to the outer realm?"

"Yes. The infrastructures are made of the same metal you saw the Charybdis harvesting. Once they are aligned with the conduits and the last of the downtrodden are transferred to their new homes, we will activate the portal and the entire city will be taken into the realm of my Elder God. The great city of New York, with its rich and wealthy will reside for eternity under its watchful eye. The rest of us will remain here, upon the backs of the *Mitsukurina owstoni* as loyal servants."

"The wealthy agreed to this?" Roosevelt asked.

"They agreed for me to take the destitute and the poor away. The chance to control this city is all they care about."

"In another realm. How will they manage that?"

"Physically, you mean? Well, I have that all figured out."

"You can't do this to me," Mayor Miles screamed. "I'll contest that document to the governor."

"You cannot promise your donors what I am giving them. Absolute control of all five boroughs by taking away the *scourge* of the city. But don't worry, I have assured them that you will still play the part they elected you for." Tyner pulled the lever. "Under the direction of my Elder God."

The liquid in the cylinder bubbled. Mayor Miles looked down in confusion before starting to scream. Tyner pressed a small button atop the lever. The engine rattled, followed by a plume of steam rising from a pipe alongside the cylinder, blocking their view of the mayor. When it dissipated, a large tentacle was sliding down around Mayor Mile's body. Another, much thinner tentacle slipped down and began to caress his face. He opened his mouth to scream, and the tentacle slid into him. Slowly his body sank into the liquid, and he disappeared.

"Sir, the last airship has left Queens and is making its way to its island," Paerdegat said as he entered the bridge. "Brooklyn, The Bronx, and Staten Island are done. Manhattan is taking longer to vacate."

"Reroute all available airships to Manhattan Island. Once the sun goes down, we make our move."

Paerdegat nodded and exited the bridge.

Tyner motioned for Roosevelt to follow him to the forward section. He took hold of a massive ship wheel, steering the airship out over the East River where they had a complete look at the city. Roosevelt marveled at the sight of the huge floating islands shadowing the world below. The sun, making its descent, slowly disappeared behind the massive Manhattan structure.

"It is almost time." Tyner mustered a smile. "I have reserved a space for you among us."

"What about your god? Won't I have to serve him as you do?"

A whistle from the engine prevented Tyner's answer. They turned and watched the fluid from the cylinder drain out onto the floor through a hole at the base.

"The mayor and his Pinkerton are nearly ready." Tyner reached into the pocket of his waistcoat, retrieved a pocket watch, and looked at it.

"Here come the airships," Roosevelt said.

Five large dirigibles with long metal noses were flying toward the floating Manhattan Island. In the middle of the island stood six tall iron spires that lit up an electric blue color as the airships floated close to them. The noses attached themselves to the spires and the ships docked.

"Perfect timing," Tyner said. "Come, I have to deal with the final piece of my mission."

They returned to the machine and Roosevelt saw the cylinder was empty. Tyner pushed the lever forward. Gears turned inside and something unlocked. The machine split open slowly, revealing two glass cylinders encased in metal. Inside were two figures that no longer looked human. Parts of their upper body resembled a tentacled underwater creature. The one to the left was Anderson. The one to the right's facial features had not yet been transformed, and Roosevelt recognized the mayor. His left eye was sealed with a flap of skin. Tendrils that writhed like small snakes hung from the side of his face.

"Tyner, this isn't right," Roosevelt said, disgustedly.

"Wiiiiilliam." Mayor Miles placed his tentacle sucker arm on the glass. "What have you done to me?"

"Prepared you for your journey. This ship will take you back to Manhattan. I have fulfilled my promise to the people, and the sacrifice to my Elder God."

Tyner took his watch out again, held it in his palm, and turned it counterclockwise. A portal opened to their right. He took hold of Roosevelt's arm and pulled him through. Roosevelt found himself standing on a balcony below the clock of the Williamsburg Building looking out at Manhattan Island and the giant *Mitsukurina owstoni* above it. It dwarfed the airship he had been on as it descended toward the city.

A loud boom sounded as the clock behind them chimed. In Manhattan below, the rooftops of Tyner's building glowed blue. A beam emitted from the one at the southern point of the island and connected to the others. Then the beam shot back into the clock. A large portal opened beneath Manhattan and swallowed the entire island. As it closed, the *Mitsukurina owstoni* let out a burst of flame from its mouth and scorched the water as it descended creating gravity waves. When it settled, a complete replica of Manhattan sat in place, indistinguishable from the original.

Rising from the new city were beautiful long schooners that had been converted into airships. Steam trains on elevated tracks rocketed along the river fronts. Fireworks burst into the air in celebration as dirigibles left their moorings and headed north.

Soon, the other *Mitsukurina owstoni* over the Bronx then Queens then Staten Island landed in holes left by the original city. Brooklyn was the last to land. Roosevelt realized then he was not in the original borough any longer as he looked down at the city streets teeming with life. People happy and moving about in steam-powered automobiles. At the base of the building, hundreds had gathered to cheer for Tyner.

The clock above chimed once more then went silent.

Tyner smirked. "I told you I would reclaim New York... for the people."

Roosevelt looked up into the evening sky with tear-filled eyes. Within a group of clouds, giant tendrils danced then faded away. The skies darkened like the world he had seen through the portal. His New York was gone. Fear consumed him as he watched people move around on unearthly conveyances like those of another world. All in the presence of the Elder God now keeping a watchful eye over its new domain.

Visions of the Manor

Carol Gyzander

Bent over her task as far as her corset allowed, the tip of her tongue sticking out the left side of her mouth, Alison focused on aligning the new lenses perfectly in the brass goggles. No ordinary lenses, of course, but ones with a special coating she had worked on for months.

She prayed the unique lenses would help her find the location alluded to in her father's journal that she'd finally discovered hidden in the basement laboratory after his passing. Not just wanted to—she needed to. Her future depended upon getting into the university, and that depended on her proving her father right. The University acted like his talk of parallel worlds was a crackpot theory, but it was the only thing she'd heard of that might explain The Mayhem.

She was determined to prove them wrong because they didn't accept many women, although she was more qualified than half of the students there, thanks to what she had learned helping Father. He'd discovered his girl child had a natural aptitude for science and taught her at home from a young age since it wasn't included in the curriculum for girls. She'd been helping him with his astronomical calculations about alternate realms of reality since her mother had passed ten years ago.

But even worse, time was running out. Unknown marauders invaded the area one night every five years during The Mayhem, wreaking havoc. Although the town put out guards and watchers armed to the teeth, no one had ever seen the attackers—they simply reported an odd sensation running down their spine or twisting in their stomach that faded by morning, and all that was left was to tally the damage. The University's bias against admitting women put the whole community at risk by shutting her out.

Alison adjusted the calibration tool sitting before her on the workbench in the dim basement. A curl fell loose from the coiled hair piled atop her head; as she impatiently pushed it away with the back of her wrist, a few blonde hairs fell onto her well-worn navy gown. She grimaced as a squeak at the laboratory door interrupted her focus. "What is it?" she snapped.

Her twin brother, Edward, poked his head inside, one eyebrow cranked upward in question. Her exasperation faded. "Oh. It's you. Okay, come on in."

Edward carried a tray with sandwiches and two steaming cups of coffee. "I said, have you eaten today? I'm just home from the office." He wore gray trousers and a white shirt, the sleeves pulled back by elastic garters to keep them ink-free as he wrote in the accounting ledgers.

She rolled her eyes. "I can't worry about that! I've almost got these goggles ready."

"Great. Then you have time to take a break and get some food in you. And I brought coffee..." He brought the tray closer so that the aroma tickled her nostrils.

"Oh, coffee. My friend and master." She joined him at the small, cluttered side table where he placed the tray. A large, intricate planetary model dominated the room's central work table, a clock bearing multiple dials ticking at its center. Star charts marked with scribbles and numbers covered the wall above the table. "I guess I could take a few minutes."

As the pair dove into thick ham sandwiches on homemade bread, a black cat jumped onto the table to join them. It sat, twitching the tip of its tail in time with the ticking clock.

Alison absently pulled out a few bites of ham and put them in front of the cat, who nibbled daintily, then sat up and licked a paw, methodically wiping his whiskers.

"You're just so obsessed with this, Alison," Edward said around a mouthful. "I know you want to figure out Father's machine, but I'm a bit worried about you. It's taking over your life just as it did his after Mother died."

About to take another bite, she paused, then sat back and stared at him. "You *know* it's important. Just because *you* have a job, you can't forget about me."

He held up a finger until he swallowed. "Yes, but that job is all that's keeping us from living on the street."

Their family's finances had been destroyed two cycles ago when attackers broke into their family's mercantile upstairs, killing their mother and ransacking the store beyond recovery. People had shunned the location in favor of one across town that was not tainted by the mark of The Mayhem. Their father had lived for nearly another decade, constantly working in the lab on his theories about overlapping realms of physical dimension, until passing from what they assumed was overwork — or a broken heart.

"If I can solve the mystery of what his device predicts, I'm sure there will be something of value in it. And they'll *have* to let me in on scholarship!" Her fist clenched around the sandwich. "The clock is ticking down to the next celestial alignment that Father talked about. His journal shows that these recurring alignments match the cycles of murders that killed Mother and are tied to a geographical location nearby. Maybe we can stop The Mayhem from repeating. It's *important!*"

He nodded and downed the last sip of coffee. "Yes, I understand that you need to figure it out. And I'll help as much as I can now that it's the weekend." He placed the cup on one of the table's few clear areas, at the edge between himself and the cat.

"Oh, I wouldn't put it—"

Before she could finish her words, the black cat stopped cleaning his whiskers and stared at the cup. His head tilted to one side, then the other, and one paw reached out. Tap, tap on the cup—then the cat knocked it off the table.

Edward jumped as the porcelain shattered into pieces on the floor. "Oh, Midnight—" At Alison's stern look, he caught his breath momentarily, then went on. "My fault. I wasn't thinking."

He reached out and touched the cat on the nose. Grabbing a broom and dustpan, Edward swept up the broken pieces before the cat could jump down and cut his feet.

"There. Sorry, Alison." He dumped the shards into the garbage bin and briskly sat down to finish his sandwich. "So, what is it that you've done here? Something new?"

"Thanks. Yes, my research in Father's journal points to a location on that cliff over the river." She patted a worn, leather-covered book. "I even found a sketch of a grand house in here and identified similar geographical features in the area… a tall rock pinnacle. I went as close as I could to view the location recently, and there is no sign whatsoever of any building or human occupation. You know where I mean?"

At his nod, she put down her sandwich crusts and rose, beckoning him to the work table. "There was nothing there as far as I could tell from a distance, but I had the most unusual feeling that something was watching me. Like something was *there*, but I couldn't see it. When I came back to the lab, I thought to alter the chemical composition of these goggles I make so that they will tune out certain shades of light and focus on others." She held up the goggles, now fitted with an array of green lenses fanned out on each side that could be rotated in and out before each eye in various combinations. "Want to try them on?"

He slipped the heavy goggles over his head, adjusting the brass buckle on the leather strap so that they fit snugly against his face. Looking around the room, he held his hands out in a defensive posture. "Kind of dark, but I can see. Um, what am I supposed to be seeing?"

"Well, let's try this." She flipped through the old journal's scribbled pages until she found a hand-drawn sketch of a huge stone manor on a cliff next to a tall stone pillar. "Father must have drawn this on the site, so I assume it's affected by whatever makes it disappear. What do you see?"

He peered intently at the image. "The whole thing has a sort of green glow… *Oh, my goodness!*" Edward leaned in. "I see… people? In the picture… and… and they're *moving!*"

"Exactly what I hoped for." She beamed as he pulled off the goggles. "So, will you join me to see it for real? I've been plotting the star charts, and Father's device agrees. Tomorrow is one of the recurring alignments of Jupiter and Mars, like when people last disappeared."

⚜

Steam trailed behind the pair the next afternoon as they dismounted from their small, rugged vehicles. After pushing them off the rutted track from the town, they donned their rucksacks filled with clothing and food.

Most locals would be locked inside for several days, expecting the unknown marauders to reappear, but that left nobody available to come over and care for the cat. Alison refused to leave Midnight home alone for what might be several days of exploration, although she worried about the rodents that might overrun the laboratory in their absence. She smiled wryly as she slipped on the pouch containing the black cat to hang in front, thinking of the "gifts" of dead mice Midnight often left at her doorstep and how she rewarded him with treats.

"I'm afraid this is as far as the steam bikes can make it. We'll have to walk from here." Edward pulled some branches over the vehicles, careful not to let them touch the hot part of the steam engines. "We actually got farther than I thought we would."

Alison adjusted her skirt's bustle so the pack fit comfortably. While she still wore a long, full skirt—her concession to public opinion, since no respectable woman would appear in trousers—she'd pinned it up in front, revealing her legs in a pair of striped, knit leggings. The net result offered her more freedom of movement.

Together, they continued up through the underbrush to the top of the cliff. Far beneath them flowed the river, the town on its banks visible in the distance. A tall rock pillar stood in the clearing—the geological feature Alison had identified from the old book.

"I really hope this works." Alison pulled two pairs of the special goggles from her waist pouch, gave him one, then slipped hers on, scanning the cliff area. "Oh my..." Her breath caught. A huge dark shape filled one side of the clearing with emerald light shimmering behind it.

"This way!" She took off at a trot, securely holding the cat's pouch to her chest, and Edward bolted to catch up.

They followed the green glow inland a hundred feet from the cliff's edge. She stopped, frowning, then adjusted the goggles, fingering a tab that slid a second lens into place in front of the first. "Aha!" She bumped into Edward as she took a step backward. "I see it! It's really there!"

"What do you see? What is it? I see nothing." Edward held her shoulders from behind as she stood pointing before them.

She reached back and adjusted the lenses of his goggles.

He looked around—and froze. "I see it. *I see it!* Father was right."

They walked together toward the massive stone edifice, their feet crunching on gravel that became a driveway. The faint aroma of ozone filled Alison's nostrils.

The pair paused at the surrounding wall, where everything seemed to shimmer and shift before their eyes. Edward took a deep breath and opened the gate, taking her hand as they stepped into the shimmer.

The cat let out a low, warbling growl, and Alison's skin tingled. All the hair on her arms and the nape of her neck seemed to stand up at once. A quick shiver and the pair passed through the glimmering wall and went up onto the wide stone steps before the front door.

"Everything seems perfectly fine here… I'm guessing we don't even need the goggles now that we crossed that shimmer." Alison confirmed her assertion by lifting her goggles off her head. "Yes! Should we go in? Perhaps better to knock on the door first. What if someone's home?"

He snorted and removed his own goggles, stuffing them in his jacket pocket. "How could someone be home when this place isn't really here?"

Alison reached up to the large ornate brass doorknocker on the wide double doors and gave three sharp raps.

Nothing happened.

She repeated the knock, and they waited several minutes, then tried the door when it became clear there would be no answer. It opened with a low creak, and they entered a huge entry foyer lined with mahogany paneling. Their footfalls echoed on the stone floor.

Before them rose a wide elegant staircase, split at the top to join a grand hallway that formed an overhanging balcony. At the base, closed doors built into the paneling on either side likely led to servant areas or other rooms.

An archway on the left showed a huge dining room, its ornately carved table surrounded by a dozen beautiful chairs that strangely had five legs, an additional one set at the back as if needing to support a great weight. Heavy closed shutters covered all the windows beneath voluminous draperies.

To the right of the entryway, double doors opened into a huge, comfortable-looking living room dominated by a stone fireplace and a pair of mahogany-framed sofas upholstered in blue velvet. Candle-holders on each end table and on the walls bore partially burned candles, their asymmetrical alignment making them difficult to look at for long for some reason. The windows on the outside wall flanking the fireplace were tightly shuttered, like in the dining room. An assortment of strange stone blocks of different geometric shapes on the stunning carved mantelpiece flanked a brass clock shaped like a cat, pulling her into the room.

"These are familiar, Edward! I saw some of them sketched in Father's journal." She ran her finger along the mantle before each one, exclaiming as she recognized several shapes from the old tome, then paused to rub her fingers together. "How utterly strange that there's no dust. And there's wood laid out in the fireplace, ready to be lit. Those logs are huge, though… can you imagine carrying them?"

Edward peered over her shoulder at the mantle. "Well, I have no idea what these shapes represent. That clock is at least recognizable as a cat sitting upright, although I've never seen one like it with a clockface set in its belly. Strange that the fur on its forehead seems to be all tousled between the eyes."

He studied the brass statue, then leaned in to listen. "I'll be damned. It's ticking." He pulled out his pocketwatch and compared the timepieces. "And it's set to the current time. Somebody's been winding it."

A book-lined library off the back of the living room called enticingly to Alison. Late afternoon sunshine played across the library's plush carpet from the glass doors set in a wall of floor-to-ceiling windows that opened onto a central courtyard. "Oh, I look forward to diving into those books!"

She slipped the rucksack off onto an ottoman by the living room sofas in preparation for checking the shelves, but her brother stopped her with a touch on the forearm.

"Yes, fascinating, but I'll never get you away from those bookshelves." Edward drew her back into the foyer and called up the stairs. "Hello! Is anyone here?"

No reply. They shrugged and started up the steps to where the upstairs hallway formed a U-shape, open to the foyer below, with presumably bedroom doors lining the two side wings. A cursory examination showed the floor unoccupied and shutters covering all the windows facing outward.

Alison led her brother into one of the interior bedrooms, gesturing through the window at the gravel-lined courtyard below. "Look, more of the same shapes." Several large stone obelisks and squat geometrical forms stood in the large space formed by three sides of the U-shaped mansion and bounded at the far end by a tall stone wall. More large stones balanced, irregularly spaced, across the wall's top, and the geographical marker of the stone pillar rose behind it.

"What do you think caused the dents?" Large depressions in the gravel gave her pause, and she frowned.

Edward shrugged. "No clue, but they seem to run in a line from those giant stones at one end to the wall and then all around."

"Let's see if we can get out there."

They met no one as they returned to the ground level, and Edward followed Alison into the living room past where she had left her rucksack. It lay toppled onto the floor, no ottoman in sight. She blinked at it a moment, then shook her head and chalked her faulty memory up to excitement. The siblings continued into the library and then outside through the glass doors.

Alison let the cat out of the pouch, stroking his head as she placed him on the ground in the enclosed courtyard, but Midnight froze, sniffing and moving his head from side to side. After a pause, the feline skulked across the pea gravel, belly flattened to the ground, and dove underneath a stone bench.

They could not coax him out, so they sat on the bench and shared some food for supper. Alison dropped bites on the ground near her feet, and eventually, Midnight snuck out and gobbled them down. The cat made a slow revolution of the courtyard, pausing in various places. He thoroughly sniffed one area of disturbed gravel along the wall, ending with his mouth slightly open and eyes almost crossed. Next, the cat turned and let loose a stream of urine against the wall.

"He's claiming it as his spot!" Alison said. "I've seen him do that after someone left the door open and another cat came into the store."

The cat uttered a warbling, deep-throated moan. As Alison approached him slowly, the hairs on her arms stood on end again. The idea that she was not supposed to be there reverberated in her head, and her vision grew more distorted the closer she got to the wall. Dizzy and slightly disoriented, it took her a moment before she could scoop up the cat, rubbing his ears as she retreated to the bench—where her head cleared.

After resting, they decided to continue their explorations of the house. Midnight refused to go inside, hissing and struggling when she tried to carry him into the library, so they resolved to leave the cat in the courtyard.

Further exploration revealed no inhabitants, although the entire manor seemed ready for someone's arrival at any moment. Fresh flowers filled urns on the dining room table. The bedding in the bedrooms all felt clean and smooth, but some nagging feeling bothered Alison until she bent to sniff the sheets. Nothing had an aroma—not the clean sheets, the flowers, or the cheese on the huge butcher block kitchen table. She lit a candle as darkness fell, and the matches gave off no sulfuric smell or smoky odor.

Edward lingered near the door in each room they entered, apparently feeling less interest in exploring than his sister. "So, have you seen enough? I'd like to get going before it gets fully dark."

She gaped at him. "But... but we just found it! There's so much I need to learn here. People who could cross the planes of existence must have wonderful information to share. And maybe they can help us decipher The Mayhem."

"We can always come back tomorrow." He crossed his arms and squared his shoulders, an unfortunate reminder of one of their father's gestures when he set his mind to something.

She wasn't about to give in after all her research finally paid off. "What if it disappears while we're gone? I can't wait another five years. And besides, it's almost dark, and The Mayhem must have started already. We can't ride around out there at night."

That convinced him to stay. Unwilling to be separated or make themselves overly at home in the strange house, the siblings headed back to the main level to bed down in the living room. She prowled around the foyer while Edward lit some candles on the end tables.

Peering into the darkness of the dining room, her stomach roiled as the furniture seemed to shimmer and morph through various shapes. She grabbed the doorway to steady herself. When she stared directly at it, she found the table as she remembered from their arrival. But had the chairs always had three legs like that? She hastened to rejoin her brother.

Midnight again refused to come indoors, so Alison left some food and a bowl of water for him in the courtyard.

She sat on one of the sofas, swinging her legs up and covering them with a lap blanket. "What do you think of this place?" She punched a velvet pillow to make it more comfortable behind her back on the burgundy horsehair cushions, trying not to think about how it hadn't seemed to be there when they arrived.

Edward paused so long before he answered that she almost asked him again.

"Well, it's definitely strange. The place gives me the creeps, and I swear it's either playing with my memory or else it keeps changing. Weren't these cushions blue? It's like the house is here... but yet it's *not*... if you know what I mean?"

"Yes! And nobody has ever reported seeing this place, yet it should be in clear view from the town or the river below. Even I didn't see it when I scouted out the area."

"So, why is it here now? Where does it come from?" He pulled a crocheted lap blanket over himself on the sofa across from hers.

"As for *where* it comes from… I have a theory that it's from another world like ours, perhaps another dimension." She sat back on the sofa. "And as for why *now*, remember what I said about the astronomical congruency? Father's machine indicates the realms will align around 3 a.m., and everything should fall into place. This place seems to be becoming more defined as the dimensions overlap."

"Huh. Weird." He yawned and blew out the candles. "Good thing we're here, then… I guess. Thanks for taking first watch. Wake me up at two…" His voice trailed off as he almost instantly fell asleep.

It took Alison longer to relax, just as it always had when they were children. In the darkness of her single candle, every little sound in the house caught her attention. The walls creaked and groaned as if rubbing against each other. A crunching in the gravel outside the library made her sit up and call out to Midnight, but when he didn't answer, she figured he was just prowling around and lay back on the sofa.

Soon, Alison's heart beat in time with the ticking clock on the mantlepiece, lulling her to sleep despite the excitement of their new find.

❧◦❦◦❧

The sound of galloping footsteps overhead, followed by a vague sense of movement, woke her. Moonlight spilled in from the courtyard. She looked over the edge of where she slept and gasped at the great distance to the floor. Everything around her now appeared immense, and the cat clock loomed on the mantle far overhead. As she moved, several cubes where the end tables had been started radiating light; a molten lava-like blob in the fireplace pulsated heat.

"Edward! Wake up!"

He startled awake opposite her, which now seemed terribly far away. "Wha… what's up?" He sat up on his stone slab.

She checked her watch: 2:45 a.m. "I think we've almost reached the congruency! But look at this place. It's not a manor house at all."

A cacophony of yowls and growls poured in from the courtyard.

"Midnight!" Alison swung her legs over her slab's edge and dropped several feet to the floor. "He must be in danger!"

The siblings pulled their shoes on and dashed to the multi-paned glass doors of the library.

"What the hell! The building is… growing?" Edward had to reach up to unhook the door handle, and they burst into the courtyard—only to stop short in surprise. The end wall towered overhead a great distance away, now tall enough to obscure the geographical marker of the stone pillar. As shadowy shapes flashed back and forth before them, Midnight streaked across the open area and jumped into Alison's arms.

Screams echoed in the distance from the direction of town.

Alison hardly noticed, however, given the spectacle before her. Giant cats taller than Edward chased one another around the courtyard in the darkness, pouncing, tackling, and wrestling each other to the ground. Alison and Edward flinched when a monstrous cat, threading its way across the top of the wall, paused and knocked one of the huge stone objects onto the ground. The massive shape sprayed pea gravel—now as large as their heads—into the air when it landed with a reverberating crash.

"Look at the size of those cats!" Alison grabbed her brother's arm.

Suddenly, another cat leapt onto the wall from the far side, carrying something in its mouth. It lightly jumped down and carried its burden to the glass doors near where they cowered, then stepped into the light and deposited it on the threshold.

It turned to face them, revealing not a typical feline face—but a weird mashup of features dominated by a huge, fanged mouth and a third eye on its forehead between the other two. It spun and growled as another creature approached from behind, swatting the encroacher in the face, apparently for getting too close to the gift it left on the doorstep, then chased the intruder away across the courtyard. Their forms flowed and morphed as they moved, changing from feline to ameboid to a multi-legged creature that made her head hurt to watch.

Alison's spine tingled, and her vision blurred. She shook her head, unable to look at them anymore. Edward pulled her toward the library door, stumbling to a stop as the… cat's tribute became clear. The limp body of one of the town's policemen lay on the threshold, bleeding from slash marks across his neck and staring at them with blank eyes.

"Oh, my God. This is what happens to people during The Mayhem. We have to get out of here!" Alison clutched Midnight to her chest, and together, she and her brother approached and then stepped carefully over the poor man's body, muttering words of sorrow and apology as they passed through the huge doorway.

As they moved, the monstrous creatures turned and focused upon them, then bounded and flowed across the space with an undulating, shrieking howl that pierced Alison to her soul. She froze in horror as Midnight yowled in response. The creatures stopped and fixed the siblings with an unblinking stare. The courtyard around her faded as the lead entity's three eyes expanded, drawing her mind into a swirling, revolving chaos of glowing green light and viscous fluid that absorbed her essence until she couldn't even remember her name. How could she have ever hoped to understand this place? Stars and planets floated beside her as she merged with the alternate realm.

Midnight's claws dug into her arm, breaking her trance. She spun with a gasp and pushed Edward through the opening. Once inside the library, it took both of them to slide the metal door shut with a reverberating clang and keep the indescribable creatures outside.

They headed directly for the entry foyer but found the journey took longer than expected. The living room stretched out before them, now many times larger than before. The sofas, now stone slabs on crossbars, stood so tall that they could walk underneath them. They paused momentarily before the carving on the mantlepiece, now a huge, fanged stone entity morphing in shape around the clock in its belly it ticked to 3 a.m. The tousled fur over the eyes formed a third opening that radiated cold light from the vastness of space, illuminating the entire area with a pale green radiance. The siblings held up their hands to block it from sight and turned toward the door.

As they crossed the space where they had just spent the night, the ceiling creaked and stretched irregularly overhead, forming an asymmetrical arched surface pocked with random craters of oozing green goo that dripped down in strings.

A huge blob landed on Edward's hand, glowing and spreading up his arm. The bone went soft, and the arm lost shape, dangling helplessly by his side. They dodged the rest of the shimmering, dripping slime and approached the front door, panting from exertion, just as it started to creak open.

Edward stopped short. "Oh no, Alison…" He shoved his sister behind him with his good arm.

Her spine tingled, and her heart lurched in her chest. "Oh my God! We've been so focused on those creatures and the building being larger.

But they must just be the pets. Now the owners are home, and just think of how huge they will be!"

As she spoke, a smaller one of the creatures burst through the library door with a clanging crash and undulated toward them like a rocket. It grabbed Edward by the head, shaking his whole body side to side so that Alison heard the immediate crack of his spine. She froze, unable to move or even comprehend what was happening in this strange place.

The front door swung fully open. Tripod legs supported a tall shimmering figure whose glowing head rose so far above them that it seemed tiny in comparison—or perhaps it actually was.

The creature laid Edward's body at the shimmering entity's feet just as it had placed the policeman's body in the courtyard. What might be the head bent down toward her brother with a gruff exclamation she couldn't interpret. Three brilliant green eyes stared out of an otherwise smooth, featureless face.

The scene so stunned her that she couldn't make a sound.

A second creature burst in from the courtyard—the one that had mesmerized her outside. Its three eyes locked her in place from across the cavern. She trembled in fear as it stalked relentlessly toward her. Alison finally screamed as its maw gaped open and descended over her head.

TICK TOCK

RACHEL A. BRUNE

The planet was dying, and only Lord Brocious Glasscock dreamed of the stars.

The fourth and only living son of a long-forgotten noble, Lord Glasscock lived on an as-equally-forgotten estate a short way outside what was left of the capital.

He prized the solitude and the darkness that kept desperate citizens from striking a path to his doorway. In the old library that now served as his workshop, he spent his days cursing the inner workings and delicate gears of his machine. Lord Glasscock's eyes strained behind thick goggles that magnified the tiny bits he strove to lay order to in the puzzle that consumed his feverish mind.

It had taken the space of a week for the skies to dim and the sun to go out. And then, the infernal ticking began. The incessant, almost soundless *tick tick tick* had driven half the population to mass slaughter, a self-purging that choked the streets and overwhelmed sanity of the survivors. Now, a scant month later, the same *tick tick tick*ing kept time for Lord Glasscock through every weld and solder and twist of the wire. Even the thick, stone walls that shrouded his work from the world could not keep out the syncopated urgency that counted down to some unknown fate.

Sweat gathered in the unseasonable heat, held back from dripping down his brow by a cloth band enclosing the top of his goggles. He worked on, clambering over the gleaming brass and copper pipes, coaxing cooperation from their gears, pausing at irregular intervals to boil an egg or take a bite of an apple.

And, as always, whether he labored in the depths of the machine or threw himself down on the chaise lounge he'd dragged into the room for a fleeting nap, he could not escape it.

Tick tick tick.

In the depths of his brain, beneath even his sense of sound, he heard it. The clock, ticking and tocking a senseless pounding. At times, the sound came as a tap, tap, tapping; at others, came the faintest hint of a whisper in the dark. But always, always under the smoke that obscured the day and the night, the ceaseless, urgent pulse beat on and on.

As Glasscock grappled with a problem of hydraulics or a gear that slipped under too much pressure, urgency drove him with every metallic oscillation of the invisible pendulum. That same urgent heartbeat drove the rest of the world into madness.

Even before the mysterious cataclysm, the skies were darkened by a soot and grime so thick that no one could render any certain judgment as to whether or not the earth remained in rotation around the sun, or if her own satellite still proceeded through its lunar phases.

Amidst the drifting black clouds, garish Airships floated. A few explorers had been hardy enough to test the heavens, rising above the scum of the vaporous murk. None had returned. Now, the Airships held steady, safe from the horrors of the ground, piloted by crews half-insane with the *tick tick tick*ing that no amount of music or dancing could drown out.

Tickets had been scarce, and more than one lady or gentleman had boarded who did not match the original name on the reservation, or who had tell-tale brown flecks smeared where the conductor punched the entry hole.

Once aboard, the Airships hosted a gay mélange of men and women dressed in fancy dress, or lingerie, or soldiers' uniforms, or diplomats' robes, or even—especially with the heat—nothing at all. They chatted and cheered and kissed under the rare, costly electric lamps, pouring their clear drinks of crystal bubbles into golden goblets, even as they passed over the darkening land below and out over the vast, dark seas, the only place they could still catch the wisp of a cool breeze of clean air.

For everyone else, the vast steam-powered factories had rusted silently shut, grinding to a halt as if some cosmic entity had thrown a continent's worth of sand in their gears. That same malaise choked the life from the fields, leaving crops wilting and petrified like so many mutated skeletons. In the first week, news came from abroad of wars and slaughter and hoarding and death. And then, there was no one left to man the telegraph stations, even if the wires still pulsed with the signal of life from beyond the confines of the dark.

Far below the gleaming lights of the monstrous Airships, heat and soot and death smothered those who remained behind. As the local remnants of social bonds crumbled, the inhabitants found their own paths through the ever-darkening, increasingly scorched cities and the lands that surrounded them. And still, the *tick tick ticking* beat on.

Some sought their own dark pleasures in the tunnels and avenues of the sweltering gloom of the great city. The waters strangled and died in the grime and profuse blooms of sea plant life, they sang and ate and drank and fornicated as if waiting for the edge of the river that bisected the ancient town to sneak over its banks and drown them in a blanket of relief.

Others grasped their children tightly, taking turns to forage, scavenge, and steal food, bringing it home with lies about how things would get better. Sometimes, a father did not return at all. Sometimes, a mother reappeared with blood on her clothes and meat for the next two weeks.

Still others struck out on the lonesome roads, seeking what they could find. Not many of those who chose this route survived the journey. One of those unfortunates found himself before the open door of an old manor, just a short way outside the city.

As the beggar ambled around a curve in the drive, the lights suddenly flared to life. The lamps lined the soot-streaked exterior, extending down the path toward the road, almost as if to lead him to the open door and the promise of perhaps a night's shelter away from danger.

For a long moment the beggar hesitated, torn between the known dangers of the road and the uncertain temptation of the manor. In the end, the hope of a door between him and those who prowled the night won out, and so the beggar crept hesitantly down the long path, past the skeletons of long-rotted trees, over stones matted with grime and soot.

Reaching the final set of steps up to the open door, the beggar stopped, waiting, listening. There were no longer any of the sounds one would expect to hear at such a manor—no coaches passed on the road, nor dogs barked, nor birds sang. Even the insects were mute in the dark.

Steeling himself, the beggar walked up the front steps and, again, hesitated, but this time for quite a different reason. He had only ever entered large estates through the servants' entrance. That had been in his former life, before the heat and soot and clouds obscured the skies and the world began its merry, clawing, mad descent into darkness.

The beggar steeled himself and proceeded, stopping in the middle of a giant, open room. A flash caught his eye and he let out a strangled sound, cringing, before realizing what he'd seen. A giant grandfather clock stood at the base of a set of stairs that headed up into a darkened upper floor. The massive pendulum hung still. No ticking disturbed the absolute silence.

Two corridors, one on each side of the entrance, ranged off, lit dimly by more gaslamps.

Debris scattered the floor—leaves and twigs and bits of paper and string. The beggar shuffled as he ventured farther into the shadowed entry, stirring up a sharp, earthy smell of old feces and moldering newspapers.

He shrank back as a shadow approached, a thin, dark psychopomp heralding the approach of a gentleman—and what else could he be in those finely tailored clothes, even if they *were* stained with the grease and steam burns that belied an engineer's vocation?

"You may call me Lord Glasscock."

He did not look the beggar directly in the face, which was to be expected from a gentleman. Briefly, the beggar wondered how someone of Lord Glasscock's means had not booked passage on one of the long-departed airships. Something of a mania gleamed in the gentleman's eye, a strangeness reflected by the gaslamps.

The Lord blinked both eyelids in quick succession and jerked his head to the left, as if someone had just come upon him unawares. A thin bead of sweat dripped from his brow.

"My... my lord?" The beggar stepped back, remembering tales of the early days of the darkness, of nobles who, having lost their herds of swine or sheep or cattle, welcomed in those who took to the road as other fare. The beggar had never believed those tales, but he already regretted his decision to answer to the call of the light in the dark, wondering now if it had been more will-of-the-whisp than beacon of hope.

"Come with... with me." Lord Glasscock turned and strode away down the hall. This time, his shadow lingered behind him, as if taunting the beggar with the promise of things to come.

Things to come?

The beggar cast one last glance behind him, at the open door that led to the road beyond. A nasty wind drifted in, carrying with it hints of sulfur and soot, barely stirring the leaves that littered the foyer underfoot.

Desperation lay outside. Could he so easily turn away from its bastard cousin, hope?

The beggar followed as Lord Glasscock led the way down the shadowy hallway, stopping at the end before two floor-to-ceiling wood doors. All the time, his fingers kept tapping against his thighs, keeping rhythm to some unheard beat. The beggar nodded in time, captive to the same ceaseless rhythm.

"My lord?"

Glasscock jolted, as if he'd almost forgotten the beggar trailing behind him. The beggar tensed, casting an eye back the way they'd come.

"In here." The gentleman pushed open the doors, and a warm, vibrant light spilled into the hallway.

Despite his misgivings, the beggar could not stop his feet moving into the beautifully appointed room. There were many fine furnishings and pieces of strange equipment, but the first thing that caught his eye was a long table shoved against a wall of bookcases. And on that table, a bowl of clean, ripe apples.

The beggar made another choking sound and stared wildly at Lord Glasscock, who nodded.

"Partake." His head jerked to the side, then back. He fixed the beggar with an unswerving glance. "Take an apple."

The beggar ran to the table, grabbed the first apple, and shoved it in his pocket before taking up a second one to his mouth. He closed his eyes as he bit into the sweet flesh. Tears salted the first mouthful. Unashamed, he let them roll down his cheeks as he greedily snatched another bite, and then another.

Opening his eyes, the beggar found Lord Glasscock ignoring him to tinker with the monstrosity that took up the rest of the room.

Gleaming pipes of copper, brass, and steel reached almost all the way to the open ceiling. The room looked as if it had once been a library. Now, the dark and the heat poured in through the gaping hole in the roof. The beggar gazed up and up, although all that could be seen was more of the same filthy darkness.

The contraption itself was set up in an oblong shape, with hydraulics and gears packed in tightly. For some reason, it reminded the beggar of a drawing he'd once seen on a page ripped out of a textbook someone had discarded—a picture that showed all the internal organs under a skinless, grinning human body.

The beggar shuddered and took another bite of his apple, thinking longingly about the rest of the fruit sitting in the bowl.

"Here." Glasscock was gesturing at him now. What was he pointing toward?

Ah, yes. There. In the center of the machine—a large, reclining seat. "Here."

The beggar narrowed his eyes. The unease returned, and he thought of the stories of those who disappeared wandering the road, and of the open door he'd walked himself through.

Then he thought of the apples in the bowl.

Snagging another piece of fruit, he walked closer to the machine.

"My lord… you wish me? To sit here?"

Glasscock was tinkering with something on the other side of the machine, and his voice came out muffled. "Yes. Please. Sit. I'm fine… fine-tuning some of…of the spec—specifications."

The beggar imagined him jerking with that peculiar tic of his. Shame crept over him, unexpectedly. A momentary seat in exchange for three apples—perhaps four and maybe one for the road, or maybe even a real bed for the night and another piece of fruit for breakfast? How terrible a bargain would that be?

Gingerly, the beggar picked his way over a few extruding pipes and clambered onto the seat. He took a bite from his apple as he settled himself into the surprisingly comfortable chair, closing his eyes again in the sheer pleasure of the soft leather cushion against his back and legs. If he were not careful, he might even fall asleep right here.

Something heavy and leather came down across one shoulder, then the next. The beggar choked and coughed and opened his eyes to see Lord Glasscock tightening and buckling the contraption to which he was now bound. The loose leather straps had dangled below the chair, unnoticed until Lord Glasscock had heaved them up to fasten across the beggar's torso and lap.

The sweet fruit turned to soot in the beggar's mouth. Surely, he'd come into a bedlam populated by one sole, aristocratic inhabitant. He chewed, nonetheless, hunger driving his jaws like an automaton. Chew, swallow, take another bite. Should he try to reach for the burnished brass buckles, so tantalizing close, their surface glistening in the gaslight?

Lord Glasscock pulled a set of heavy goggles over his eyes, peering intently through the thick, amber lenses into the gears and workings of the machine, his fingers tap, tap, tapping in time with a beat that the beggar could not hear, no matter how he strained.

"Please, my Lord." There was freedom and there was the apple, and the beggar cut off his own soft plea with a crunching bite that left little in his hand except seeds and stem.

"Don't move." The Lord turned to him with a gaze magnified through the thick lenses. He twitched again, his fingers tapping to that invisible beat, journeying along the gleaming copper fixtures that framed the machine. "Delicate."

With a flourish, he pulled on a pair of soft leather gloves. Grimacing, he stilled the fingers of one hand with the other and rested them both on a series of knobs and pulleys.

"You will see," he said, in a tone as flat as the river on a dull day. "And you will tell me what you see."

With that, he pulled a series of complicated buckles and levers. The beggar, finally, understanding it was too late, struggled against his bonds, straining to reach the buckle, the gentleman, anything.

Lord Glasscock stepped back a careful few inches from the machine, close enough to observe the gears and lights that took on a life of their own now that he had set them in motion, but not so close as to be enveloped by the sickly green aether that glowed around the entirety of the machine.

Under the straps, the beggar's body tensed, knuckles, neck, jaw, every bone and limb going taught and clenched as if possessed by an electrical tremor.

Tick, tick, tick…

The machine picked up speed, its engines accelerating into a rhythmic cacophony that sent a deep, thudding percussion throughout the room, matching perfect time with the tap, tap, tapping of Glasscock's twitching limbs.

Above the machine, the green aether gathered itself into some semblance of order, fanning out in spiral arms like the tender shoots of early spring ferns. Among the arms emerged specks of red and yellow and other colors Glasscock's mind could not put names to.

A wordless pulse emanated through the room, thrumming through the soles of Glasscock's boots, vibrating the body of the beggar that still flexed against the restraints. His jaw clenched and seized as his entire body stiffened and bucked. Then, the vibrations stilled. The beggar fell back, collapsing in on himself. The beggar's mouth dropped open, but the voice that came through was made of sharp glass and the twisting of broken, fragile springs:

EeeE'rghothane… wayfarer… türR'noth… release…

Layered through these words, as if an echo reverberated through them, Glasscock saw the stars, felt his hands itch to make the adjustments the voice commanded. He understood the final, finite adjustments needed for his machine to make its leap to pierce the darkness and dreamed, once again, of the stars beyond.

The voice choked off. The beggar's mouth hung wide now, bleeding freely. Glasscock noted in disgust the pink tip of his tongue hanging by a thread. The man choked again, and his body went limp.

The beggar rolled his head, his nearly-severed tongue flopping with the movement.

His eyes fixated on Glasscock, wild, bloodshot as the capillaries broke and flooded the whites with blood that looked black under the green miasma.

"The stars…" The words, muffled with deformity and the blood that flowed down his throat.

"Yes?" Glasscock's fingers tapped ever faster. "Yes, tell me!"

"The stars… they are ready."

The discolored eyes went blank with a familiar emptiness. The remains of the apple, slightly brown by now, fell to the floor, freed from the beggar's lifeless grasp.

～⋙⊙⋘～

The machine slowly returned to its idle state, gears and pipes popping and hissing as they released the last bits of steam into the room. Once he was satisfied that the green aether had dissipated, Glasscock grabbed an apple from the table. Taking small careless bites, he bent to unbuckle the body from the straps.

Hoisting the corpse on his shoulders, he strode out of the room and down the hall, snacking as he went. At the end of the hall, he paused. Habit had brought him to the solarium.

Glasscock had perfected the bulbs that adorned the ceiling of the room. The shrouded sky had almost killed the stunted fruit trees that grew there, but he had brought the room back to life with his bulbs, and with the barrows-loads of soil he'd carted inside. But there was no need, now, to bury the last experiment.

Chuckling softly, he dropped the body and the apple core to the ground and headed back out, turning the lights off after himself.

In the same fashion, Glasscock ventured back to the foyer, switching off the lights that lined the exterior, that had brought the beggar, like the ones before him. They had been welcomed in, fodder for the machine.

In the utter silence of the house, the ticking began again, the silent, urgent pulse that tapped his fingers along with it. That calling from beyond the darkness. That—

Glasscock shook his head. He had a few more measurements. One last fine-tuning. Returning to the room, he set a kettle on the portable burner and dropped in an egg. Setting a timer, he returned to the machine.

He had not always thought to use the unfortunates who still fled along the roads, as if there was something to flee. The first being to fuel the machine was a cat that had once belonged to the son of the old housekeeper.

It hadn't died after that first trip. Oh no. Glasscock hadn't yet come close to perfecting the connection that his machine would later achieve. Instead, once he'd powered down the machine and the green had faded away, it had leapt at him, scratched his face badly, then run off to its own dusty death.

The *tick tick tick* of the egg timer wound down, and Glasscock shut off the burner. He took out the egg with a pair of tongs and rapped it sharply against the table, then peeled and ate it, ignoring the burning sensation.

The ticking continued, underlying everything, unmuffled by the stillness that hung in the air. Glasscock sweated under his clothes as he made one final adjustment in accordance with the observations the beggar had revealed.

It was ready.

Had any Airship been passing over the Glasscock estate at the time, even the rowdiest partygoer would not have been able to ignore the green light that leapt into the sky from the shadowy landscape below.

But no gleaming Airship sailed over the cities anymore, having all deserted land for the ocean's more welcoming currents.

And so, there was no one to witness the silent glow that pierced that darkness, rising like a sallow green ball over the curve of the horizon, growing so hot that the center turned white with heat. As it rose, creeping ever higher, light flared at its sides as if seeking to pierce the air.

A thunderous sound accompanied the white-green orb, rumbling like twenty of the stoutest steam engines, more powerful than the most monstrous of any airship built by man's technology.

Inside the machine, Lord Glasscock felt the forces of nature strain against his body, holding him in place almost more firmly than the straps he'd buckled around himself. The green aether, as he'd designed, protected the machine and the fragile human body inside as it ascended through the layers of filth and grime that polluted the atmosphere.

The air would be getting thin—the first aeronauts had discovered the details of the sky through which he now ascended, although he would soon leave behind even their highest-flying descendants.

Resting on the controls, Glasscock found his fingers once again tapping to that incessant, ceaseless *ticking*, the never-ending pulse that had settled itself in his ears since the dark and the heat had grasped the world in their blanketing jaws.

That ticking had spurred so many to hedonistic mayhem, madness, despair, desperate acts of murder and survival. But for him, he had always heard *something* behind the ticking, something that spoke to him, that called out to him.

It was too dark now to see anything beyond the soft, green glow. By his calculations, Glasscock must be on the edge of the known limits of the atmosphere.

Gasping, he threw his head back, straining to see through the whirling arms above him, through to the stars that called to him.

The machine strained higher and higher, a precious green dot carrying one single heartbeat.

Into the darkness.

It has been so long…

The leviathan let the tiny green crumb settle before yawning wider. In all the millennia, in all the galaxies, it was rare but not unheard of for one of the creatures inhabiting a world below to mistakenly attune to it.

It had happened before. It would happen again.

That spark of connection, a sharing of dreams. Of course, it would drive any of the minute inhabitants mad, but given a world with beings arrogant enough to pursue the dreams of the gods, and it wasn't unheard of for one of them to rise to meet him.

Tick, tick, tick…

The leviathan had warped time along with the light, twisted and churned them around this once-blue morsel, counting down the heartbeats until it slowed almost to a standstill. The waiting was almost at an end. From the depths of the leviathan's being, waves of heat settled and cooled. The creature's vastness had brought the stygian murk to bear on the world below, and the sweltering incandescence of his essential energized matter had done the rest, simmering the world to his patient satisfaction.

With a vast ponderousness, the leviathan brought its appetite to bear on the world below.

The Eye at the Center of Existence Never Blinks

Maxwell I. Gold

i. Tick

Closer, drawn inward passed the steel, bone, and rickety pieces of
thought-clumps that collected at my feet I watched the old stars
wither below me — whisper and cough, their metallic innards too
soft to churn, too slow to push one moment longer.

Tick,

throb,

and crash,

Followed the rhythmic mechanization of the stars around spherical
sundries of a lost rust-ball that was the universe, empty and
something else staring deeper, strained, and cracked like my body
as I walked along the old staircase listening to the music of
old forges and forgotten places —

ii. Throb

Where some ancient mass, yes, too familiar and anxious, wider with
undulating quickness, it blinks, and twitches, covered in thorns and
emerald shields — prepared to welcome me beat by beat, minute by
terrible minute as if my soul were composed of copper or nickel, and
surreptitiously stripped of its elemental reason, oxidized by that
which was most terrible and indifferent.
Too soon I felt the unreasonable weight of existence press upon
me like a glaive as I was cut down — another thought-clump,
trapped betwixt the hands of that old clockface;

tick,

throb,

and crash.

iii. Crash

Past the old crumpled arms where below me — no whispers or coughs
escaped — embers of smoke bent upward from the scarred time-body.
Forsaken by the dark umbrage of an unspoken terror I saw the
shattered clockface swallowed by a horrid mass whose lidless form;
ne'er shut compressed at the center everything, endlessly beating,

tick,

throb,

and crash.

About the Authors

Marc L Abbott received his MFA in Creative Writing from SNHU. He is a Brooklyn native whose work includes *The Hooky Party & Etienne and the Stardust Express*. He's the co-author of *Hell at Brooklyn Tea and Hell at the Way Station*, the two-time African American Literary Award-winning horror anthology. His horror short stories are featured in *New York State of Fright, Even in the Grave, Under Twin Suns: Alternate Histories of the Yellow Sign & Blackened Roots An Anthology of the Undead*. He is a Moth Story Slam and Grand Slam Storyteller winner and an award-winning actor. He is one of the hosts of the podcast Beef, Wine and Shenanigans and a member of the Horror Writers Association.

Find out more about him at www.whoismarclabbott.com.

Award-winning author, editor, and publisher **Danielle Ackley-McPhail** has worked both sides of the publishing industry for longer than she cares to admit. In 2014 she joined forces with Mike McPhail and Greg Schauer to form eSpec Books (www.especbooks.com).

Her published works include eight novels, *Yesterday's Dreams, Tomorrow's Memories, Today's Promise, The Halfling's Court, The Redcaps' Queen, Daire's Devils, The Play of Light,* and *Baba Ali and the Clockwork Djinn*, written with Day Al-Mohamed. She is also the author of the solo collections *Eternal Wanderings, A Legacy of Stars, Consigned to the Sea, Flash in the Can, Transcendence, The Kindly Ones, Dawns a New Day, The Fox's Fire, Between Darkness and Light,* and the non-fiction writers' guides *The Literary Handyman, More Tips from the Handyman,* and *LH: Build-A-Book Workshop*. She is the senior editor of the *Bad-Ass Faeries* anthology series, *Gaslight & Grimm, Side of Good/Side of Evil, After Punk,* and *Footprints in the Stars.* Her short stories are included in numerous other anthologies and collections. She is a full member of the Science Fiction and Fantasy Writers Association.

In addition to her literary acclaim, she crafts and sells original costume horns under the moniker The Hornie Lady Custom Costume Horns, and homemade flavor-infused candied ginger under the brand of Ginger KICK! at literary conventions, on commission, and wholesale.

Danielle lives in New Jersey with husband and fellow writer, Mike McPhail and four extremely spoiled cats.

Rachel A. Brune is an Army veteran, former military journalist, novelist, and editor of the creepy and macabre. She is the founder and chief editor at Crone Girls Press, an indie horror micro-press specializing in anthologies. In 2022, she became Senior Editor of Falstaff Books' new horror imprint, Falstaff Dread. She lives with her spouse, two daughters, one reticent cat, and two flatulent rescue dogs. The first book in her werewolf secret agent series, *Cold Run,* was published in 2022 by Falstaff Books.

James Chambers received the Bram Stoker Award® for the graphic novel, *Kolchak the Night Stalker: The Forgotten Lore of Edgar Allan Poe* and is a four-time Bram Stoker Award nominee. He is the author of the short story collections *On the Night Border* and *On the Hierophant Road,* which received a starred review from *Booklist,* which called it "…satisfyingly unsettling"; and the novella collection, *The Engines of Sacrifice,* described as "…chillingly evocative…" in a *Publisher's Weekly* starred review. He has written the novellas, *Three Chords of Chaos, Kolchak and the Night Stalkers: The Faceless God,* and many others, including the Corpse Fauna cycle: *The Dead Bear Witness, Tears of Blood, The Dead in Their Masses,* and *The Eyes of the Dead.* He also writes the Machinations Sundry series of steampunk stories. He edited the Bram Stoker Award-nominated anthology, *Under Twin Suns: Alternate Histories of the Yellow Sign* and co-edited *A New York State of Fright* and *Even in the Grave,* an anthology of ghost stories. His website is: www.jameschambersonline.com.

Teel James Glenn has killed hundreds and been killed more times — on stage and screen, as he has traveled the world for forty-plus years as a stuntman, swordmaster, storyteller, bodyguard, actor, and haunted house barker.

He is proud to have studied sword under Errol Flynn's last Stunt double and been beaten up by Hawk on Spenser for Hire TV show. He did over two hundred episodic appearances on Soap operas, 70 feature films and 60 renaissance festivals all over the country.

He has published dozens of novels and his poetry and stories have been printed in over two hundred magazines including Weird Tales, Mystery, Pulp Adventures, Space & Time, Mad, Cirsova, Silverblade, Heroic Fantasy, Blazing Adventures and Sherlock Holmes Mystery.

His novel *A Cowboy in Carpathia: A Bob Howard Adventure* won best novel 2021 in the Pulp Factory Award. He is also the winner of the 2012 Pulp Ark Award for Best Author. And he was a finalist for the Derringer short mystery award in 2022. His short story "The Clockwork Nutcracker" won P& E's best steampunk story and has been expanded into a novel. Epic ebook award finalist. P&E winner "Best Steampunk Short", a P & E finalist for "Best Fantasy short, Collection" and his novel "Callback for a Corpse" was a second-place winner in the CWR Poll as best mystery.

His website is TheUrbanSwashbuckler.com.

Maxwell I. Gold is an acclaimed Jewish-American cosmic horror poet and editor, with an extensive body of work comprising over 300 poems since 2017. His writings have earned a place alongside many literary luminaries in the speculative fiction genre. His work has appeared in numerous literary journals, magazines, and anthologies such as Weird Tales Magazine, Startling Stories, Space and Time Magazine, Other Terrors: An Inclusive Anthology, Chiral Mad 5, and many more. Maxwell's work has been recognized with multiple nominations for both the Rhysling Award and the Pushcart Prize. Find him and his work at www.thewellsoftheweird.com.

Bram Stoker Award® finalist **Carol Gyzander** writes and edits horror and science fiction, frequently with a female-centered perspective. She calls her work "twisted tales that touch your heart." Her short stories appear in various magazines, including *Weird Tales 367* and *Weird House Magazine*, and dozens of anthologies—the latest is *Tangle & Fen*.

Her novella from Systema Paradoxa, *Forget Me Not*, features a cryptid creature near Niagara Falls in 1969 with a family twist. She co-edited the ghost anthology *Even in the Grave* and *A Woman Unbecoming*, the horror anthology inspired by the reversal of Roe v. Wade that benefits reproductive healthcare services.

Living in the NYC suburbs of northern NJ, Carol is Co-Chair of the Horror Writers Association NY Chapter, co-host of their monthly Galactic Terrors online reading series, and helps oversee HWA chapters in the US. HWA, MWA, SFWA, SinC. Her website is www.CarolGyzander.com.

Jeffrey Lyman is an engineer in the New York City area. His work has appeared in the anthologies *Sails and Sorcery* from Fantasist Enterprises, *New Blood* from Padwolf Publishing, and *Breach the Hull, So It Begins, By Other Means, Best Laid Plans*, and *Dragon's Lure* from Dark Quest Books. He was co-editor of *No Longer Dreams* and all four volumes of the award-winning *Bad-Ass Faeries* anthology series, several of which won awards. He is a 2004 graduate of the Odyssey Writing School and won 2nd place in the fourth quarter of the 27th Annual Writers of the Future Award.

Will McDermott turned a love of science fiction and games into a writing career. He has published nine novels, more than twenty short stories, and helped create numerous worlds, characters, and stories for card, board, and video games. His fiction is often set in gaming universes, including *Magic: The Gathering, Warhammer 40K, Renegade Legion Universe*, and *Mage Wars*. He is known for bringing larger-than-life characters alive, including Warhammer's Kal Jerico and Mad D'onne, Magic's Balthor the Stout and, more recently, Night Stalker's Carl Kolchak. Check out willmcdermott.com, w_mcdermott on Instagram or willmcdermott.author on Facebook.

F. R. Michaels is a nice, normal person who happens to like weird and scary stories. Seriously. His work has appeared in Alfred Hitchcock's Mystery Magazine and Haunts (as Frank Michaels) as well as the anthologies Strangely Funny II, Mysterion, Wicked Weird, Wicked Creatures, Monstorm, and SVP's Little Black Book of Terror. His jazz-age pulp horror novella "The Blood of Saint Vera" will be available sometime next year. He dwells on Long Island and writes horror and dark fantasy.

Much to his embarrassment, **Bernie Mojzes** has outlived Lord Byron, Percy Shelley, Janice Joplin and the Red Baron, without even once having been shot down over Morlancourt Ridge. Having failed to achieve a glorious martyrdom, he has instead turned his hand to the penning of paltry prose (a rather wretched example of which you currently hold in your hands), in the pathetic hope that he shall here find the notoriety that has thus far proven elusive. His work has appeared in a number of anthologies and magazines, including *Bad-Ass Faeries II* and *III, Gaslight & Grimm, Betwixt Magazine, Daily Science Fiction,* and *What Lies Beneath.* In his copious free time, he published and co-edited *Unlikely Story* (www.unlikely-story.com) and the ever-timely *Clowns: The Unlikely Coulrophobia Remix,* as well as editing *The Flesh Made Word* for Circlet Press. Should Pity or perhaps a Perverse Curiosity move you to seek him out, he can be found at http://www.kappamaki.com.

Jody Lynn Nye lists her main career activity as 'spoiling cats.' When not engaged upon this worthy occupation, she writes fantasy and science fiction, most of it in a humorous bent. Since 1987 she has published over fifty books and more than 200 short stories. She has also written with notables in the industry, including Anne McCaffrey and Robert Asprin. Jody teaches writing seminars at SF conventions, including the two-day intensive workshop at Dragon Con, and is Coordinating Judge for the Writers of the Future Contest.

Hildy Silverman writes speculative fiction of all kinds, primarily for anthologies. Her story, "The Six-Million-Dollar Mermaid," was a finalist for the WSFA Small Press award. Her novella, *Invasive Species,* was released in 2023 as part of the Systema Paradoxa/ Cryptid Crate series published by eSpec Books. From 2005-2018, Hildy was the publisher and editor-in-chief of Space and Time, a venerable magazine of fantasy, horror, and science fiction. She is a past president of the Garden State Speculative Fiction Writers and a frequent panelist on the science fiction convention circuit. For more information about Hildy, please visit www.crazy8press.com and www.hildysilverman.com.

Our Calm Amidst the Chaos

We could not have done this without:

A.S. Etaski
Alexander H.
Alicia M Rabb
Allyn Gibson
Alp Beck
Amaia Belasko
Andrew Cook
Andrew Hatchell
Andrew Kaplan
Ann Stolinsky
Anonymous Reader
Anthony R. Cardno
Avatar-of-Chaos
Avis Crane
Aysha Rehm
Becky B
Beth (Peldyn) Sparks-Jacques
Bill Kohn
BOBBY ZAMARRON
Brad Goupil
Brad Jurn
Brad Kabosky
Brandy H
Brendan Lonehawk
Brendan Pease

Brian, Kay, and Joshua Williams
Bridget Engman
Brooks Moses
Caitlyn Price
Carol Gyzander
Carol Jones
Carol Mammano
Chad Bowden
Charlie Russel
Chris Newell
Christopher D. Abbott
Christopher J. Burke
Cindy Matera
Coleman Bland
Crohnicgamer
Crysella
Cullen Barr
Cynthia Radthorne
Dagmar Baumann
Dale A Russell
Danielle Ackley-McPhail
Danny Chamberlin
David Keener
David Lahner
David Myers

Denise and Raphael Sutton
Dianne Nicholson
Doc Coleman
Donna Hogg
Douglas Yeager
Dr. Nina B. L. Urban
Dusk Zer0
Ef Deal
Elaine Tindill-Rohr
Elizabeth Crefin
Ellery Rhodes
Eric P. Kurniawan
Eron Wyngarde
Frank Michaels
Fred Bauer
Fred Rexroad
Gail Z. Martin
Gary Phillips
Gav I
Gene Mederos
Gina DeSimone
GraceAnne DeCandido
Greg Levick
Hadrosaur Productions
Ian F Bell
Ian Harvey
J Piper Lee
Jace Chretin
Jacen Leonard
Jack Deal
Jacob H Joseph
Jakub Narębski
James Johnston
Jeanne M Hartley
Jeff Young
Jenn Whitworth
Jennifer L. Pierce
Jeremy Bottroff
Jessica Fortin

Jim Thornberry
John L. French
John Markley
John Ordover
Jon Quigley
Judy McClain
Julian White
June Chase
Karen Mitchell Carothers
Kate Cserjes
Kate Tabor
Kathryn Black
Kathy Brady
Keith R.A. DeCandido
Kelly Pierce
Kevin A Davis
krinsky
Lara Beneshan
Lara Struttman
Lauren O'Byrne
Lilia Millner
Lillian Taylor
Lisa Kruse
Liz DeJesus
Lori Beard
Lorraine J Anderson
Louise Lowenspets
Luis Leal
Lynn Pottenger
LZ
M. T. Hall
MAllder
Margaret Bumby
Marie Devey
Mark E Thompson
mark roth-whitworth
Mary Ann Shuman
Mary Jane Hetzlein
Maureen Hart

Megan Struttmann
Mel Follmer
Melissa Honig
Michael Axe
Michael Barbour
Michele Hall
Morgan Hazelwood
Mubarak Sadoon
Murky Master
Mustela
Nathan Turner
Nova Sisk
Otter Libris
pjk
PunkARTchick "Ruthenia"
Raphael Bressel
Regis M. Donovan
Richard Novak
Richard O'Shea
Richard Parker
Robby Thrasher
Robert C Flipse
Robin Lynn
Rusty Waldrup
Ruth Ann Orlansky
S. Evans
Saul Jaffe
Scantrontb
Scott Pearson
Scott Schaper
Shawnee M
Shelby Elenburg
Steph Parker
Stephanie Lucas
Stephen Ballentine
Stephen W. Buchanan
Steve & Beckey Sanchez
Steven Purcell
Susan J. Voss
Tawney Cooper
Therese Moore
Thomas M Karwacki
Thomas P. Tiernan
Tim DuBois
Tim Lonegan
Traci Belanger
Tracy "Rayhne' Fretwel
Tracy Popey
Trainor Houghton-Whyte
Trip Space-Parasite
Walter J. Montie
white beard geek
Whysper Wude
Will Gunderson
Will McDermott
william myers
Wingnut
Xanthe W.
Yosen Lin